OCEANSIDE PUBLIC LIBRARY
330 N. COAST HWY
OCEANSIDE, CA 92054

Big
Big
Sky

D1532986

YA
SF

Big Big Sky

Kristyn Dunnion

Red Deer PRESS

OCEANSIDE PUBLIC LIBRARY
330 N. COAST HWY
OCEANSIDE, CA 92054

Copyright © 2008 Kristyn Dunnion
5 4 3 2 1

All rights reserved. No part of this publication may be reproduced, stored in a
retrieval system or transmitted, in any form or by any means, without the prior written
permission of Red Deer Press or, in case of photocopying or other reprographic copying,
a licence from Access Copyright (Canadian Copyright Licensing Agency),
1 Yonge Street, Suite 1900, Toronto, ON m5e 1e5, fax (416) 868-1621.

Published by
Red Deer Press
A Fitzhenry & Whiteside Company
1512, 1800–4 Street S.W.
Calgary, Alberta, Canada t2s 2s5
www.reddeerpress.com

Cover design and image by Jacquie Morris and Delta Embree, Liverpool, Nova Scotia
Text design by Tanya Montini
Author photo courtesy of Jen Black, www.jenblack.net
Printed and bound in Canada by Friesens for Red Deer Press

Financial support provided by the Canada Council, and the Government of Canada
through the Book Publishing Industry Development Program (BPIDP).

Canada Council   Conseil des Arts
for the Arts   du Canada

Library and Archives Canada Cataloguing in Publication
Dunnion, Kristyn, 1969-
Big big sky / Kristyn Dunnion.
ISBN 978-0-88995-404-5
I. Title.
PS8557.U552B53 2008   jC813'.6   C2008-900070-6

United States Cataloguing-in-Publication Data
Dunnion, Kristyn.
Big big sky / Kristyn Dunnion.
[240] p. : cm.

Summary: Rustle is a young scout of a tight-knit female warrior group,
but somehow the group is falling apart. The team finds their way in a totally
unfamiliar world where they must learn to survive—or not.

1. Fai

3 1232 00863 6807

AUG 1 8 2009

Dedicated to the pitbulls of Ontario
and in loving memory of
Mark N. Karbusicky
(1971-2007)

"And round about in reel and rout,
The death fires danced at night."
— Coleridge —

Book
1

Rustle: Convulsed!

Sometimes it's harder to kill than pod might think.

I crouch in the dark, staring into the manimal's shining eyes. It blinks right at me. It shakes in fear. Its thrumping furred chest quickens my own pulse. It licks its full lips and I feel the send. *Or do I?* It's not Loo, and it's blaaty not me. The thing wave-sends a sonic roll of pure emo: terror, disbelief, and a wee glimmer of hope. That's when I, like, completely lose it. I drop my crossbow, and the filthy thing scampers into the darkest corner of the cave. I freeze.

"Blaaty whafa, Rustle?!" It's Loo, yelling and pushing me forward. "Be fit!" she shouts, but there's no use.

Over there, somewhere, marked and quivering, the thing is waiting to die, and it's my turn and I'm, like, totally convulsed. Hundreds of kills with nary a winkle of glum glum, and now this. I weep quietly, while inside, the hunters' dread sickness paralyzes.

"She's—," I start to say, but Loo interrupts.

"*It.* It dies in the now. ScanMans' orders."

"It's wary scary Pod-like, Loo," I say. "I can't do it."

Loo snarls. She unsheathes my long knife, presses it into my hand, and hurls me into the corner, practically on top of the target.

Her. *It.* Panic-scent fills the cave but there's nowhere to run, so the thing just stays curled up. My visionquest goggles track her thermal map. With the hyperspectral drive, I can see her skeleton, her nerve weavings, and the layered muscle tissue, all just like our own. Rivers of blood pump through her, some to the heart center, some away. My knife hangs high above.

One Pod, she sends.

"Whafa are you?" I say.

But it's too late. Loo leaps forward. Loo's silver dagger is already dancing under the dirty chin, opening the neck to a bright hot rush that pours its way down her matted hair and over her furred fleshcore.

"She sends," I yell. "She Pod-sends!"

It's over in a milli. Loo sinks her teeth into the wound and claims the deathmaul spirit as her own. Her strong jaws mash the flesh while she drinks her fill. Later, she checks the corpse for weapons, for jewels, for hearing helpers, or mole droppings.

"In case it was a fakie plant," she says pointedly. "In case ScanMans were testing Allegiance and Obeyance." She doesn't find mics or cams, and absoblaaty no weapons. Only the shredded clothes on her back and one tarnished ring. Loo tries it on and tightens it around a slender finger. "My kill," she says, "my trophy."

I couldn't agree more.

Loo: Blood Smothered

"Bag it and tag it!" I toss the kill onto the floor of our shuttle. I'm bouncing, full-on revved with adrenaline. Since I scored, Rustle has to clean up. But she doesn't move. She slouches all glum glum in her Scout's chair.

"S'alright," says Solomon. "I'll get it." Solomon drags the body over to the storage area in the main hold. I hear her opening and slamming cubby doors, stowing it safely away before take off. I wipe the sticky blood from my face and neck with a wet towel and wash my stained hands in the sink.

"Nice work, Loo," says Shona. She's up front, finishing her Pod Leader report, texting Controls with my rating.

"Good one, huh?" I do my victory dance: fists up, pink hair swinging, bum shaking.

Shona interrupts. "So, like, whafa happened to Rustle?" Her eyes narrow. She's looking past me, back into the hold where Rustle is still slumped in a mopey pile, blanked.

I shrug. Like I'd nark my own unit, right?

Solomon calls out that she's ready. "Is Roku on board?"

"Yeah," croaks Roku as she jumps into the shuttle heavily. She slams the main door and secures the bolts. "Lockdown complete," she says, and then takes her seat at the shadowy back of the small craft. Rustle straightens up and belts herself in, too, right across from Roku.

Solomon slides in beside Shona to help steer the way with her Healer's gifts. And I plop in my Hunter's chair, the swiveling perch attached to our missile launcher and the magnifying scope. The shuttle rumbles into action. Engines fire themselves up; the control board flashes. Then we're up and out, speeding back to StarPod.

My new badge shines on my puffed-up chest. I swig Dreamy Drops and belt out cheersongs with the rest of the scouts. It's roasty warm in Canteena Time, and we Warriors fill the air with our jubilant voices. Dozens of units crowd the feed line, piling up hot plates of mash, and refilling mugs with foamy brew. A few others are also honored for their recent Kills. We get to wear the shiny pins all night while everypod shouts our praise. They'll give us regular badges that we can sew on our unis in a few days' time. Prolly we'll get a day off training, too. And in the meantime, we get extras of all the best feed there is on offer, and so, by default, do our Pod units.

An older Eighth Level Scout comes to our table and pats my shoulder. "Super fit," she says into my smiling face. "You're on my ScanMans' recommend list," and that swoons me even more. I can't wait to move up a rank and wear their solid black unis, instead of our lavender Seventh ones.

"Brag much, Loo?" Shona shovels piles of sweet root into her mouth.

"Don't even have to," I say cheerfully. "Everypod's too busy bragging about me." I punctuate that with a belch.

"Like, ewww?" says Shona.

"Like, you should be thanking me, since I'm the one who got us the top feed tonight, right?" I imitate her perpetual upward inflection. Shona glares but I don't care, Leader or not.

"Way to go, Loo," says Solomon in her low voice. "Thanks." She raises another full cup so Shona is obliged to cheers me again. *Snort snort.* Solomon tosses her dreads. She swallows half the mead.

Shona grimaces but joins in. "Here's to the others' leaving more feed for us." She toasts the two empty seats where our Scouts always sit. Roku claimed some type of illness and refused to feed. Rustle is outside, earning discipline for her mistake on Mission.

On cue, we all look out the glass window to the outer corridor. An Eighth Level Scout barks orders into Rustle's muddy face. She is paying, all right, forced to run short relay stints under the dripping rock fissures while the rest of us feed and drink. She jumps, dives, races. She re-loads her weapon and drops to the ground for more sweaty push-ups, no doubt. We can't see her when she's down on the ground, but I bet that's whafa doing. The black-clad Scout blows a whistle and Rustle jumps up, more ragged than before, and races the length of the hall again, more drips streaking the dirt on her frowny face.

Poor Rustle. I chug more mead. I wipe my chin with my sleeve. I take a nappy when nopod's looking and pile some protein pals in, add some sweetroot, then wrap it up. I tuck it in my pocket to give to her later.

Another cheersong bursts forth at the front of the room, and a new Dreamy Drops barrel rolls our way. I burp loudly and lift my glass. The same Eighth Level Scout fills it happily. Scouts shout and pound the tables, rattling the spoons and spilling their feed. I stand and raise my fist. I do my dance to thunderous applause, while Shona growls at my side, irritated that I'm in the spotlight, once again.

Who cares? I think. Then I drain the liquid from my victor's cup.

Rustle: Lonely Night

I squish through the mud and stand at attention forever, while the sadistic Eighth chugs a big mug of frosty mead. It smells so good. She wipes her mouth, and when her fusion friend sneaks some more drink out to her, she finally lets me go. I drag my sorry carcass down to travelshaft, away from the lusty Canteena Time shouts. I go straight back to our unit's lair, trembling with exhaustion.

Swoosh.

The port opens and I'm home alone. I cross the star-shaped chamber and stumble to my point. *I love you, cot,* I think, as I flop onto it. I am sapped: cold and lifeless and dirty to the core. I mute the volume on the giant monitor that takes up the whole ceiling center. It flickers its blue nonsense. Autotron updates race across in capital letters; images blink mercilessly. Heads talk; faces smile. To shut it off completely would be a kronking dream. To have stillness here, for once, would be divine.

I look around the four other points, each with a wee cot and storage trunk beneath. Each with a few shelves for precious belongings, and each decorated to perfectly reflect our individuality. Practically our mindcore prints, ya? Ever since we'd first core-fused as a unit, we'd lived here together. Now, after all that training, we're the top in our Level: the highest-ranking Seventh Level Assassins.

On my left is Solomon's point, painted red with pieces of treeskin and twiglets glued to the wall. She collects samples when we scout new territories. She binds them and dries them, and sometimes shares them around with the Healers in other training units, learning all kinds of secret uses for them. She also keeps pebbles and shining metals found tunneling during her free time.

Loo's Hunter tip is painted silver with pink sparklies, just like her hair. Her weapons rack perches above the cot with her fave knives, her long bo staff, tonfa, and nunchucks. Her crossbow hangs on the wall. A bar is suspended further along so she can do chin-ups whenever she's restless, which is often. Her point smells good, like her skin. Like candy and wee flowers, all crushed up together for a good snort. *Mmm.*

Next is Shona, Pod Leader, with her perfect regulation bunk reinforced for her broad frame. She has extra storage units for all her Leader blaat, I spoze. Other than that, her walls are bare. No images, no colors, no special things up on display. Wary weird, but then, that's Shona.

On my right, all the way full circle, is Roku's point. She built a top level above her cot. She hangs long fabric down to the lower level, for privacy, I spoze, although some pods find it a bit rude. Roku roosts in there most nights with hardly a wink of rest. She reads old handheld text copies from the Intelligard Center. Kronk knows whafa, exactly, but she is serious mindtuned, especially for a Scout. Roku has texts stacked on her shelves, around her cot, falling out of the bottom layer. A giant copy of our base mantra, the original command, hangs on her wall. Now, after all these years, I think it whenever I see her: a solid black background with the ominous orange eye in the middle. Spelled in large letters around the top of the eye is, *ONE POD*. In smaller, menacing font it says, *Until she may Decline, Deform, or Disobey.*

Back at my point, it's a complete mess. I'm buried alive by dirty laundry. I clutch my cloth foamie, the one thing I've had since I was small. Since before the Treason Times. Before I was Found and delivered to ScanMans, before I was trained and tuned and fused here at StarPod. I should clean up, but I've been so distracted with more important things. Like why I couldn't perform the kill today. Why I'm second-guessing everything, full-frontal paranoidal.

And I think on the deeper secret I have that grows bigger every day, threatening to destroy me: the poison that trickles through my veins, the convulsions that hit me with increasing regularity. My whole core betrays me, betrays our unit. *I'm Deforming!* I think in a panic, *and this growing Aberration is prolly killing me from the inside out.* I must tell the others before I become even more of a liability. *Shh,* I think. *Shh.* There's my pink feather, a love gift from Loo that calms me the way she often does. Now I touch it lightly on my face.

Swoosh.

The shadowy center of the floor spins open; the floorport rises up. The others are singing loudly off-key. Solomon hoists Loo up and dumps her on top of Shona. "Arg," they holler, laughing. They stop when they see me, lumped in my dark corner.

Shona hits the volume and our ceiling screen screeches back into effect. She gives me a dirty look, crosses her arms in front of her ample chest. "How are we spozed to hear ScanMan updates if you're, like, always muting it, Rustle?"

I shrug. Like I give a blaat. Like ScanMans would actually let us sit around missing out on some completely important event, just because our monitor volume was turned down.

"'Ssup," says Solomon, and I nod to her. Loo's silver stare rakes over me. She doesn't fuse-send like usual. I sigh. She's mad about my freak-out on Mission. My Kill Op disaster. They shuffle into their personal points, disrobing. They toss dirty unis into the bilge bag. I watch Loo strip out of her sweat-stained uni and slip into a fluffy robe. That precious milli in between, when she is full-frontal naked, is the one that sets me quivering. *Twitchy fit.* Even if she hates me now, even if she's, like, completely blanked to me, I love her muscular core, her long limbs. Even more, I love to rememory the way they crush me to her in fusion.

Loo scowls like she is reading me—she prolly is!—and she turns away, tightening the belt on her robe. She stalks back to floorport, and—**swoosh**—she's gone, down to the showers to share her nakedness with all those other soapy pods.

"Still blanked?" says Solomon gently. Her voice soothes my ruffled self.

"Full-frontal," I say, grim meeky.

"She'll get over it."

I smile, grateful for her kindness.

"Ha, wish much?" Shona's shrill notes pierce my hopeful bubble. "But realistically, Rustle, you're, like, out-synched. The least you can do is clean up your mess and get adjusted. And, like, maybe bathe?"

"Shut it, Shona," I growl. But when nopod's looking, I sniff under my muddy arms and reel back with the awful truth. *I stink!* I do need to shower, but how can I without stripping down in front of the others? I can't let them see me, see the strange new changes that have been rippling through my core.

Solomon swings her long dreadlocks up and ties them with a scarf. She is the tallest, and even more imposing now that her snaky hair is piled up high. She pulls a big towel around her brown shoulders and heads to the floorport.

She smiles at me again. "Coming?"

"Naw," I say. I decide to creep down alone after they drop.

"Wait, Solomon," says Shona. She quickly wraps her blue self in an ugly regulation robe and hobbles after Solomon, who fuse-sends warmth into the chamber before disappearing, **swoosh.**

It's only then I wonder: *Where the blaat is Roku?*

I lie blanked when the others return, filling StarPod with their fruity cleanness and their good humor. They crawl into their cots and, one by one, extinguish the light in each point. Then the Sleep drops start. Shona sucks the amber liquid slowly into her mouth. She tries to outlast the rest but falls quickly. Solomon slams it into her dark muscled arm after she ties it off. And Loo. *Oh, Loo.* Most nights she'd crawl in with me for some suckly fusion, for mindaltering wrestles, and often we'd drop together in the same instant, in the same wee cot. But not tonight. Now the needle glints at me when she bangs it fast fast and lonely over yonder.

Still no Roku.

I mute the volume as soon as they're down. It's as if I can breathe properly again; I can even *think,* maybe. I gather my own blaat and creep to floorport. **Swoosh.** Then I'm inside travelshaft, churning down to the right stop. When the door slides open, the hot steam from the long line of shower stalls hits my skin, fills my happy lungs. Water pools in places on the floor; it gurgles down the center drain. Soiled towels clump wetly on the tiles. The cams are fogged, as is the long wall of mirrors, thank Kronk, so I don't have to see myself reflected there in all my Deformed glory. I scuttle to the farthest stall and turn on the taps. Hot water revives me. Nary a strong blast left, but enough to chase the dirt from my hide, enough to send the filth flying. Pure soapy goodness coats my skin. I work the bubbles through my thick, purple hair before rinsing it away, down the metal drain. I shut the taps off. I'm naked, standing in front of the mirror. As the steam dissipates, I can't help but notice the thickening muscles in my shoulders, my arms, my thighs. My hair and skin suck up the water droplets so that I need nary a towel to dry myself. The wetness brings my skin to life, sets my long hairs twitching, and soothes my swollen lips, my lidless eyes. The long trails on the backs of my legs and arms, like hair but also not like hair, they thrill to the watery rush. So do my strong hands with their curious webbing between the fingers, so different from the others in unit. Although I wasn't hatched with them, these webbed parts have been my own for almost as long.

Kronk.

I stare-send into the clearing mirror before me. It's obvious that I'm sick, that I'm Deforming in a completely convulsive trip. *Molecular mutiny!* My chest aches and I touch myself where full gynolumps—like the others have—used to gently swing. I now have tightly packed muscles instead. More muscles line my aching bellyparts and lower, down to the feverish gynos below. I can hardly bring myself to look at their strangeness, at the skin grown recently different: skin that tingles to every touch, jumping to even the slightest breeze that blows past. Before, all was tucked away and cupped with a plump mound of flesh. Now these smallest and most private of parts seem to be swelling, outgrowing their place, no longer hidden but almost *spilling outside.* Wary weepy, it makes me. And angry, too. I lean toward the great mirror and hate it; I strike it with my fist. *Ow.* A cold feeling settles into my throat—it's fear that chills me so.

I wrap my Aberrant self tightly in my robe and run back to travelshaft, which takes me straight to our floorport. It's all quiet, dark except for the blue light flickering overhead. Shona snores but nopod else stirs. I pull on some nightclothes. I lay there, heart thrumping, mindcore racing; I'm shaking in my cot.

"Rustle?"

"Roku?" I whisper, although the others can't even hear a cot crash when they're nuzzling the foam. Roku moves toward me in the dark. She sits heavily on the end of my cot. Her frame, formerly the slightest of our unit, seems bulky. I wonder what she's wearing, what in Kronk's name she's got going on to make her feel so—so big. There is a faint light coming from the bottom of her cot where the long drapes are opened a bit. There's the blue light overhead, too. But it's still so dark I can't see much of her, nary a feature but the whites of her eyes when they roll back and forth over me, probing. She smells funny. Whiffy. Not like Roku.

"Not dropping?" she says in a raspy voice.

"Naw," I say. I try to make it sound casual, like I've got better things to do. Truth is, I can quadrenkle the drops but still the yellow liquid doesn't work anymore, doesn't send me anywhere close to Sleep. Not since the changes started chugging along my genestrands, rattling my nerves and bursting up through my core.

"Are you alright?" I say. "You sound sick."

She shakes her head, no. **Not sick,** she sends, no longer using her voice. **I'm getting better. Like you, too, I think.**

"Whafa?" I keep mouth-speaking, trying to maintain that distance that evaporates when Pods mind-send. Roku is freaking me and I fear her intimacy, now that I have so much to hide. "Where did you go after Mission?"

Why? Roku leans closer. Her breathing sounds ragged.

"You're always disappearing lately," I say. For weeks, she'd been crawling into our lair long after lights out, after the others had dropped, while I lay wide-eyed, faking my own rest. No drops for her either, I noticed. No dreamyweaves, no snores.

I've been learning, she sends. **Finding answers. And I've been growing stronger every day with new powers. Just like you, Rustle.**

But I'm getting weaker, I think. Before I can say a word, Roku begins wave-sending all kinds of weirdness. Like, I can feel her mental *self* pressing into my mindcore.

"Stop it, Roku," I hiss. "Whafa doing?" It's some strange intrusion, completely uninvited, and not at all twitchy–fit, like when I fuse with Loo.

Mindsweep. She's sending like before, but it's as if her words are my own thoughts. Like the words are deep inside my mindcore, but it's her raspy voice that planted them there.

Convulsed!

I jump away—as if that would help—and make some squawking noise. "Get out of my mindcore, Roku," I cry. "Get out of me!"

"Sorry, Rustle," she croaks. "Shh, shh." Still she doesn't stop this mental invasion. It fills me: whirling, clicking numbers, whooshing patterns of programming, planted deep in my barren soil by Roku's cold, stark mind fingers. I rub my head vigorously, uselessly, trying to get rid of those ghostly codes. I'm paralyzed while she keeps pressing inward, filling my mind with her contraband download.

"For Kronk's sake," I say when she finishes. I switch from mouthspeach to mindtalking, to keep safe from the intermittent clicks of the hearing helpers planted around our cabin. I send, **That's, like, Aberrant enough to get us** *both* **Deplugged, so cut it out.**

"Rustle," she says, "Listen." She sends the rest. **I need you to keep that safe for me, that program.**

"Blaaty whafa?" I don't get it.

It's about our new powers, Rustle, she sends. **It's about how we can reprogram podselves, for a whole new way of living. I need to hide it safe from them.**

Full-frontal paranoidal!

"Safe from who?" I ask. "How can it be safe in there?"

From ScanMans, from the Pod Leaders. Nopod will prolly think to look there, she sends.

This must be some kind of joke, so I try to laugh, but it's not actually that funny. Kronk knows I don't have the biggest intelligard model around, but it still hurts to hear that sort of thing, ya? Like, *here's a blaaty secret that nopod must know, so we'll just hide it in wee Rustle's meek mindcore where nopod would ever think to peek.* Then I think, *Aha! I may be stupid, but not* **that** *stupid.* I'll not fall for that one coz spozing it's all a trick for her to, like, scan my Deformity so she can nark me to ScanMans, right? A blaaty trap, whafa.

Roku tries to calm me down. She knows I'm right convulsed. Things are not going the way she'd like them to. She's good, though, with all her quiet murmurs, her sends; she almost has me convinced that somepod *is* after her, like she claims. She asks me taboo questions. She sends me all her bizarre thoughts. Like: **ScanMans are exterminating us, Rustle. Come away with me before it's too late.**

"No, Roku," I say. "It's so unlike you to be all weird and that, but really, I'm, like, completely blanked."

She prolly thinks she's found me out but I'm not budging. And that's it. I stop talking. I refuse her sends. I'm sealed up in my own mental space, and none of her words can hit me, poisoned darts that they are.

Finally, she sighs loudly. She gets off my cot and rummages around in her point. She snaps off her light and lifts a pack onto her back. She stands, facing me silently, her dark shadow taller than it should be, wider than it's ever been, her features shadowed in obscurity. She doesn't speak. **One Pod,** she sends. Then she leaves.

Swoosh.

Then, nothing. All night, while the others sigh and wriggle, I wait for the big bust. I wait for ScanMans to arrive with Eighth Level Scouts to drag me from my cot, screaming. I wait for the interrogation, the torture, maybe even a full-frontal old-fashioned Send Down. A chronic Deplugging. *Could I leave like Roku? Might I creep the long underground hallways and find some forgotten place to hide?* I think of all the clicking, whirling cams, the screens and monitors, the hidden mics tracking our movements when we least suspect it—the never knowing when or if they're watching. And I surrender to my own inevitable defeat. A tear rolls down my sorry cheek as I flashback to the Treason Times. I rememory all those twisted cores, those poor broken specimens struggling, impaled on their death sticks, waiting for the pain to end. Our ancestors, the human mothers who bore us, ridiculed 'til the very last milli and Beyond. That'll be me soon. *Sniff.*

Then I rememory Loo, and that stops my heart. That I should be Deplugged and never again be hers. That she might never make up with me, that I might go forever unforgiven—that sends me howling into my pillow, weeping for shame. And, that afterwards, I'd also be completely erased and never thought on again, not even by my own unit, my only kin. That breaks me. Like, completely.

Loo: Mock Evac

I wakey fit and fine. The shiny victor's pin smiles at me from the wall above my head, where I stuck it last night before I dropped. I roll over, looking for Rustle, but she's not there. *Oh yeah,* I think, *I'm right mad at her.* I almost forgot! But it's hard to stay mad when I'm so proud of my pin. Another whole day waits—training and target practice, big feeds in Canteena Time, and maybe a cheersong competition in the Grand Hall tonight, if we're dandy good, right?

"It's about time you got up." Shona's grating voice startles me.

I sit up tall and rub my eyes. She points to the autotron update, which blinks and bellows: *…one bag only. Prepare for Mock Evacuation. Warrior Scouts permitted one bag only.*

My balloon of happy thoughts pops. Mock Evac is long, tedious, and boring. I'd rather train hard and roll in the mud as per usual. Besides, Shona kronking irks my core.

"Guess we won't have time to pat your back again at First Feed," Shona says cheerfully. "Better get ready. You, too, Rustle." She says this while packing her things, methodically wrapping items, labeling them, and stowing them safely in her survival bag.

Rustle groans unintelligibly. She's flopped on her cot drinking Fizzy Drop. "What the blaat fits in one bag, anyways?" she says.

Then she mutes the overhead screen with our remote. Rustle is full-on tweaking, if you ask me.

Shona says, "Rustle, you should really—"

"Shut it!" she yells. Rustle throws her Fizzy Drop can at the monitor's sensor pad. Angry pink bubbles foam over the keys. They sizzle. The giant ceiling screen wilts; the blue lights flicker—it disappears. It's still.

Rustle blaaty turned it off! Our chamber is suddenly larger and lighter, less dense without the constant droning and overhead blinking.

"That's, like, pretty extreme?" says Shona, licking her lips nervously.

"I guess, like, I'm feeling pretty extreme?" says Rustle, imitating her perfectly.

Nopod's ever turned it completely off, I think. I look around nervously for Roku or Solomon, somepod with better sense who can calm Rustle, before ScanMans order an Eighth Level unit over to rearrange our wiring.

Shona says, "Great. So now we're, like, disconnect?" She drops the pack she's holding. **Plonk.**

Rustle says, "I'm sick of training, sick of Mock Evacs. I don't want any more autotron updates, and I hate the Crusades!"

"We need to keep the monitor on, Rustle, for, like, future updates?" Shona clomps over and stands under the blank ceiling screen. She reactivates it. She mops up the sticky liquid spill. She drops the Fizzy Drops can down the reconfiguration chute. Whirling, clicking noises chide us for shutting it down. Words spell themselves across the screen. An angry red light glows at the top left corner. Somepod in Controls is scanning our system.

Do not disconnect your monitors. Prepare for Mock Evacuation.

I clear my throat loudly. Rustle looks at me for the first time today. "So now they're tracking us," I say. "Great."

Rustle starts to tremble.

"Whafa wrong?" I say it a bit meanly, since I'm still cross about the Kill Op disaster yesterday. But I'm also worried. Something is seriously wrong.

Rustle shrugs.

Shona resumes her packing. "This has canteen and glowball attachments on it, right?" she says.

Numbing my mindcore.

"You can clip a pullout sleep mat here. It's like ScanMans knew we'd need these exactly for Evacs?" She waves the yellow sleep mat toward Rustle. She looks flushed with the effort of getting ready, I spoze, but she's also excited. She's already wearing her uni, and it's a snug fit. Two lavender mountains loom above Rustle's frowny face.

Wary scary.

"You two really should get going," she says.

"And you really should get a minimizer, Shona. Are those things getting their own shuttle, or what?" Rustle snorts and rolls over, ignoring her.

"Shut it?!"

I laugh out loud. Rustle is bramy hilarious, even if I am mad at her.

Shona huffs loudly and gets back to her preparations. I jump out of my cot and pull on my cleanest uni. I can feel Rustle peeping over at me, at my nudeness, and I send a sharp message: **Zlota!** Even with my back to her, I can feel the sad, sorry waves, wiffling around her dejected core. I open the packet I brought back for Rustle from Canteena Time last night. I nibble a piece of the freshroot.

Shona hums some loser bopcore hit from the noventas. She dusts her lightweight precision-tool kit, then packs it. She lays water-resistant tarps, ropes, pulleys, and a glowball all out on the floor by her cot. She shakes out large hemp-blend briefs, snaps them in the air, and folds them.

"I hate that song," I say, but she keeps at it, cheerfully dementoid, humming off-key and busying herself with the neat piles she's making. Everything always seems so clear to her. Everything always has its own place.

Rustle, as if to act on my own private thoughts, whips a rolled-up dirty sock at her head.

"Bramy!" Shona's nostrils flare with annoyance, and that makes me laugh even harder. "Departure's in, like, now and you've got a mess to go through, if you don't mind me saying." She resumes humming, but it sounds a bit forced.

"Loo," pleads Rustle, before the smile leaves my face. "Come."

Why not? I think. She is so funny, after all. I dive onto her cot playfully. I offer her a bite of the sweet orange stump I've been gnawing. She takes it in her mouth gently, and I bite her arm instead. Her skin is soft over rippling muscles. She must have showered late last night. Soapy smells linger in her sheets. I lick her arm where the small, round marks from my teeth appear in sharp detail.

"Don't be mad at me." Rustle sounds all leaky emo. She's still chewing the same orange mouthful slowly.

"I'm not. Not any more, see?" And I kiss her, soft and deep, like I mean it. The sticky suction of her tongue tickles the roof of my mouth.

"Why not blanked still?" she says quietly.

I say, "You've suffered enough. I'm sure you learned your lesson. Plus, I dreamed wary well last night but I missed you." I squirm close and wrap my arms around her. Oh. She's warm and clean, finally, and I've missed her so much.

"I missed smelling you," she says into my tickly hearhole. Rustle nuzzles my pink curls and sniffs the pretty stuff I drip into my hair to make it radiate. "Smells like those hard pink candies with the goopy insides from when I was small," she says and I nod.

I also rememory those treats, suddenly, though I might not

have if she had never mentioned them. I close my eyes and I can almost feel one in my mouth, the sugary crunch when I bit down, and the soft perfumed hand that gave it to me. I roll on top of Rustle, kissing and touching, but she pushes me away. I sit up.

"We should get ready, ya?" she says.

I shrug. "It's only Mock. Nothing chronic." We'd been doing those since we were hatchlings. I straddle Rustle and pin her arms above her head. She resists, but even with all these new muscles of hers, she's still weak to me. My other hand moves down the length of her core but she twists her lower half away from me. I growl softly.

Please don't, she sends. She waits. Her eyes move from mine up to the overhead screen, to the tracking movements of the infrared lights, to the cams, the hearing helpers sprinkled throughout our lair. My eyes follow hers. Only Kronk knows if they're actually watching us, or if we're only mindfreaked into believing it so as to behave better when we're on our own.

But *I get it,* I think. Something is going on with Rustle and she can't let anyone else know.

"Whafa—"

"Shh," she says.

She shakes her hands loose from my hold and grips me about the waist. She settles me square onto her torso and I feel it right away. I wonder: *Whafa in Kronk's name?* She looks down to her own bellyparts, whafa cradled underneath me, and the frightened look on her lovely face saddens me. Some new weirdness lumping up from her gynos—it's unmistakable, right? I can't hide the surprise on my face: it's reflected in her shining eyes. I try to pull back the sheets, to tear down her flimsy sleep clothes and have a look at this strange thing, but she grips my wrists hard and shakes her head, *No.*

Whafa this? I send silently. If it is a Deformity, it feels pleasant enough. I rock forward slightly and the thing gets even harder beneath me. Her mouth falls slack, as though from pleasure waves.

I don't know, she finally sends back. **Wary scary, ya?**

Shona clears her throat and shrilly says, "Like, you two better cut it out. This is not the time or place for fusion."

"Right," says Rustle. "We better get ready." She pushes me to the edge of her cot, but the worry doesn't leave her eyes. I blink, speechless for once.

"Seriously," says Shona.

Rustle smiles that wide phony smile she uses when she is trying to be brave. She says loudly, "Well, Loo, I believe we're on the verge of mock planetary exile. And I've, like, nothing at all to wear."

"Zlota!" I laugh and skip back over to my own cot. I chuck stuff into my hand-decorated metal kit, but I can't meet her eyes again.

You won't nark me, Loo. Will you? Rustle sends this to me rather than mouth-speaks it so that Shona can't hear.

And I honestly wonder. *Would I, in spite of our synch?* My belly-parts tighten. For deep down, I know that it doesn't really matter. Either way, it's only a matter of time before some other pod discovers Rustle's secret.

Rustle: Plan B

"Where the blaat are Solomon and Roku?" says Loo. She's over at her cot, packing quickly. She's talking to Shona, not me. It's the first thing she's said since feeling up my lumpy self. Since I showed her part of my secret.

"Haven't seen Roku since yesterday's Mission. You?" Shona peers sharply, her eyes narrowing at me.

I shake my head no. Still too choked up to make sounds with this scratchy throat of mine. I think on my strange meeting with Roku last night, but I decide then and there not to mention it.

"She'll prolly meet us at the shuttle," says Loo.

"And Solomon's still out tunneling," says Shona. "She should be back by now."

But it's like Solomon is more podself, picking through crumbly fissures in those dark, underground, winding trails than she is here with us in training. Somehow, and it doesn't seem right, but when we blast off on Mission, poor Solomon gets all long-faced and gray, like she's afraid she'll never land back into these drafty shifting holes, and, although I'm not a suck, I feel for her.

A **bleep bleep bleep** summons Shona. She lunges to the manual-punch handset. She peers around to make sure we're not scenting her out. She blanks a wall, a telepathic block, then taps in her secret special Pod Leader code. Loo and I grin snaky. *Shona is chronic paranoidal!* She puffs her lavender chest higher and juts her chin forward whenever she scores the miniman scoop.

Meanwhile, now that things are under control in the deformed frontals department, I'm up and about. No way of avoiding the blaating Evac, so here I am, fluffing through my mess and stuffing my pack. I shove in a shiny can of Fizzy Drop, a couple of beat mags, and some gaming cartridges for if we get bored waiting our turn to dock back in when the whole procedure's done.

Swoosh.

The floorport slides open and Solomon's dreads elevate into view. "'Ssup?" She nods to the three of us.

"About time," says Loo.

Solomon hugs a rubberized sack filled with sand and rock specimens. She carries it over to her star point and gently sets it down beside her growing collection of labeled samples. Then she peels out of her filthy crawling gear, balls it up, and fires it into the bilge corner. She zips on a slightly cleaner uni. Then she dumps Mock Evac stuff in her survival pack.

Shona is ready first. I'm crouched behind my cot, trying to slip into my blaaty zlotan uni without anyone looking my way, when

Shona tightens the straps on her pack and announces it's time. "We've got less than three millis, unit. Solomon, do you, like, need any help with anything?"

Loo stifles another snort and I raise my eyebrow, but Solomon doesn't even blink. "Naw, Shona. I'm fit." She hoists up her bag.

Shona clears her throat. "Good. Change in plans, unit. Drop your survival packs, and unload your weapons. You won't be needing them. We're going straight to GeneScan."

"GeneScan?!" My mouth dries out and my bowels cramp. Roku's narked me after all, I think. *No wonder she's hiding.*

Loo says, "Yeah, that's chronic. Didn't we just Scan a few weeks ago?" Loo steps in front of me, blocking my pheromone waves from Shona.

"Like, that's our updated pre-boarding order. Some Hybrid scaled the Deformity Zone, but they're not saying who. What's wrong, Loo? Anything I should know about?" Shona steps closer and her mouth drops open slightly. She takes quick, shallow breaths and sniffs the air. She's blaaty panting, senses carnage already. My mindcore fritzes. "We wouldn't want you to be deep-scanned and, like, permanently Deplugged?"

Loo hisses, "You get up in my face and I'll zlotan claw you full-frontal." Her anger fills the room, masking my panic-scent.

Nopod moves for a milli. Solomon, ever the peacemaker, says, "Nopod's gene deficient in our unit, Shona. We're all Level One Heterosis." She claps them both lightly on the back, shaking away the tension. But I feel her eyes rest longer on me, probing.

I broadcast neutral waves as we drop our packs and stand at attention on floorport. Solomon touches my hand lightly but I refuse to look at her. Loo leans into me, sending warmth and fusion, and, although it won't blaaty save me, it does make me feel a bite better.

Shona, still with her survival bag strapped to her shoulders, taps in our code, and the engine whirls into motion. There's the **Swoosh,** and we descend, feigning confidence and steeling ourselves for the Gene Trial ahead. We stand tall, muscular, highly schooled in the Military Defense Arts, survivalists every one.

But none so terrified as me.

Loo: Mantra

Inside shiny travelshaft, we stamp and stare and twitch. We speed along together: Solomon, Shona, Rustle, and me. We're breathing, swallowing. It's hot with tension. I blank to Rustle's badness, to her frowny face. I flex my strong muscles. I shake my arms out long and loose. I shake Rustle off in the same milli.

One Pod. The commandment monitor flashes Rules and Regs over and over, one blink at a time. The repetition quiets me, somehow, helps me focus.

Usually I love speed rushing my veins, the blue screen flickering on my skin, and the metal grated walls. I still rememory my first trip ever, rememory thinking, *Chronic fit!* No more trekking along the dark earthen tunnels like the low-grade hybrids, those disposable foot soldiers. No creeping about like slavey dronebeets in the stone-lined shafts and vent trails. But today there's no victory in it. It's more like we're trapped and summoned. Travelshaft carries us direct from our own floorport, down, down, and away. Past the shuttle loading dock, down to the depths of GeneScan. Right next to Living Lab.

One Pod. That flash again.

It pains me to feel Rustle's hackles rising, all her nervy woffles. Her eyes roll toward me. I look away. I read the autotron text instead. There's the GeneScan update—Deformed Warrior warnings with lots of exclamation marks. Then there are blinks about a new flavor of Fizzy Drop, our fave iced protein drink that increases nerve-receptor reaction time. *Yum.* Then back to our base mantra.

One Pod.

We are far from One in the now. First, like, Roku is not even here. Second, Rustle is a blaaty wreck, and Shona is a high-strung, accusing mess. Solomon is fit and so am I, mostly. We four are more like a manimal, but one that would gladly chew off its own leg to avoid capture or contamination. I stamp my thermal barbarian boots, feel the pulse and grind of the travelshaft move through me.

Living Lab. It still scares the bramy wire out of me. It's the ultimate, unimaginable threat, looming since our small times. *Be good, or else? Off to Living Lab with you!* Roku says we're over-programmed, well-behaved tools, but I know lots of gynotype who were sent there. And nopod ever came back.

Let's run, sends Rustle.

"Where?" I hiss softly. It's a risk to send in such tight quarters, as the others can prolly feel it. I scan the sealed air-pressure-controlled cabin of travelshaft: stainless-steel walls, bolted floor panels, and the impressive dome roof. We've never had cause to break through it before, and even if we could, there'd be millimiles of inlaid tracking to climb back along. Prolly we'd be instantly flattened by other units' travelshaft cabins, hurtling along the passageways over to GeneScan.

Autotron texts our arrival. Rustle shakes. I wave-send confidence.

Swoosh.

Our door opens to brightly lit confusion in the cavernous stadium. Sirens slice through all the competing noises. Autotrons flash text instructions to Pod Leaders from every angle. Shona preens, revving into gear. She signals us to prep. We'll run in formation around the stadium to Basic ThermScan, as usual. ScanMans sit up above, watching us from behind tinted bullet-proof windows. A helmeted line of Eights fence off the main exit from the stadium. They look so much bigger than us, though they're only a bite older—so anonymous and powerful in their slick black unis. *I can't wait to be one!* The rest of us lower-level scout units have to move into the more invasive levels of genetic cellular testing, each grueling procedure followed by verification or re-routing. Verified pods keep moving onward. Re-routed pods get detained and removaled. And then, Kronk knows whafa.

Rustle wobbles weak beside me. I wonder how far we'll get before they detect her secret. *Whafa become of her?* It's not like we're disposable. Not after all the years of training, all the programming and the gene-pool tweaking we get. We're fully expensive to make and maintain, so ScanMans don't like to Deplug unless it's absoblaaty necessary, right? In Deplugging, all rememories are wiped clean from the rest of the unit; pod's artifacts are all destroyed. It's like pod was never even hatched in the first place.

Oh, Rustle. I touch her arm gently.

The autotron signals us to begin. Red letters spell out our command, but Shona hesitates. Her flank trembles. Roku's not here to meet us. Roku's never late.

Our autotron letters blink more quickly. Shona scans left to right and back again. She almost growls as she searches for Roku in the surrounding chaos. There's the angry red eye monitoring our Pod now, and a new siren bursts forth directly above us. I push Shona. We trot forward, then to our right, along the far wall of the stadium. A powerful spotlight follows us, illuminating our movements, heating us up fast, keeping us visible for ScanMans.

"So much for flying under the radar," I say, gritting my teeth.

Rustle is fully overnerved. When we tight-turn to the right, I catch a glimpse of her. Sweat glistens along the scar line on the shaved part of her head. We run through our paces in tight formation, but it's weird with no Roku. I'm supposed to be able to lift my right arm and reach it out toward the tips of Roku's left fingers, more or less. We are meant to run parallel, like Solomon and Rustle in back. Shona's boobs always lead. At least, that's what Rustle says.

We approach Basic ThermScan. Hyperspectral rays sweep over us, head to foot. We salute the omnipresent ScanMans, wherever they are up in the tinted rooms that overlook the stadium. We wait for more autotron orders.

Entry denied. Incomplete unit.

This has never happened in all our years of training. Shona signals us to repeat. So we trot around in a tight, dancing circle and swivel back up to ThermScan. We salute.

Invalid unit. Entry denied.

Scouts from other units are starting to really notice us now. Whispers ripple from the ones nearest us. Shona's head starts to shake, light and quick—her almost imperceptible nervous tick. She's convulsed. Shona's never had a single word of conduct analysis in her entire training, and now it's like she's targeted as Leader of some Aberrant Pod, or something. If we weren't on the verge of, like, total extinction, Rustle and I'd be loving this. *Full-frontal ironical!*

"Run for it now?" Rustle says, loud and clear.

I groan. At this rate, we'll all be tossed up for Deplugging.

"Be fit," says Solomon.

I normalize with Solomon and send calming waves to my unit. It helps block out all the hostile stares from our so-called sistren, all our rivals in Seventh, who would love to see us take a fall right about now.

Rustle, Solomon, and I step in time. But Shona's leg is full-on jigging and she's growling again. She emits panic-scent before shaking her head back and howling. Eighth Level Scouts respond on signal; they hoist their weapons in one choreographed arc and stamp their terrifying boots. They quickly file toward us, marching in time with the pulse that pounds in my own veins.

"Get blaaty fit, Shona!" I say. But no.

Solomon, Rustle, and I regulate. We mask our fear and disjunct from Shona in the same milli. I fuse-send to Solomon and Rustle, strengthening our sonar bond. We stand tall. *We are settlement warriors.*

A metal cage drops over us with a loud clang. The black-clad Scouts surround us completely. Full-on profesh, they are, and I'd give anything to be in their fearless line-up rather than in our mess of a disastrous unit. They silently secure the thing, and that's it. We're in lockdown. They don't speak or text. They don't even really look at us. It's over in a milli.

Shona whines through the bars. She pleads with the nearest Scout, reaches through, and gets ShockMauled back into place. She falls to the ground, clutching her wounded arm. I scent burnt flesh.

They get to carry ShockMaulers!

Black-clad Scouts jog along, pulling us in the cage. They keep the other Warriors back, and it's a blaaty good thing, too, as there'd be a kronking riot, otherwise. The lower-level Scouts look frightened by this upheaval—poor weenies—but our rivals in Seventh are licking it up. They shake their heads and chirp at us; wail as though we're contaminants or Aberrant low-grades. Some spit clear into the cage. But we are blanked to them. Solomon, Rustle, and I hold hands and high-step in place as the cage moves forward. Shona rolls in pain at our feet. We mantra solid and grow stronger, storing up energy for whatever lies ahead.

We will need it.

We are heading straight for Living Lab.

"Blaaty Kronk," I say to nopod.

Solomon, Rustle, Shona, and I are forgotten for the milli. Still trapped in the metal cage with no way to escape, but ignored, at least. Our cage is parked in the Grand Hall, the mammoth cavern right in front of Living Lab. Where we usually meet for updates before major Ops; where we do some of our regular training; and where we have our cheersong competitions. It's also where we get parceled off once in a long while, when there's a new flick to feed us on the big big monitor. Only if we've been very good, right?

Shona lies in a useless, blubbery pile on the cage floor. *Wahhh.* The older Scouts scurry around, deactivating alarms, unfastening giant pins on the reinforced metal wallport before us.

They get to do so much more, I think. *Blaaty unfair.* "I better not be getting demoted," I say to Rustle and Solomon. "I better be getting to Eighth, or else."

"Check the wallport," says Solomon.

She and I scan, but it's, like, completely solid. There's no way we could ever break it down, no sign of weakness from this side. Once we're locked in, there'll be no hope. I crave my weapons stash, my faves back in our lair, the rest all locked on board the shuttle, whafa spozly waiting for Mock Evac. I keen and call to them now, to no avail. All I have is one wee slingshot at my hip.

I say, "For serious. This is not happening, unit. We are so not going in there, right?" I swallow hard. Nopod who goes into Living Lab ever comes out. Not in one piece, anyway.

Then Solomon says, "Maybe it's not the end. Maybe other things are going on, like Roku says."

"Like blaaty whafa?" I say. "Think we're getting medallions? Maybe a set of hand-husbands for our trouble?" I stare at Rustle. I fuse her core-deep, but if her secret keeps me from advancing in the Warrior levels, I don't know whafa I'd do.

Rustle clears her crackly throat. "Well, Roku would know, since she is prolly full-on narking the rest of us out right now." She looks about wildly when nopod agrees.

Solomon says, "Huh?"

"Where else do you spoze she is?" Rustle looks at me frantically, as if I'd back up any random accusation she flipped out of her mouth.

"We don't know where Roku is," I say in a warning voice. "No point mutinizing everypod."

The big scouts stamp and stamp. They pick it up a notch, surround our cage again, and prepare for some new order.

"Shona," says Rustle.

Shona is still a pile of flesh in a soiled uni. I nudge her with my boot. "Get fit," I say. "Full-frontal." I kick her harder. She ignores me so I text-send, **Urgent,** exactly like her fave bureaucratic memos, the kind ScanMans send around to all the Leaders. She opens her eyes, at least. **Get Up. On Boots,** I command. She looks confused, so I do it with more Authority. Of course, it works! Shona stands tall but in the altogether wrong spot. I push her into formation and notice the ugly wound on her arm. The flesh is blackened where the uni burned clear away. In the center of the angry gash there are balled-up bits of melted uni mixed into the bubbling layers of skin.

"Poor Shona," says Rustle. Prolly the first time anypod ever felt sorry for her.

I step into formation with Solomon. Rustle steps, too. Shona blanks, but we feel her pain rolling underneath. I am pure battle-fierce, wave-sending for Roku in sonic distress. She could help us, right? Solomon joins in, exponentially increasing our range.

Roku!

We funnel energy into surging waves, build intensity; the older Scouts shake with it. Blaaty right we'll give them a run for it. Scouts nearest the cage fall back. Pulleys that hang loose by the giant wallport start vibrating, then swinging. A rumble echoes in the cavernous Great Hall.

ROKU!

Rustle joins in, finally, fuelling our wave with some unexplained over-emo, some angry-hurt waves. But at least she's helping. The cage rattles dangerously. Scouts scramble closer, waving their butchering ShockMaulers and, **blink!** We stop. Solomon, Rustle, and I stare ferociously. Inside, I'm still crying that *they* get to use Electortures while we do not. Solomon makes a sonic-wave barrier inside our cage in case they shoot voltage between the bars. But the Scouts put down their pretty weapons. They back away. Instead, a sudden blast of cold air pours into our cage. Our breaths come out in clouds. Sharp, frozen stings in the eyes and nose tell me: *IcyFreeze.*

We're blaaty useless and done for!

And that's when we hear the sickening scrape, the big big screech of metal on metal. We clutch our hearholes with freezing hands as best we can. Living Lab's giant wallport is opening right before us.

IcyFreeze.

Fleshcore frozen but mindcore full alert. I struggle to breathe, to gain control of my joints, to move appendages. My blood pumps slow slow but strong. I hear it loud inside me. I'm bramy wired from the IcyFreeze dose, but dandystill admire the weapon, right? Originally it was developed for use against electrolls, but who knew they liked subtherm? Now we use it against each other. *Full-frontal ironical!*

In Level Five, we had wee training doses to play with. We got to fire on dronebeets, huddled up and quivery, all winging and weepy. Set them up, knock them down. Then we shot podselves with the leftovers for fun, right? Today, they are not blaating around with teeny weenies. They have these meg pellets the size of our fists. They completely kronked our militia unit right up. Completely! I wonder about long-term side effects and make mental to ask Roku. If we ever see her again. That's just the kind of thing Roku rememories. Random facts, stats, quotations, lectures: Roku has chronic sharp mindcore. A full-frontal think tank!

One Scout lies broken on the cold ground, accidentally frozen in the blast. She doesn't move, not a twitter. Two others carry her away. The Eights still preside over us. ScanMans, I note, haven't so much as made an appearance yet, but they like the elders to do their dirty work. We get carted in, cage and all. Scouts scurry around like slavey dronebeets. They scrabble at a hidden hard drive. They fire it up and one—clearly a Leader—texts Controls. Then she hides the contraption away again and marches most of the Scouts back outside to the Great Hall. Their heavy boot steps echo off the stone floors and up around the high, vaulted ceiling of Living Lab. Four stand guard inside while the wallport closes behind the others, slow slow and soundful.

I start to thaw. Ice sticks hang from our cage bars. They drip and melt. My skin burns as it therm adjusts. As soon as I can lift my frozen boots from the platform, I shuffle closer to the others to share the warmth. The others have been worse hit. *Or more susceptible.* Prolly depending on our Ancient Swarms, our hybrid modifiers. Shona's face is bluer than usual and, when I lean forward to touch her, part of her hair breaks and shatters on the cage floor. **Zlota!** Rustle is dandystill frosted, not a twitch from her.

Weak, I think, with a certain amount of disgust. *So not her Warrior self.*

But Solomon glows steadily warmer. In a milli, she can scan. We both track calculations of the huge room we're in.

The barren walls are smooth stone. There are no windows, no portholes. No trail tracking for travelshafts. Just those walls, the flattened stone floor, the stone ceiling high up above, one massive wallport with two armed guards in front of it, and a large white double door leading to the rest of Living Lab. Where ScanMans commit their scientific acts of horror. Two other guards walk the perimeter slowly. The air in here is somehow easier to breathe than in the rest of the underground chambers and tunnels. It seems cleaner, less dusty than our training tunnels. But there is a bad feeling to this place. Against the far wall, lined up neat as pins, are dozens of elevated cots. Above them hang mini-screens. No autotrons like in StarPod but the screens reflect live feeds from the fleshcore below.

Whafa!?—I send Solomon.

She growls. She's still recovering a bite from the icy blast.

These cot bundles seem very Pod-like, but they emit chronic low energy. Rows and rows of cots with straps around them, with metal stands beside them, and sheets whiter than teeth. The screens flicker: shadows moving slowly. Tubes go in and out of the lumpy fleshcores. I send, but nopod returns. Their fleshcores are laid out in rows, but their mindcores are stolen. *Chronic.* Some greater force lurks here. I catch fear-scent. Behind me, Solomon makes a sound. Then she points to a cot near our cage.

"No," I say, as the horror of it sinks into me. "Oh no."

Solomon and I coo. We wave-send Pod-style. We get no response. We stare and statue. For there lies Roku, still as stone.

Rustle: Living Lab

So weak. That's me, lately. Weak and Deformed and blaaty frozen, ya? I wakey feeble, like from coma-state. I shake off this ice, this coldness that sits on my chest and siphons my lifeforce. I'm thawing into a puddle at my own feet. I sniff but can't smell a thing—my nostrils are still subtherm. Ice melts and drips off my face. My eyes burn and sting.

Where are we? Oh yeah. Living Lab.

I look around the locked cage. Loo and Solomon—they're calling for Roku. I swallow hard. *Roku won't save us,* I think. *That's who narked in the first place!*

Shona stands, frozen, before me. I scan her pulse, quietly thrumping in her neck. Her hair is a bramy mess: parts broken right off, piles of it thawing on the floor beside her. *She will so convulse!* When I can lift my feet, I step close to share my warmth with her, as she's in worse shape. Her arm is a painful ooze, but her eyelids flicker, and soon she'll wakey. Then her mouth will thaw and, in a milli, I'll be back to getting zlotan wired from all her whiney blaat. I glory silence in the now.

Solomon and Loo are not cooing now, but keening. Their melancholia hits me in wrenching waves. I follow their feel-path over to one screen, where somepod lies tractioned on a white cot, eyes closed, face still. Tubes taped to her temples, the left side of her head shaved. I run my cold hand over my own baldness, rememory my own scarline and the things they did to me then. I squint hard. *It's Roku!*

I'm chronic slow. Questions fire in my database, too much for my frozen frontals. **Loo,** I send. I can't mouth-speak with my frozen tongue.

Loo is saying, "Maybe it's not our Roku. Maybe it's a fakie." Solomon says, "If I can get close enough, I can find out for sure." She looks down at her powerful hands. All Healers can handscan internal damages and help repair the hurts. They read secrets deep below the skin's surface with their big hands.

When I shake my head, I hear the tinklecrash of tiny icesticks shattering on our cage floor. I'm still thawing. I look away from Loo and Solomon, away from Roku, and into the shadows of the Living Lab cave. It is big in here. Two of the guards don't move a winkle. The other two guards march the length of the main hall we're in. They pull open a set of heavy white doors. I can see a long white hallway on the other side of the open doors. The two guards march away from us, down the long hall, their dark shapes getting swallowed up in all that white. The doors swing shut.

I look back to the rows of cots. There are dozens of others like Roku, all pinned back and tucked in. *Chronic blanked.* I gag. So unfit to lie there, broken.

"We have to get out of here so I can check Roku," says Solomon, firmly. Like everything's so simple.

"What about the others?" says Loo. "There are so many." She counts the beds quickly.

"Whafa are they?" I say. "And what about the guards?"

Loo says, "The other two will be back soon." She yanks the heavy decorative buttons off Shona's Leader uni. She waits until the two guards in our sight put on hearing helpers to check in with their Leader, who's prolly back in Genescan with the other big Scouts. Loo lines up her slingshot and stretches the band back, aiming for the closest hidey-cam perched just outside our cage.

Thunk. She hits it clean, smashing the lens. *Thunk.* She disables the recording device. *Thunk, thunk, thunk.* She is our best shot in unit and she gets those other cameras quick. The guards haven't even noticed yet. Meanwhile, Solomon opens Shona's survival bag. She rummages around for some easy tools. She busies herself with one of her specialties—disabling the alarm system in the cage corner.

Loo scales the bars. "Require assist, Rustle."

I'm still standing, doing nothing. "What about Shona?" I ask in a feeble voice. She *is* Leader, after all.

"Zlota!" says Loo. "We should get the blaat out, before the guards come back." She disconnects a live-wire tape-send and swallows it whole. "We might be completely off-line now, or not," she says tersely.

Only Kronk knows whafa other spyware they have set up.

"Rustle," says Loo. "The guards!"

They're heading our way.

Meanwhile, Shona starts to move her fingers. Her database is chronic iced so she can't talk or even send yet. But she knows whafa going on, coz it looks like she wants to extinctulate us with her bare hands! She is prolly planning to sit and wait and whine to whatever PsychPod arrives to rearrange our wiring. She'll say how she's such a dedicated Leader but ended up with some Deformed Defiant Warriors. She'll preen and pluck while we all grind to a horrific halt. Shona shakes her good arm slowly and starts to move her fingers. Her mouth will liberate any milli.

I swing upwards to assist. Solomon and I power-surge the bolts right out of the cage hinges. The running footsteps of the guards get louder.

"Freeze!" they yell. One stays back, weapon raised; she covers for the other, who rushes the cage. Sounds come from behind that white door. The other two are heading back, as well.

Solomon and I raise our arms in a surrender pose. Loo is above us, her back flattened against the cage ceiling, her strong calves hooked through the metal bars, her hands with the slingshot steadying her against the ceiling. She swings forward from the hips so that she hangs upside down, her legs still holding her in place. She shoots between the bars like this, from the space between Solomon's and my shoulders. I can hear her laughing at the disbelief on the guards' faces.

Thunk! Loos' aim is true. She knocks the first guard right between the eyes, stunning her solid. Solomon and I lift the metal cage door off the hinges. We leap out. *Thunk!* Loo gets the second guard, too. Solomon and I roll toward the white door. Loo dives for the closest ShockMauler. It's now in her happy arms, pointed right back at the bewildered first Scout. **Blam!** She's down, singed and convulsing. Loo leaps and shoots, and—*sizzle*—the second stunned one writhes in a pile. Loo keeps the scope trained on them, and even a seizure twitch grants them more blasts. Loo is having a great time, ya?

Solomon and I leap when the double doors burst open—we nab those two guards and wrestle them to the floor. Solomon squeezes the breath right out of hers with those huge, huggy arms. I slip and tumble with mine, who lands right on me, nearly knocking me out cold when I smack my head on the polished stone floor. Solomon almost pitches in to help but, just when I'm about to roll this one over and get a leg up, that's when Loo blasts with the Mauler.

"For Kronk's sake, Loo," I gasp. "Nearly blaaty got *me* that time!"

"Well, get your sorry self out of the way, then," she shouts back, cheerfully.

We harvest the Scouts' weapons and strap them all on. Two ShockMaulers, though the one Loo had is nearly empty. She takes the remaining pellets out of the first and re-loads the second one. She tosses the useless one in a corner. There are four repeat-fire guns, a couple of thermal tracking masks, and a pretty dagger, much like Loo's favorite, back in our lair. Loo takes the dagger, a gun, and a mask. Solomon takes a mask and a gun. I get a shiny gun, too. I lean the extra gun against the smooth wall. We drag the Scouts back into the cage. I take ropes from their kit bags and tie them up tight, wrists to ankles, and drop them several paces apart from one another. Two of them writhe on the floor. Two are down for the count. Solomon lifts Shona and carries her out of the cage. Shona groans. I carry her bag.

"Leave her in there with the others," barks Loo.

Solomon hesitates.

"We can't," I say. *She's our Leader, after all.* "Maybe we might need her?" I don't sound very convincing. I jump down beside Loo. She's stroking the full ShockMauler, smiling at it like a new lover.

Solomon lays Shona down on the floor outside the cage and turns to reinstall the wee bolts, locking the Scouts in tight.

"Bunch of Low Grades."

We swivel. Shona is finally alert. She limps past Solomon and me, over to the Eights. She yanks up the sleeves of their unis and injects them all with quick doses of Sleep. The amber fluid rushes their bloodstreams and they are down. Then Shona limps back to her bag. She finds some chem samples. She mixes liquid from one tube with powder from another. She pours the whole thing over the metal hinges, covering her mouth and nose from the sudden putrid smoke. We watch as the compound coats and welds the metal shut tight. Shona wipes the edges of the containers, places them back in her bag, tidily.

The rest of us are speechless. We watch while she does it all herself.

"That should shut them up for a while," she says. "And Loo? For the record? Just, like, rememory who your Leader is." Shona thanks Solomon and then says, "Unit, you, like, quadrenkle owe me this time."

Loo: Fakie

Shona blaaty well revives and becomes her useful, rusty self, minus a good chunk of her formerly long hair. I glare, waiting for some comment on my mutinous programming, but no. Not a word-sound or thought-send. She's blanked to me and the rest, limping and sniffing. I caress my new weapons, sniff the oiled chambers of the gun, make sure I learn it solid. Rustle and Solomon push some of the cots over and block the great white doors with them, in case there are other Scouts to come rushing out at us.

"Now whafa?" says Solomon. "We can't just sit here waiting for the next guard shift."

The hairs on the back of my neck bristle. I scan all the way around the room. I cock my new ShockMauler high and peer through the sight chamber. Shona drops to her fours. Rustle freezes. Solomon holds a fully loaded gun. She taps my shoulder and we move as one, focused and intent. We scan the perimeter of the large stone space. Our steps echo. There are no other guard sets coming, not from the large wallport, not from behind the solid white door. *Not yet.*

Solomon nods and we turn, not perfect, but fairly in tune. Roku is my usual pair, and I am so used to her dark, slim frame in my periphery, her noiseless crouching and stealth. Solomon is much more solid. She has an entirely different spiritwind. I have to take longer steps to match hers, make bigger movements to shadow properly. When we make a round near the cots, I shiver. So unfit.

"The Eights didn't deposit us and scramble away for nothing," Solomon says.

I say, "We don't have much time. The next unit will pour in once these Scouts don't call in on command." I dream their serious shiny unis, imagine myself wearing one now. *I better be bumping up a Warrior level.*

"Whafa thinking?" asks Solomon.

I blush with guilt. "Why is nothing happening? You'd expect some hands-on torture," I say. "Or something." *Something immediate and terribly painful. Something Beyond.* The tingling at my hair roots grows stronger. "We can't just sit here."

"Sure we can," says Shona.

Solomon shrugs. "There could be more surveillance. Hearing helpers, hidey-cams, Kronk only knows."

Rustle says, "Prolly studying us like experiments." She sighs loudly. "ScanMans blaaty programmed us to survive or die trying. We're not wired to self-destruct. They *know* we'll do anything to escape."

I say, "Maybe this is some surprise skill tester? Hey, this is prolly the secret ranking test for Eighth Level." I dream being welcomed in, awarded my black uni like the other solid keeners. Embraced and slapped on the back, I'd be knocking back the Dreamy Drops, shouting cheersongs. *There'd be more medals,* I think. *Prizes.*

Shona snorts. "Like, I think I would have been completely informed?" she says.

I say, "That's debatable, Shona." She ignores this comment and, instead, investigates her various wounds. She takes ointments and bandages from her bag.

"Rustle, stand guard," I say. *I'm not missing out on this chance, not for nopod.*

Solomon and I walk straight over to Roku. Solomon lays her big, dusty hands above Roku's head. She is scanning, trying to sense familiar patterns. The healing powers of her large hands radiate warmth.

"Whafa?" I say.

Solomon shakes her head slowly, passes her hands over the closed face, the throat and chest, down along the whole length of the flesh-core. Solomon frowns. She says, "It's an empty core, a replacement fakie. This is not our Roku. There's nothing to rescue."

I blank for a milli, re-program myself to not rememory Roku when I see the stolen copy that looks like her. *No sense getting over-emo with a fakie.*

Solomon moves to the next lumpy cot and pulls back the white sheet that hides the face. This one looks exactly like Solomon. We both freak. Solomon quietly gags. Then, in a few millis, she's back and focused. She starts moving her hands carefully down the fakie core. I sidle away: I am an invader in this strange selfness. Instead, I move from one cot to the next. I pull back sheets, blink, and reel with each new discovery. Some are faces I do not rememory, but there's the blond Hunter who filled my mug in Canteena Time last night, and a couple of Eights I've admired from a distance. I don't see a Shona anywhere, not in any of the cots.

I take my pretty dagger from the leg holster. I go back to the bedside of Solomon's fakie first. I tell Solomon to walk away. I sever the head completely, even the tough tendons and the silver-white nerve strings, the spinal column bones and the thick muscles. Stinks! Same to the blond Hunter in the next cot. Same to Roku, though I hesitate, not having her here in the flesh to be sure I'm not exterminating her solid. Solomon joins in now and we keep at it, destroying all of the fakies. There are only two more left in this section, two that draw me close and tingle strange thrills under my skin. I tug the white cloth. I know what I will see before it even falls away.

There lies Rustle, long and stretched; the taut muscles I fuse so well lie still, waiting. Her strong webbed hands drape across her chest like some robe worn in the ancient times. This one's eyes are blanked like all the other fakies, but the rest of her face is luminous. I stare at her beautiful fleshcore. Strong cheekbones and a square jaw frame full lips. Her long, natty purple hair seems even more energized. The main difference is that this smooth scalp is unscarred by mindcore tuning. Also, this one's finely arched brows are not furrowed like Pod Rustle's have been lately. She looks re-modeled—stronger, more muscled, less gynofleshy—and as though she is sleeping coma-style, deep and dreamless.

I breathe in sharp, exhale loudly. I'm bramy wired, right? My Hunter survivor training commands to walk away from the next cot, to not look at the Aberration I know must lie in it. But something deep and deadly calls me forward. I rip the fabric away and stare into the copy of my own silent face. That sends my organs lurching to my throat. I don't know why, but looking at this fakie, this pretend me, I am hit with a rememory from long long ago. It's a snippet from an ancient swarm song, a lullaby that was prolly de-programmed back when I was a wee hatchling. Just the melody and none of the words come back, right? The tune builds up inside me and pushes out my surprised humming mouth. I drop the sheet.

I go back to fakie Rustle. I do it. I use my dirty knife, and it pains me full-frontal. She is even more beautiful here, fresher and stronger, and I wonder whafa *this* one, this fakie Rustle would be like. Last of all, I pull back the sheets again on my own fakie, but I don't know if I can do it. It enrages me, and I stab at the pillow beneath her head. Feathers fly around us, fill the air. I pound that fake flesh with my fists. Feels not too different from our own, and that scares me. My rage wanes. I raise the knife. Then I think I hear that song again, humming from her lips.

I can't. I run to Solomon, run anywhere, before the wash of stinking vomit shoots from my own mouth.

Now I'll never get promoted!

Rustle: Distract

"So, Shona, whafa now?" I swing the shiny gun, keeping watch out the sides of my blinkless eyes. The Eights will be down for a good long drop. Loo fried them full-frontal before Shona gave them the Sleep. I wonder how long we have before the dozens of Warriors that line the Great Hall will burst in and fight us, one after the other. *How many corpses will pile up before the day is done?*

Shona hovers near the edge of one mammoth stone wall, ignoring me. She is trying to find something. Another chunk of her thawing hair falls to the ground.

"Oops," I say and snort.

"Stop blaating around and help me," she snaps. "You low grades dumped all the Scouts' gear in the cage with them, so I can't even call in on command. Their handsets are in their packs."

"So?" I say.

"So, I'm looking for, like, a monitor handset or a direct link to Scan Central, or something."

"Why?" I say. "Huh?" And I think, *Well, I guess Shona's never been here before, either.*

"Maybe it's, like, hidden along the wall?" she adds.

I say, "Like, why would you text Scan Central? ScanMans *know* where we are. That's who blaaty put us here!" My mouth hangs open. "That's who ordered your arm ShockMauled practically right off, and that's who called out the IcyFreeze. You're going to ask them for help? You, like, totally convulse me!"

"Blaaty help and shut it?!" she says.

"Whafa going to tell them, huh, Shona? That you Sleep-dropped those Scouts and fused them shut inside the cage? Think ScanMans will like to hear about that?"

"They'll thank me, you stupid Scout," she says, "Otherwise Loo would have slaughtered them completely. At least, this way they're safe."

I can't even believe it. "Just when you finally impress me with your Warrior training, it turns out to be a complete sham," I say. *Unreal.*

Shona keeps feeling along the wall. She is focusing very hard. I can tell because the tip of her blue tongue sticks out.

"Hey, is that it there, Shona?" I point to a pile of dronebeet dung on the ground.

"Very funny, Rustle," she says.

"Why do ScanMans let dronebeets inside Living Lab?" I say.

Shona says, "For experimentations, duh. Plus, they do all the stupid menial stuff. You know."

I poke the dung with the tip of my gun. The outer layer is dried and darkened, but it's still soft and whiffley on the inside. *Fresh.* Where is the manimal that made this now, I wonder? Without taking more steps, I scan the ground around it, scan for tracks, for any clickety claw marks. I catch a faint pattern in the dust and follow the scrabbles over, up the sheer side wall, and higher. There is a strange dust disturbance on the rock face about two podlengths high.

"Hmm." I turn one long lab table on its end and climb up high to get a better look. I brush away layers of dirt and grime from the wall. Dust flies and I start coughing. I'm wiping madly at the wall. Underneath all that blaat is a wee metal grate. Those scratchy, pale track marks lead right into it. I dig the faceplate out and blaat falls right into my surprised face. "Aha!" I jump back down.

"This is all Roku's fault," Shona is saying, "for turning you against me with her ancient-day rhetoric. I'll explain the whole thing to Controls, and we'll be back in StarPod before Canteena Time. Out of my way, Rustle."

She tries to push past me, but I spread my arms wide. I plant myself, leaning in toward her. I can't think of any other way to stall her. "Shona, don't tell Loo, but I'm bramy wired about you. That's

Book 1

41

the real reason I've been all glum glum lately. Give us some twitchy-fit, ya?" I wrap myself around her and make kissy, try to steer her away from the hidden wall panel, but she's having none of that. Shona sputters and chokes. She pushes against me hard. I clatter to the cold ground.

"Whafa?!" She wipes her mouth where mine attacked and looks at me like I'm full-frontal dented. "Rustle, are you, like, totally Deformed? You're convulsing more with every milli!" She turns away in disgust, still wiping her mouth with the sleeve of her burnt uni. And that's when she notices the disguised monitors and control panel the Eighth Leader had fiddled with during our big freeze. Shona shrieks with joy.

"Zlota," I say to nopod.

Shona fumbles around until she glimpses something shiny—a tiny ring fastened to the stone surface. She pulls on it and a square-shaped part of the wall pulls out like a little port. Inside, there is a mini-screen and a handset. "Super fit," she says. She starts to punch in her secret Pod Leader code. I'm so there in a milli, hanging over her shoulder, peering at the blaaty contraption, wishing Solomon and Loo would hurry up and intervene.

"Uh, like, Rustle?" she taps her foot impatiently and raises her eyebrows at me.

"Uh, like, whafa?" I imitate her, toe tapping and all.

"Don't try and get touchling with me again or I will text Loo for real," she snarls. "And get out of my mental range while I, like, code in?" She nods to dismiss me and turns back to the memo box.

I sigh. "Okay, Shona. No more kissy touchling for you. But I really love what you've done with your hair. Don't forget to thank the ScanMans for that when you're, like, texting them, ya?" I'm still snorting when Loo and Solomon come running toward us. They are super-freaking for serious. Loo looks wary scary, more than I've ever seen her. Solomon's skin is gray, her eyes wide with fright.

"Stop, Shona!" yells Solomon.

Shona is clearly enunciating into the handset. Solomon rips the thing right from her hand. Solomon punches in a sequence of codes, scrambling the hard drive and overloading its system. Then she does the absoblaaty most unthinkable thing. She pulls the whole contraption out of the wall and severs all the cords with her new hunting knife. She drops the broken mess onto the floor with a clatter. She sweeps Shona with those big hands of hers and stops around the waist to remove a series of mini hearing helpers and one mole dropping.

"Whafa?" shrieks Shona.

Solomon grinds them down, one by one, and stamps them into the dust.

"Seems like Shona has some explaining to do," says Solomon.

"You set us up, Traitor," says Loo. Her silver eyes flash. She snarls like a wild thing, full-frontal Defiant. Loo's claws slash. Shona stands white and stunned. Blood drips down her face.

Solomon holds Shona, arms pinned behind her back, and tells me to get her bag. "Get the ropes, then dump everything else out. Let's see whafa Shona packed."

I do as Solomon commands. I'm confused, feeble, and missing most of the story, as usual. I untwine the carefully piled ropes and measure out a length. Solomon binds Shona's wrists together behind her back. Solomon pushes Shona onto the ground face first. She's bound hand to foot in a painful arch, just like the Eights. Shona lies on her bellyparts so her chin rests on the stone and dirt, snot dripping from her noseholes. Her mouth is zipped up with a piece of sticky. Loo rifles through Shona's bag like somepod possessed.

I'm saying, "Whafa?! Whafa?!"

Loo hurls the bags of dried feed out from Shona's bag, chucks them right at me to shut me up, like. She shakes out the giant hemp bloomers, the tool kit, and everything else. Loo stares at Solomon. They private text each other, and then Loo burrows away inside the bag again, carefully feeling the sides and the lining. Shona grunts and wriggles. Loo sends some extreme viol to Shona and digs back into the bag. Loo finds the proof she's looking for under a false flooring. She shakes out the carefully wrapped package and shows us a ScanMan textsend capsule—a tracker, alive and blinking. Solomon steps up and rips away a piece of Shona's bloodstained uni. Underneath it is another stickied hearing helper, fakied onto a patch of uni fabric.

"Mmr, mlaat," says Shona.

And that's how Shona went from, like, Leader to Traitor in one-half a milli, flat.

Loo: Interrogation

Ah-hah!

Shona blaaty excretes when I slap the tiny text-send capsule in Solomon's hand to reconfigure the data, as well she should. She smells the mutinous rage whafa simmers inside and bubbles over, and zaps out my angry fists once in a milli. I rip off the sticky that covers her drooling mouth. Shona gags but stays quiet otherwise.

Solomon reads the secret messages back and forth. She pauses as the sent and received texts filter through the tiny monitor. She reads some parts out loud: "Unit very quick to mutinize. Rustle is too stupid to avoid extinction. Loo is a bramy spietchka. Solomon's the only one worth saving. Roku is stellar dangerous and still missing."

"Bramy spietchka?" I slash her zlotan face again.

Rustle throws her hands in the air. She says, "I'm too stupid? You think I'm too stupid? Like, if I was really too stupid, how would I have found our escape path? I'm not too stupid, right, Loo?"

"Shut it, Rustle," I say.

But she doesn't. Rustle keeps blaating on and on, saying,

"Shona, you almost lost your whole arm for a set-up. How stupid is that, huh?" Then she yells, "I'm so stupid I actually felt sorry for you!"

Shona's noseholes drip. She says, "I was, like, *sniff sniff*, just doing my job, *sniff sniff*, okay?"

"Since when is it your job to get us all Deplugged?" Rustle crosses her arms moodily.

Solomon interrupts. "Whafa mean escape route, Rustle?"

Rustle points to the mess she made with the up-ended table. Solomon climbs up and peers into the opening left by the grate.

Rustle says, "Think it leads someplace useful?"

"Anyplace is better than where we are," I say. I spit at Shona.

Solomon pulls podself up toward the opening. A slight draft blows dust into her face, lifts the wisps of baby hairs that don't tuck into her dreads. She looks hopeful. It's a small space, hardly wider than her shoulders.

"I didn't know they would use ShockMaulers!" Shona is saying. "And nopod texted anything about IcyFreeze. They just want to run interrogations."

"Interrogations?" I say. "And you think *I'm* a bramy spietchka?" I step on the back of her neck with my boot.

"Stop," she chokes and sputters, her face squished into the hard floor. "Please."

I kick the side of her head. Solomon jumps down from the table and pulls me away. I lunge, but Solomon wraps me in a tight lockdown. She sits on me. I am full-frontal raging; my face is hot and slobbery; my limbs thrash against Solomon's solid weight. She flattens me. I fight but it's no use. Millis later, the kill pulse wears thin. I lie panting and shaking but still angry. The others look wary scared of me.

I breathe deeply, stand up, and walk away from them all.

Solomon says, "Shona, you say ScanMans want to interrogate us, but we have nothing to tell. Nothing we're aware of, at least. They'll torture, electromangle, and debilitate us. They prolly plan to harvest our organs and replace us with those fakies. That's why they're all laid out, ready to re-program. Right?"

Shona blinks but doesn't say a word.

Solomon says, "Our entire unit will be destroyed, Shona." She tosses Shona's RouteFinder to Rustle. "Pack it up. We're moving out."

I say, "Or maybe not the *entire* unit, right? That's why Shona doesn't have her own replacement." I move closer to her and the urge to hurt her grows. "Think you'll get another crack at it with a bunch of retouched fakies?"

Shona's blush deepens.

"Think you'd be able to handle the next unit any better?" I sneer at Shona. "Think you'll even get a chance, once we've all broken down and admitted that you held regular secret meetings with Roku—"

"You wouldn't lie!" Shona shrieks.

"I blaaty will. You'll be ripped limb from core, just like the rest of us. You'll go way worse than us, Sent Down in eternal disgrace as a Defiant Leader."

Shona's face trembles. She cries in despair. More than her fear, I love that all she holds sacred in her mediocre mindcore will be destroyed.

Easy, sends Rustle. And her gentleness surprises me. Annoys me, too. **Her faith in ScanSystem,** sends Rustle, **is like mine unto you.**

I scowl. For being chastised here, even silently, even gently. For Rustle's generosity and for her stupidity. Rustle fuse-sends, but I blank. I check Shona's ropes. Her head hangs to one side. Tears roll down the cheek that I can see.

Solomon, meanwhile, is ready to leave. "Shona will tell us all she knows," says Solomon. "She owes us that much. But first, we have to get out of here. Now."

Shona sniffles. "Whafa doing with me?"

Nopod sends or says a thing. We're undecided. Shona's upturned nose leaks. Her eyes bulge more than usual and her cheeks are flushed deep blue. The ropes still hold her firmly in place, arms tight against her side. Her large chest heaves with each difficult breath.

"Well," Rustle says. "She can't climb all tied up. And I'm not blaaty hoisting her."

Solomon handscans Shona. Solomon looks conflicted.

Rustle says, "Rock, paper, lasers?"

Shona grunts.

I laugh and say, "Just kidding, Shona. It's even worse. We'll vote; majority regs. I'm for killing her, that's what. If ScanMans are spying on us now, they'd intervene, right? It'd be a good way to find out if they're still watching. And either way, we win."

Solomon says, "I'm for keeping her. She must carry her pack and all the rations. We'll need them. And I think we'll need her expertise yet."

Rustle withers under my glare, so I know already how she'll vote.

"Shona," she says, untying her. "This time you quadrenkle owe *me.*"

Rustle: Tunnel

I smell manimal. Prolly a dronebeet passed this way not too long since. And farther, even fainter, there is a tiny tremor of air. A current from somewhere in the passage stirs the thick dust and—whafa!—I pass Shona's hand-sized glowball. When Loo presses it, the thing shines steady like our moon. Its light fills the tunnel, up and up.

"Bramy filth," says Loo, as a clump of blaat falls out and smashes by her boot.

"Come on," says Solomon. Her left cheek twitches. She loves

creeping in this rocky stubble.

Dust and dirt fill my nostrils when I look up. Solomon is already millimiles ahead, the first pod in, joyful. She's the expert—she clears our path, moves blockages and rock crumbles. Next is Loo, who keeps an eye on Shona. Of course, Shona can't go last as she's still the blaaty big traitor, and who knows what she'd get up to. So I'm stuck at the end. Me—the pod to clean up the floor, replace the lab table, and quadrenkle-check for footprints, for forgotten tidbits, or signs of scuffle. To fake our tracks near the wallport and divert ScanMans from finding our true exit, *if* they haven't got this whole drama on cam, that is. Our new guns and the ShockMauler don't fit in the opening, so I have to toss them all together in a lonely pile. I'm the pod to stick dirt and dust over the ventilation grate, covering our print smears. The last pod to climb up our blaaty rope ladder, made from whafa formerly held Shona. I pull it up behind me and wind it tight. I tuck it into my utility belt. I reinstall the grate from inside the vent shaft, then scramble, wary scary in the dusty dark, trying to catch up to the others.

No pressure. Like, none at all. Me, blaating around with Solomon's tools. Me, endlessly alone in the black black night, straining for a glimpse of the glowball ahead. Wish I had my nocturnal vision mask, my laser globe, anything. I crawl and swoon.

Suddenly, there is a sound. My heart thuds heavy. My large tongue bakes in my oven mouth. Sweat trickles down my scalp. I am so thirsty I try to catch the drops as they roll down my face. *Nothing.* So I start to crawl again, forever on sore knees and blistered hands. *There!* Again that sound. It's a scratchy claw sound. Not wiring twitches or motor rumblings or hard-drive hummings. It is a hollow tapping sound of bone on stone. The sound slithers into my hearholes and shivers a path up and down my spine. It twitches the back of my scalp.

I rub my face with my fists. I tremor when I stretch my hand out in the black black air. A rush of movement pushes air over my skin. There is a *chirruping* and a scramble scratch. Something speeds along the tunnel ceiling, right above my head, above my back, and now it chirrups from behind me. I spin, but get stuck in the tightness of the shaft. I swivel onto my right hip and scan for movement or hearsound, for pulsing vitals of any kind. *Wish I had a thermal mask cam now!*

"'Ssup?" I say. My voice cracks.

Nothing.

"Hey, whafa?" I force more air through my lips and teeth, grip the small knife from my leg holster.

My jaw falls open. The small thing starts to glow. A light radiates from within it, and soon I see a dronebeet, nary one podlength from me. It backs up a milli, glows brighter still. It's looking at me, maybe even *considering* me. I twitch my knife hand and—*zappa*—the light extinguishes itself. The thing scuttles farther away. I shookashake my dented head. I've never even been this close to one before.

"You should blaaty thank me," it says.

I lick my cracked lips. I am prolly dehydrolizing and inventing this whole thing. Or my Deformity could be shorting my wires and causing this hallucination.

"Dronebeet showed stupid Scouts the way out."

The thing starts to glow again and, although it is absoblaaty freaky, the pale green light comforts me some this time. I'm still not convinced that this manimal is generating text. It seems to have two round eyes that roll and focus, separately mobile. One chronic fixes on me, the other roams and whirls. The whole thing could maybe fit in Solomon's large cupped hands, not the feelers, ya, but most of it. Sets of legs glint like metal. Prolly whafa makes the scratchy clickclaw sounds. Its wandering eye zips back to me. The feelers undulate. The green illuminates inner organs and fluid travel paths, wiring circuits and whafa.

"Are you, like, speaching me?" I'm completely freaked.

"Don't you forget it," it says. "Dronebeet dung saved your sorry carcass." It chirrups and caws, and then the light vanishes, and the clickety clack scratches hurry scurry and fade in the direction of Living Lab. I dandystill sit until the tunnel returns to eerie quiet. I rub my sweaty head. I am, like, full-frontal tripping in this hotbox trap. I push the strange meeting far from my mindcore. Then I start crawling again, away from this imagined thing. Far far away from it.

I crawl at least a hundred millimiles of rough vertical tunnel, and there's not a pulsing send from anypod. No light and no more hallucinated dronebeets. Only the odd distant quake, thumps of movement muted by millimiles of dusty space trapped inside endless tonnage of ancient rock. Sometimes I stop to rest, panting and heaving and listening. My hearholes ache from the nothingness. *Do I even have hearholes?* There is a sharp turn, more level now, and I drag myself along fairly easily. That's when I finally see a glimmer of glowball ahead. I pull myself by the bleeding hands the last bit of the way. My unit sits and sips precious drips from Shona's water bottle. They rub protein powder on their gums and on the backs of their tongues. I collapse, gasping. Loo sprinkles water on my lips.

"Did you dust-brush the cover? Quadrenkle-check for prints?" Loo fires questions at me like from one of her automated weapons.

I croak and she offers me more drops. I suckle them up hardcore. How to speach that I had been certain I'd never see them again? That I feared the absoblaaty worst: an endless crawl in the black black, only to shrivel and die alone, Podless. Loo sends a warm fuse-wave, in spite of the already hot air we suffocate in. I suck it up and sigh.

Solomon says, "Scouts must be back inLiving Lab by now. They prolly know where this tunnel leads, but we don't. There could be an ambush waiting ahead. We got to keep moving."

The large shadow between Loo and Solomon is Shona. She sits silent except for her sniffling. Those three start to crawl again, but I just stay put, dreaming of those comfy cots back in Living Lab, dreaming of a long and uninterrupted rest. Loo chucks a clod of dirt back to smash by my head, and sends, **Bramy move it, Rustle!** So I do.

We continue along and veer to a gradual incline. Hours of hot, sweating work have left me with ripped fingers, shoulders shaking from exhaustion, and crusting bloodied knees. When I think I cannot move even once more, Loo gasps.

"There!" **There Light,** she sends. The emo-wave is almost a sob, a sheer pang of relief.

I collapse. I push myself along on my back, using my booted feet as propellers to give my hands and knees respite. Finally, I push my head out from the tunnel and suck in the cool, moist air beyond. I, too, cry out.

The others have straggled onto a sandy loam surface. We are inside a hollowed-out chamber in the mountain. We stand in a cave, the mouth of which is a watery inlet. There is a wide expanse of sand that leads to a careful pile of slippy black rocks. Then an endless shining body of water laps and kisses back at the pebbled shore on which we stand.

"Whafa," groans Loo. In the fading light, I see how covered in blaat we all are. Dirt and other filth cakes our skin.

Water, I send. I lick my cracked lips.

"Wait," says Solomon. She leans carefully over the liquid. She fills one of Shona's anti-contaminant containers. It doesn't melt or dissolve. A drop hits Solomon's skin and we jump and hiss, but nothing happens. No acid burn, no skin peeling. We set the timer, add the sterilization pills, and try to not stare while we wait for the bacteria to die.

The air is cool and dank, and is so easy to breathe it almost shocks my lungs, my wind pipes, my cracked and peeling lips. The sand we stand on is just as strange. Not hard-solid like the walls of Living Lab. Not metal like the furnishings we know. It feels cool and damp to touch. When we walk, we leave soft, smudgy imprints behind. Moisture in the air and in this soil suffers me even more to drink.

So much blaaty water, I send. It's the one element we've never conquered. We've never seen so much of it in one place before. I rememory the training tanks we submerged in, rememory blowing bubbles under water and feeling so alive. The others dreaded those sessions, even nightmared them, while I had to hide my secret delight.

How travel? I send cautiously.

Shona starts to cry then and Loo looks bleak. She and Solomon limp along the sandy shore in opposite directions. They scout as far as they can along the edges of the cave walls. But on both sides the path disappears beneath the chilly liquid. Solomon drops wee stones, then larger, heavier ones to measure deep depth. So does Loo. They freak when they cannot scan the bottom, when they cannot even sense the stones landing. Loo lurches vertiginous and turns, carefully creeping beside the cave wall until she is back with us on the sand.

It's like the inside of the mountain contains our whole world, minus the shuttle launch pads and, of course, all the places the shuttles take us. On the outside of the same mountain, there is this mysterious body of liquid, endlessly deep and bone icy. And out there, not two millimiles away from us, lies the big big sky. We've never seen it like this before: bright gray with drifting patches of clouds. Anything is possible out there. We have crawled our way out from this mountain like the ticks that infest dronebeet nestlings. Our broken, bleeding fleshcores pile here, not another creature in sight. The air is salty, stinging almost, when we get to the edge of the terrifying water. Standing here, we could maybe almost imagine a future for ourselves, a future we've never seen on a monitor or in autotron updates. One we've never even really wanted for ourselves. We can almost taste it—one part dread, two parts fear, one part curiosity.

But between us and our freedom lie the big black sea and no other way out.

Loo: Water Trap

I almost faint when I peer into the strange liquid. Like the water-spirit is pulling me down, twirling with my battered core, and singing some poisoned love song to lure me to my own smiling death. An image of my fakie comes unbidden, and I hear that ancient tune again. I hear it in a ghostly whisper, like it's *her* familiar and frightening voice embedded deep inside me.

I cough, hack up a dry crackle in my throat and grind those teeth. I wave-send rage back to the water's deadly depths. When I open my eyes, it is my own filthy face I see reflected. I look wild— terrified, like some hunted thing I would break with my bare hands. I stumble backwards against the stone wall. I straighten my spine. I breathe deeply, in out, in out. Out.

Solomon stands across from me on the other side of the inlet. She is also leaning against her side of the rock wall. We face each other. Shona and Rustle lie collapsed in piles on the pale sand. Solomon sends, **Easy, Loo.** So mirrored, we climb our way amongst the shifting rocks and sudden cold splashes, back to the wider section of sand where shallow waves rush forward then trickle away. Back to where the others wait.

Rustle is dandystill collapsed. She is a bite damaged from our long crawl. The trailing wisps along her powerful arms and legs are speckled with blood and dirt. Her fingers still bleed. Shona's face is covered in dirty slime, and crusty scabs grow from the slash points I made, but otherwise she is stable. Not bad, considering. Solomon is dirty and sweaty, but looking strong. I'm tired. I sit on a large, flat rock. After a milli, I touch one dusty toe to the water and draw back instinctively.

"Cold," I say.

Solomon shrugs. Rustle feel-sends confidence.

I bring my toe back to the water and hold it there this time. I slowly submerge it down to the sand. I flatten my foot so that the water covers it completely, so that the little waves rolling toward the beach push up around my ankle. It feels good after all that crawling, all that dirt. I wiggle my toes in the grainy bottom and rub against small pebbles. Rustle watches me. I smile. It feels good, I decide, so I plonk the other foot in as well. I tap and splash them, pointing toes and then flexing them out ugly, like dronebeet feelers. I begin to kick the water. I laugh and splash, and send icy drops up the sand, all the way over to Shona and Rustle, and they shriek—Shona in terror and Rustle with joy. Rustle gallops toward me. I kick harder now, sending fountains of water thundering high up into the air. Rustle grabs my hand and pulls me into the black pool. Watery waves rush against my calves, up around my knees, freeze my muscled thighs, and then, the bottom suddenly drops away, and the painful shooting ice water numbs my gynos, my bellyparts, my chest. I panic. My feet scramble for the bottom but there is no sand anymore. Just a watery grave and my thrashing limbs, and my body slipping down.

Loo, sends Rustle, calming me. Rustle's arms are around my torso, my back hugged against her chest, her core pressed to mine. Her strong legs move rhythmically under the water, keeping us both afloat. Our heads break the surface. I gasp. Water pours off my face.

"Follow me," she says, so I try to hang limp, try to not kick out of fear, try to feel the movements she is making that keep us balanced in the water. Rustle unzips her uni and struggles out of it. She throws it back toward the shore. She tugs on my zipper next, pulls it all the way down. The water feels strange on my bare flesh.

"Relax. Breathe," she says, and then she counts out loud, numbering her swift movements, and telling me how to swirl my legs so I can bear my own weight. I hold my arms out front and wavel them around the surface, back and forth, back and forth, like I'm smoothing wrinkles from my foamie. It seems to help hold me upright, although Rustle's webbed fingers work better at this than mine do. After a while, Rustle lets go. She twirls so that we are face to face, making our strange and tiring water dance, our shoulders bobbing up to break the surface, our faces full of wonder, so close together.

Wary scary, I think.

But then Rustle comes closer, licking her lips. "You're doing it, learning fast fast," she says. She smiles and nudges me. She wave-sends fusion right through me and opens me up. Her flesh rubs mine. It heats and melts me. *Here in the kronking water!* She is so strong now, all of a sudden, seducing me in my weakness. Zlota! She laughs out loud and moves against me, touches me, holds me. Her core presses into me, and the heat from her swollen gynos stirs me. Those strange protrusions. I touch her parts gently. They are different, right; in some strange way, the flesh is pushing out and also dropping down below.

Does it hurt? I send.

But she shakes her head, *No*, and her cheeks flush with want. I touch her below the water while we balance. She reaches down to touch me, too. Soon we press tight, moving together more urgently. She is on me and near me, around me and in me, fusing strong strong. Not like other times, but in some new way that surprises me. She pushes into me. Still it makes me pant and sigh, and then at last cry out. She smiles, makes kissy with me, sloppy and rough in all this water.

"Ah, Loo," she says in her throaty voice. "I've missed you."

Solomon and Shona stand on the shore, mouths hanging wide, arms loose at their sides. Rustle snorts and blushes. I yell for them to stop staring and join in, but Solomon covers her eyes, laughing.

ùAnyways, I realize I am big big tired whafa all the exertions we've had today. I lean forward on my bellyparts like Rustle does, arms in front, hands digging the water, and my legs stretched long behind me, kicking to a steady beat. My gynos tingle. They are tender. Rustle kisses my shoulder. I bite hers back. Our knees and fingers graze the sandy bottom when we get close. I pull myself along the bottom and straggle out onto the rocky edge, shiny and wet, and somewhat cleaner than before. My uni is tangled up with Rustle's. I hang mine out to dry and stand naked on the sand. Rustle stays crouched in the water so I toss hers over. She rinses it out and then tries to wrestle podself back into it.

Rustle lurches out of the water, weeds stuck in her hair. "Rustle swimmy Loo," she says, smiling. She shakes the millidrops off her limbs and hair. "Loo swimmy Rustle!" She laughs out loud.

"That was, like, not just a swimmy?" says Shona. She sniffs.

Solomon now walks toward the water edge and drops her biggest toes in there. A strange look flutters over her face as she waggles her foot. Shona stares and swallows when Solomon cups her two large hands together and swoops the water out and up and over the air. It lands right on Shona's prudish head, splooshes over her frowny face, and makes her shriek. The shriek stretches out and turns into a belly laugh, one we haven't heard since forever, and finally she starts to share in our new wonder.

Rustle: Handscan

"Handscan?"

Solomon amazes me with her gentle offerings. There is a patience underlying the moment, a tenderness that seeps out to unruffle my tightly wound self. We're sitting apart from the others—me dripping dry from my recent water adventure, Solomon still reeling from our swimmy discovery.

I say, "It's all mixed up now. No Rules and Regs. No real Leader, no ScanMan orders. We're not on Mission and I don't know whafa do. Just want to figure out my insides, ya?"

Solomon smiles. "Your poor, tormented fleshcore."

"Have you known all along?" I say, quietly.

"No. Only started wondering just before GeneScan. You blank pretty good, Rustle. And everything's been so chaotic lately. They work us so hard. There's almost no time to sit and send like this."

"You could've narked me," I say. I look closely at her face.

"No, Rustle, I never could. We're unit-fied." Solomon smiles.

"Roku knew," I say. "She tried speaching me about it the night she disappeared. I denied her solid."

"You had to be wily, Rus."

"I didn't have to be so cold. Roku was prolly changing, too. She sounded strange; she smelled different. She was talking all kinds of weird blaat, but maybe it made sense. I just wasn't listening, really. Too caught up in my own self."

Solomon sits quietly for a bite. "Something is definitely happening. Our training is full-on intense. Units are separated most of the time now, and we get Assassin Ops almost every day. Sometimes more. Ever really wonder who the targets are?"

I rememory that quivery manimal, the one I couldn't kill. She was Pod, all right. She knew the base mantra. But why was she so filthy, so wild? Then I look down at my own mess, at our whole scraggly, bruised-up unit. *We're just like her now,* I think.

Solomon says, "Now that Roku is missing, some unit will be out hunting her, thinking she's some vile monster. They won't know she's Pod. They'll believe ScanMans' lies. They'll exterminate her solid."

It takes me a milli to think this through. "So why those fakies?"

"I think they're replacing us with newer versions. The empty cores were ready to load and program." Solomon drums the skin of her legs with her fingers as she thinks. "There was one for each of us, Rustle. They'll hunt us down, too."

"Ya," I say. I rememory the terrific stamps of the senior scouts' boots, the way they didn't even *look* at us before firing. "Roku said we were being exterminated. I thought she was convulsed, but prolly not, right?"

Solomon exhales loudly. "If our cost exceeds our worth, they might. If we weren't performing right." She is quiet for a milli, then says, "If ScanMans could no longer control us, they would definitely want us gone. Blaaty dangerous. Imagine, Rustle, if we were out of control. That'd scare the piss right out of them."

Out of control. Exactly how I feel.

Solomon lies back on the rock and looks to the water. "Rustle, how swimmy like that, so fit?"

I shake my head. "I don't know. Just seems right. Like walking, breathing, fusing." I blush, rememorying Loo and me in the water. I shrug. "Why do I dream and crave water? Why do you all fear it?"

Solomon's careful face shows that she's still working through the possibilities. "Well, your webbing, it makes you better suited to water. But maybe with the newer changes you've been having ... maybe it has to do with that." She stands in front of me now. "Ready?"

I nod. Solomon closes her eyes, breathes deeply, and passes her hands over me. She starts up in the active air space above my core, in the electrically charged particles all around me. Her hands radiate a warm path, a tingly new awareness of being, as they make their way down my core. She slows down around my temples, covers my whole torso again, and freezes at my gynos. Solomon's hands warm my flesh through the wet uni. Even this simple attention has got the Deformity worked up again. The blood flow makes a small lump in the front of my uni. I breathe heavy and shiver. Solomon pushes me back gently and works quietly, breathing deeply, touching and not touching me. All those flesh parts I've been hiding lately. Then she focuses on my battered hands and on the long flimsy trails that have been multiplying down the backs of my legs. I give myself up to her inspection, full-frontal and in the now.

After, we sip powdered root and algae in treated water. We're blanked but not in a mean way. She's prolly interpreting the handscan info, and I'm dreading hearing about it. Loo and Shona stay at the far side of the gravelly beach, treating more water, and arguing about whafa happened to Roku.

"Blaaty Kronk!" shouts Loo.

"Like, I don't know where she is? Fine, don't believe me."

Even from here, I can see Shona's heaving podbumps.

"Hah!" Loo runs and dives into the pool. She swimmies to cool off and also to get away from Shona.

"Well? Those two will extinctulate each other if we don't interrupt soon," I say.

Solomon speaks slowly, ignoring the Pod squabble. "Rustle. You are not complete. Whatever this change is, it is not finished."

"Am I dying?" I say.

"I don't think so. I don't read death waves. I read birthing, growing waves, like."

"Oh Kronk, I'm not flowering am I?" The panic of blooming and flowering and dropping my own pod smothers the other worries in a milli. "I thought we couldn't do that. I thought all bio-pioneers were sterile!"

"We're supposed to be. Don't worry. I don't really know what's happening, especially with your gyno changes. In the ancient times, there was more than one gynotype. They had another species and, when the two mated, that is how they reproduced. I wonder ..." Solomon's brow creases deeply.

"Wonder whafa?"

"Well, it's as though you have some dormant parts inside, organs maybe, getting ready to open. Does it hurt much?" Solomon's eyes glide all over and through me, softly.

I shrug. Even when I could still drop, the night pains tore me from Sleep. For weeks I'd wake with that dull ache inside my bones, the tight crimping of muscles. Worst of all, the general uselessness, this overwhelming fatigue, had been taking the life-force out of me for longer than I cared to admit. "I'm in Decline, aren't I?"

"I don't think so, Rustle."

"I'm all three. Declining, Deforming, and Disobeying. I never meant to— ." I choke on the last words.

"Hmm." Solomon looks down at her hands, turns them over to look at the palms, stretches her fingers long. "Wary scary, ya?"

"Ya." I sigh. It would be even harder to admit that, in spite of the pain and the fear of not knowing whafa happening, I have the uncanny sense that these strange new yearnings, these new demands that call from deep within, will lead me forward, closer to some inevitable destiny. The water all around us pulls me closer with every step. I hunger for it in some strange new way.

Solomon says, "You know, if they wanted to Deplug us, they could have done it easy while we dropped."

"Well," I cough. "Sleep don't drop you when you're changing."

And that information perks her up a bit. Then she says something else about the ancient times. That we should try to think back on them, dig up our crusted rememories from that ghostly time before our training began. She says something else about Swarms, our hybrid parentals. That maybe my changes relate to them, and maybe we all have some developments in store. "Yours just might be full-frontal intense, ya?"

I snort and agree. "They're full-frontal, dandystill!" I am so fit to have Solomon here. I could go all over-emo, ya, but instead I head butt her playful-like, and we ruffle each other's hairs and smoosh noses together. When I finally tromp back toward the others, I feel lighter, more fit. Something is definitely happening inside me, but whafa?

Maybe it's not the end, after all.

Loo: New Regs

Solomon tracks the dronebeet scratchings. She stands apart from us. She frowns and tugs her dreads. She's thinking. She walks around a pile of large rocks and stands there some more.

"Whafa," I say, then look to where she's pointing. "So we completely will not starve," I say, happily. There are several bundles of waterweeds hidden behind the largest rock. We could ground this lot up and have enough protein powder to last us a long long while. I say, "Dronebeets must have gathered these, so where are they now?"

Solomon shrugs. "I scanned the rock face, the sand, the shoreline. I don't see any nests or other portholes. They must use the tunnel we crawled through."

"How about tracking units?" I say.

She nods. "Wary weird, but I didn't find any hearing helpers. No scan-cams either."

But I can't shake the feeling that we're being watched and played. Wish they'd come forward and fight me straight on, coz I'd rip them open or die trying. I pick up a parcel of waterweed and chew on it thoughtfully.

Solomon rubs a dry strand of it between her fingers and, sure enough, a soft green powder forms. She licks it up. "Just like Canteena Time, only it tastes fresher. More green," she says, smiling.

We sort through the piles and take some of the best parts for podselves.

I say, "Strange that this is here, though, right? This isn't an official feed station or anything. So why would dronebeets want to work here?"

Solomon says, "First of all, dronebeets don't want to work; ScanMans force them to. I'd like to know whose feed piles these are and why they're hidden out here."

I say, "How do *you* know dronebeets don't want to work?"

"Would you like to do their hard work?" Solomon asks quietly. "For that matter, do we like doing our work?"

Duh, No, I think to the first question, and *Kronk, Yes!* to the second. I don't say anything out loud, though. Solomon sounds more like Roku with these questions that spin my mindcore in a few directions at once, with no clear answers waiting at the end. Like, I never even thought whafa we do as being called *work.* Or that it's lucky I loved the Warrior life, as I prolly didn't have a choice about it.

"So, dronebeets don't like to work—maybe—and are forced to gather and ground the waterweeds into powder, and that's our main feed source. But this isn't a waterweed harvesting station, clearly. There's no machinery or travelshafts, or even tools. This is an undercover feed stash," I say, as I pick up two dried bundles to take back to our temporary camp. "These won't take long to pound and pack away."

Solomon brings one more for us. She stacks the rest neatly back where they originally were. I light a firestick and throw it down. The dried weeds crackle right away. Solomon shrieks and pulls the fiery parts out from the pile and throws it in the water.

"Whafa doing, Loo?"

"Feed raid," I say. I shrug. After Kill Ops they're my specialty.

Solomon frowns disapprovingly.

"So now you want to feed the enemy?" I say.

Solomon says, "We don't know who gathered these piles, Loo. We don't know if she's a friend or an enemy. Kronk, *we're* the enemy now, according to all those other Scouts."

"Oh," I say. I scuff my boot in the sand, breathe loudly through my noseholes. I don't say anything else but my mindcore pulses: *Who disjunct and made you Leader?*

"New Regs for new times," says Solomon. "We just have to think differently now. The rules are all changing." She brushes my back with a big forgiving hand, which I ignore, and we walk back in silence to where Rustle and Shona sort our supplies. I pick a stone from the shoreline and use it to grind the weeds into a soft powder. The steady work keeps me focused, keeps my muscles moving, and my mindcore quiet. I try to keep calm. I think and think, but I don't say another thing.

Rustle: Raft

"That'll take forever," I say. I stomp away from Shona. We're making a device for our escape. I curse some more. Then I kick the thing and hurt my foot. I hop and hold my sore webbed toe.

Shona keeps blowing into the dirty little nozzle on her sleep mat. Finally, it starts to move on its own a bite. Not much, though. The thing is only starting to fill with air and there's a whole lot left to go. Shona stops blowing and starts blabbing again. She pinches the nozzle shut while she talks. "Way to go, Rustle. Maybe if you put some of that muscle into your mindcore, you'd be able to help out for once. You're, like, completely—"

"Save some hot air for the big inflation, Shona," I say.

She swings what's left of her demolished hair. "Anyway, if you want to get out of here alive, you better start blowing." She holds the thing toward me.

"Look, you've got slobber all over it now," I say, pointing. "That's completely saliva, ya."

"Why don't you both shut it and get cracking." Loo growls this from her powder-grinding station. She has kept one eye on each of us as we pull and heave and blow into Shona's mat. "We're trying to escape here, rememory?"

"You could help us, Loo," says Shona. "I'm already out of breath. You're stronger than I am, so why don't you—"

Loo says, "You're not Pod Leader any more, so shut it."

"Like, I know? I'm just saying—"

Loo interjects. "Seriously. I am sick of hearing your whiney voice."

I keep my mouth on the nozzle. Loo is wicked pissed, and I am staying right the blaat out of it.

"Whafa joking?" Shona's eyebrows crinkle in the middle and her bottom lip juts out.

"How is that thing spozed to help us, anyway?" Loo sounds angry, but also a bit worried underneath it all.

I wonder: *Is she scared?*

Shona says, "We're turning it into a raft. If you paid attention in Level Four Wilderness Ops, you'd rememory that inflated sleep mats can float," says Shona. "Good thing I packed mine."

"Ya, good thing." I gasp. I pinch the nozzle and wait a couple of breaths. For once, I'm glad that Shona is so organized. I start blowing again.

Then Loo says, "So, how are we all going to fit on it?"

Shona rolls her eyes. "We're not. Of course we won't all fit."

Loo stares at the yellow mat. "Our pack will have to go in the middle while we all hold onto the edges of it and kick."

I say, "Why not just swimmy?" But even as it comes out my feedhole, I know that it's impossible. It's tiring, for one thing, and we have no idea how far we'll have to go. Or if other creatures might be lurking underwater—a new disturbing thought to choke on. "Never mind," I say. "I just hope there are no holes," I add, morbidly.

Shona swallows hard. "Thanks, Rustle."

I keep blowing. I feel sparks burning my lungs from effort.

Loo says, "Why don't you tether it with a piece of rope? You can test it out better that way."

Shona agrees, so when we finally get enough air in it, we lay it flat on the sand. I find a piece of the rope that held Shona's wrists together not so long ago, and attach it to the mat. Shona plops the thing onto the water and guides it gently with the tether. She pushes the whole thing further out. We hold our breath while it bobs on the rolling water. "It's working," she says.

Loo takes the rope from her and walks along the shore so the wee rafty follows after, like a cuddly dronebaby on a leash. "Somepod still has to test it out. It's your sleep mat, Shona, so get on."

Shona says, "Rustle should; she swimmies the best."

But Loo says, "Rustle and I already tried out the water. Solomon, too, a bite. But not you, so hop on."

Now that Shona is not our Leader, Loo is so dishing hardcore.

Shona says, "All right." She bites her bottom lip and her skin pales, but she doesn't whimper. Loo and I hold the thing still, and Shona carefully eases her fleshcore onto it, head first and belly-parts down. At once, the whole thing woffles dramatically one way, then the other, then it stabilizes as her weight spreads out evenly. It sags a bit where her huge chest makes a giant indent. Shona clutches the front edge with frantic hands, and her ramrod-straight feet trail behind a bit in the water. Water splooshes up, especially in front. A small wake forms behind

Shona when we pull the rope along the shore. Water splashes in her face and rolls over the mat in places, but she's not sinking, that's for sure. She looks so scared that even *I* don't make fun of her.

"Try looking down through the water," shouts Loo.

"No!" cries Shona, and she scrunches up her face, trying to hold her head away from the splashes that fall over it.

After a bite, Loo pulls her back toward the sand. Shona waddles around, growling, trying to get off the blaaty thing without ending up in the soup, ya? She shrieks when her whole leg flops under, but she scurries out and onto the sand quick enough. Loo claps, and I even give her shivery wet fleshcore a hug.

"You done good, Shona," I say to her.

Loo smiles. Shona is unsteady but proud. "Did you see me, Solomon?" she hoots, as Solomon approaches us at the shore. "I swimmied with the sleep mat." She looks triumphantly dazed. She thinks she has survived the worst.

Solomon smiles wide, more at the moment our unit is sharing than anything else. "Big fit, Shona," she says. Solomon investigates the raft. Shona and I pack all her stuff. We waterproof whafa can. Loo pours the ground waterweeds into two extra containers. We pack them at the top of the bag so we can reach them easily when we get hungry. Shona's cheeks are flushed, and she hums while she works. The wet parts of her uni squish when she walks past me briskly.

I smile weakly. Because the things about Shona that usually annoy the blaat out of me are suddenly reassuring, whafa all the scary newness of our situation. For once, we're fully **One Pod**, only minus our beloved, mysterious Roku.

Loo: Swimmy Out To Sea

Solomon lays an uncommon hug on me. I shrug it off.

"Don't get all emo," I say. But I can't stay mad when her big smile cracks open and she laughs, low and throaty.

"Who you calling emo?" she says, walking back to the water's edge.

We're ready. We push the yellow raft into the cold water. Our pack is as waterproof as we can make it. It's tied to the mat, and the weight of it sinks the raft down unless our bodies are counter-balancing around the edges. We are knee-deep in water, moving quickly, silently. Each step takes us deeper into the wet until the ground is sharp gone beneath us. We hang half on the raft, half off. We kick and kick. It takes a few millis to realize that we're working against podselves. We have to learn how to coordinate our kicks, how to get some timing.

Rustle says, "You're doing good, Loo," and I know it's true. I'm not as scared as before, and I'm loving the feel of the water swirling past my strong legs.

We head out past the little line of sand, past the piled-up rocks, and out the mouth of the hidden cave. Wind hits full hard in the face, and whafa seemed like tiny ripples when we stood on the sand are actually currents, surges of power that pull us, and waves that sploosh up, sometimes over our heads. Out on the open water, we just keep kicking. It is all around us, almost all we can see. The only other thing to look at is the big big sky, gray and thundering, massively cloud filled. We swimmy float, swimmy drift; we bob and twirl and steer. Each time I look at them, they are either leaning back their heads, staring up into the shocking newness, the bigness of this unknown sky, or they're peering down through the splashing waves, down through the darkening greeny-grays of the cold water, wondering at the deepness of the sea.

We, holed up for years inside the solid rocky caves of StarPod, except for our routine blast-offs into the unknown terrain of our

Missions, we are full-on freaking with all this space. And all I know is this: we are tiny specks, insignificant shadows, bouncing between these strange new worlds, and we know almost absoblaaty nothing about either.

Rustle: Rupture

Our eyes meet.

Loo's and mine. Hers—wide, staring silver—reflect my own horrified expression. It's late. The sky is green now, darker than the water. The rough waves grow in number and strength. The pack is washed apart; most of our survival gear is long gone, underwater. We stuffed whafa could inside our soggy unis. After these long hours, the raft can no longer hold us all. It sags and sinks. The wind batters it. The water tries to swallow it whole. There's yelling in the background: Solomon and Shona, I spoze. Splashing and yelling, and always the water.

Icy water rolls over my skin, in all my face holes: hearing, feeding, breathing, and in those tiny microscopic ones along my jaw, close to my hairline. Water stings my lidless eyes. Water slops around and splashes up over Loo's whole face. She blinks rapidly; the lids meet halfway in the middle, her mouth hangs open. Water pours out of it. A wave hits the back of my head. I sink. Everything is blurry, all sonic boom and gurgles.

Another monster wave curdles around. We sink even lower.

Now, I think. *Chronic!*

And I loosen my arms, sliding below the surface. I boost Loo up so her neck easily clears the water line. I'm below, hair fanning out, mysteriously alive, looking up at Loo, who's looking down through the water at me. Her face contorts; her mouth moves wider, longer. It shapes out the sound of my name as the water rolls over and through me, strangely. She clamps hard on me with her muscled legs and drags me back up so my head breaks the surface again, so we are entwined, so our faces are milli-blinks apart, so her breath warms my skin. Our lips press together, her skin and mine meant always to fuse.

I send, **Let me go, Loo. Or we'll all drown.**

I have no words. No words to transcribe the enormity of Loo. Her essence fuels me when nothing else can, when nothing else matters. I wave-send all my dented, inadequate feelings, wrap them up and gift them to her in the now. I gather them all and heave them into her beautiful face, into her terrifying predatory mindcore, and into those clammy, careful, and vulnerable sections deep inside her flesh: her organs, her wiring, her programs. Her heart, I know, is reserved for me.

Another massive wave. Loo bobs up to grapple with the raft. The momentum pushes me below. I press her legs open firmly and slip down between them, away. I hold terror in my mouth. Shock. My fleshcore rips away from hers, possibly forever. It is the longest milli, the slowest milli, of all existence. I still see her from underneath the water and she me. The fusion tear stabs and pains me. It skewers my spiritwind, and the only sound I hear is the thump of my own heart as I sink through the icy black waters.

Down and away.

Down and away.

Down.

Time passes.

Underwater, things are much calmer. When I come to, I feel the rhythmic beat of my own core. All else is changed, but I can't exactly think how. My eyes are moist and relaxed. They are growing used to this new substance. They scan through columns of water, detect pattern variances in rock, weed, and fish flesh. Shapes and colors distinguish themselves, movement and flickerings of movement. Light filters down where I hang suspended in the liquid. Light from the surface. From where my unit is. *From Loo.* A tiny bubble breaks from my nostril. It floats up and away, up through the lightening shades of gray, up to the eventual surface.

I look away from this light, look around me, look at all the parts of myself. I am not frightened. I be fit, with a sureness I haven't felt in a long time. Not since before the Aberration started up. I chew at the filthy bandages wrapped around my hands. The salt water feels good on them. The dirty rags float away. Small shadows flit toward the unfurling scraps. My hands drag and flow when they move through the water. The webbing between my fingers swells and grows beautiful, like it's never been before. I wobble, but quickly learn how to propel myself, how to stay upright in the water. How to extend and push myself, how to align myself with the current. I tilt and steer instinctively, rock with my torso, and flap and balance. Even my hair feels electric, full of life and purpose. Its tentacles browse the water with their own agenda. A deep sense of comfort comes over me. Somehow, I know this place. I know whafa do here, how to be.

More bubbles escape from my mouth and nose. All my oxygen is gone. My lungs ripple and burn; they hang useless in my chest, flapping softly. I seal my lips lightly and feel the strange suction of water enter, in me and through me, down my sides and behind my hearholes, through things unnamed but somehow not unknown: inside parts that first announced themselves months ago with dull throbbing aches and, since the Aberration, started growing with cantankerous throttles.

All this, all these, open up and begin to work. I breathe. Alone, I breathe anew in this strange and wonderful undersea planet.

Loo: Star Bright

Disjunct!

One milli, Rustle is crushed between my thighs, lips on my lips, face breathing my air; the next she is gone. *Nowhere.* Nothing but the aching feel-send song of goodbye.

Solomon's squeezes me. I choke back the sob that burns the back of my throat. Solomon fights to keep us afloat. She kicks strong and steady, keeps us chugging through the raging waters. I hang listless, sick with grief. Shona kicks half-heartedly; she is also despondent. We sway and roll with the massive waves, meg drenched by splooshes and dips. Shona shrieks staccato hiccups of fear. Solomon sends a healing wave to help us focus. There's another terrible, sad sound. I realize it's pouring out my own mouth.

Stop it! I think.

I pretend it's just a Wilderness Op with another hard lesson. Hunters and military Scouts cannot be fusing the day away, cannot be distracted the way I've let myself become around Rustle. *You pay for this exquisite joy some time,* I think.

Rustle—just her name flares a painful rip right through me. Rustle—slipped away so that I might survive. Gone, before any of us could guess or argue or pull her back up from the sea.

All in front is the cold, black water. Below? Only Kronk knows what lies beneath us, beneath the oily, churning waves. What creatures lie in wait, ready to tear her limbs from the sockets? Our raft bobs unsteadily in the gathering current, and we struggle to hang on. We float dizzily, circle wildly. We spin in sudden eddying swirls.

"Bramy!" shriek-sends Shona.

Her torso, rigid with terror, drags the raft even lower. Ice water pools across the whole mess, splooshes in our unis, up our faces again.

Breathe, Solomon sends. **Breathe and kick your blaaty feet.**

And so I push my own boots up and down in the water, motor us along in time with Solomon's legs, in time with her internal pulse. Every few millimiles, I pause and peer over my shoulder behind us, but Rustle is not there. We inch farther away from the looming points of the mountain range through which we made our escape. Maybe we are moving, after all.

Solomon nudges me. **One Pod. Be fit. Be free.**

I nod. But still the salt runs from my eyes and joins the vast pool we find ourselves in.

"It's, like, getting big big dark now?" says Shona nervously.

Nopod answers. We float and drift, and sometimes spin in a softer current.

She says, "At least it's not like before. No more storming, huh?"

We don't speach back.

"Solomon?"

There is a catch to her voice at the end of each word, and the sound rememories me of deathmaul. Like when a kill is down, you're eye to eye. It's bleeding and cowering. You're standing above with your weapon and your strength, your power coursing through, and you wave-send it all in your final blow. You seal the kill complete and suck up all that hysteria and terror and those intense survival waves, and you churn it into your own lifesource. You suck the lifeforce right out. Exactly whafa I want to do to Shona.

"I know I'm, like, not Pod Leader anymore and, like, none of this was my idea or anything but, like, somepod still has to answer me. Whafa we float swimmy half-dead until we, like, starve to death? Is that the big big plan?"

I'm too tired to talk and too tired to even text: *Shut it, for Kronk's sake!* So I bite my own forearm instead. It's a new and different pain from the chronic numbness in my cramped limbs. My hand slips off. It flops around. I force my pruney, claw-shaped fingers to open and stretch, open and then close back tightly on the sagging raft.

Shona licks her lips for the millionth time and breathes loudly out her noseholes, and even Solomon grimaces slightly. I imagine Shona suffocating underneath the raft, her blue face bloated and ugly, staring back up at us through the yellow rubber, her flailing core kicking up one last twitch, the wheezing, rattling sound of her nose air silenced for good.

"Aren't you guys, like, even thirsty?" she says.

"Yes!" we both snap.

Blaaty spietchka. Of course we're half-dead thirsty, hungry, and lost in this bottomless ocean. Practically our only feed floated away, unnoticed. Twice we stopped to try and cup up some of the water and add sterilization pills to make it drinkable, but it was impossible to keep the containers level, and we feared losing the precious contents for good. Shona had been sneaking mouthfuls of water, mouthfuls that Solomon predicts will have her pulse-puking in a matter of millis.

"Okay, I don't care whafa you two say. I'm drinking it," says Shona. She sneers defiantly, lowers her mouth and fills it. She gulps greedily. She plunges down again. Not even Solomon protests this time; that's how tired she is. The water slopping in Shona's mouth, the happy sounds that murmur out from her rubbery lips, are enough to drive me chronic mental. Rage shakes me. And when I turn my head away in disgust, that's when I see it: a short triangular fin poking above the water. It trails at a steady pace behind us. It seems to be attached to a large ocean manimal.

"Uh, Solomon?" I whisper.

She doesn't say a word. But I know she is on sudden alert. We stop kicking. We draw our legs up instinctively. I unsnap the holster from my soggy boot and pull my silver dagger out from its casing. I hold it ready. Shona is mad-sucking back water and hasn't even seen the thing. We cling and float, and we can only hope.

Time outruns us. Nopod knows where we are, whafa doing next. The big big sky blackens itself, leaving high-up twinklers and a few glowing planets to light our passage. Light pools along the watery expanse, dribbles down our frowny faces, lights the last sparkles in our shining wide eyes. The manimal is still out there, biding its time for our eventual defeat, but we can't see it now, and that helps us pretend it is gone far away, forever.

Solomon says, "I never saw so much sky before. So many twinklers. I never knew it could be so big."

"Blaaty big," I say quietly. "Breathey."

Solomon murmurs in agreement. The air is so changed from whafa we sucked up all those years in training, down under the earth. We never had it like this—cold and clear and minus the dust. Minus the dirt filters. No nose tubing, no oxy tanks like the ancients wore.

Shona hums a funny tune, one of her fave bopcore hits, but it sounds alright with us, floating quiet in the dark. She has puked endlessly after drinking up so much water, and the song is the first other sound to come out of her. *Even Rustle wouldn't kick her now,* I think.

Rustle.

And just like that, the lump inside my ribcage triples in size. It squeezes unbearably at my lungs. I gasp. Solomon moves closer. She's looking at me now. There's a dollop of skylight on her lower lip. She shapes the sound of my name, sends me fusion waves, soft and tender. They woffle through my muscled skin, break through my chest pains, and tinkle with that hard, suffocating mass inside. Again, water leaks from my stinging eyes.

Shona, oblivious, says, "If we can see them, then they can see us, right?"

"The manimal?" says Solomon.

"Huh?" says Shona. "No, up there." Her head is tilted back. She is looking at the sky. From where I am, I can see right up her noseholes.

Solomon says, "Oh. Well, prolly."

We'd always assumed we'd get to go there, all of us, together, as part of the Crusades. That was the plan all along: to travel into the big big sky, land on some contaminant or hostile twinkler rock, and maintain a pilgrim program until the host stabilized for our eventual domination. Once we passed into Eighth, our unit would have been in the first departure wave. That's how good we were. *How good we are.* Still existing. Just without an authorized Star Plan.

We stare at the innumerable clusters; some, no doubt, marking galactic collides from long long ago. Maybe our very own first planet has left some glowing nebular spill, some radioactive and pretty sky rocks, to help us guide our way tonight. Just maybe.

Rustle: Gurgle Gloop

Glug gurgle gloop.
Bulgey bleep, feathery sweep.
Swoony blop, swivelly drop.
Swimmy shimmy down the deep.
Bubble bubble bloop.

Loo: Feeding Frenzy

Much later, I snap my head back. I nod and blink. I've been zen-tuning, right blanked. Darkness leaves in streaks. Now the sky lightens, and we are even less of podselves today: tattered, dehydrated, exhausted. Full-frontal glum glum. Somepod bumps my dangling feet, glides and rubs against the length of my submerged core.

"Quit it, Shona," I snark.

"Whafa quit?" she says.

A strong undercurrent almost pulls me off the raft. Solomon bobs up and back down sharp. She shock-sends the precise sensation outwards, a reflex only, but it chills us both. Shona squeals in terror. My head swivels. I notice a series of gray fleshflags, skimming above the water many podlengths away, circling. They are like the lone scout I saw last night. It must have sent for them. They must have been calling back and forth and trailing us throughout the night.

One is right behind Shona. Water churns, it foams, and I see the great gray manimal, its slick core chugging through the oily water. Its strange triangular fin grazes my flailing arm when it descends. I feel it against my flesh, an unholy interspecies friction. With a shriek and a jerk, Solomon disappears below.

"Help her," Shona screams.

My insides quake. I blank-wave. I stare back at Shona.

"One Pod!" Shona screeches to try and make me move.

I'm stronger than her. I'm the best Hunter. I make the most lethal kills. Her face twists when I hesitate. That self-preservation program, the survivalist training plays out; I look to the empty place on the raft beside me. Shona flails and kicks. She clumsily slips away and burrows under the next great wave while I cling to the raft. I tread my aching feet underneath me, spit out more of this salty water. I watch in horror as the other fins circle closer. Some millis later, the dark water bursts with a sudden bright red stain.

Podtraitor.

The name burns itself into my giblets.

Another manimal noses me, a third dives down to my right. My innards crinkle in terror. The next bump knocks me right off the raft. I curl into a ball, try to roll, suck big big air when my face breaks the surface. On one downward plunge, currents push me millibeats from the broken lines of flashing white teeth. Blood blooms from its massive mouth. Scarlet petals trail along its corelength and, though I wriggle away from it, swivel and turn violently, I cannot tell where lies the sun, the raft, my podmates, or the unimaginable bottom of this vast sea. I feel for my hunting dagger, strapped back tight in its holster. In a heartbeat, the beast flips around and comes back to attack. I detach my silver blade, grip it tightly, and when it draws close, I push off its open jaw, hold fast to a large tooth from the top rung of them. I reach high, and when its great rolling eye bulges furiously, I stab. My slender knife pushes through retina. I'm wrist deep in eye jelly and membranes. I twist the blade, sever those tangled nerve cords. I push deeper and twist as the last bubbles leave my lips. The kick-back waves of shock push me when the beast shakes its massive self. It bucks and contorts in a violent surge of bloodied water.

I hang limp—play dead—and breathe in a burning lungful of salty air when my head breaks the surface. Another long snout nudges me. I float, hang my head. I will myself not to splash or kick or scream. The thing stiffens, catches the blood-scented trail of its mate, and speeds after it. In my next labored breath, I watch the other fins sweep past me, following the trails of crimson tide. They dive down. A furious fountain explodes. Tails and fins and foaming pink torrents mark their feast.

I move farther away from the carcass, the bloodletting, as quickly as I can. My cramped hand, tight like a fist, is empty. *My dagger?* Gone. Now my two hands work to sweep water away, to pull my bruised core farther from the carnage, weaponless. I stare into the gray horizon, alone.

Solomon, I send softly, **and Shona. And Rustle.**

Have I betrayed them all?

Rustle: Silver Glinty

Blaaty heart shock.

A shining glint twinkles through the dark water. Something about its lazy funneling course tells me it is not alive. Not one of the wary scary long fishies with tricky light-ups that lure a pod close, only to sting and strangulate her. Not a streaky clump of the electrocuting seagrass either, all twitchy and scratchy, whafa scraped up my legs full-frontal. Whafa tricks wee fishies into its glitzy meadow, then sends their small fated corpses floating toward the open mouths of camouflaged predators, way bigger fishies.

No. It is the free-fall dance of a precious thing that calls me. It tugs at some dying part of my rememory banks. It is a tiny sharpened tool. It cartwheels and twirls, eddies up on a small current, draws small darting fishies to it, scares them away when it turns, falls, draws down toward unknown sandy floors. I watch it, hypnotized, and somewhere inside me, the taut string of nerves that allows me to function in this strange new place, that allows some plodding rational mask of sanity to corral all those other dangerous flights of passion, somehow, this cord snaps. For when I look and see and rememory it, I know.

This is Loo's pretty silver dagger!

I singlemindedly push to catch this piece of metal, this thing of Loo's, infused with her warmth, her strength, even with her scent, although I can't track that in the wet. Encoded with the history of its own usage, it sings its own stories and battle songs. Even in this underwater planet, it could prolly lead me back to her.

Loo.

And as I swimmy steady on, quick and strong, I see only the silver flash of the knife and think on her same-colored fierce eyes. I trace the silver outline against the dark wall of some underwater mountain, its deep and mossy shadow tones a perfect foil for the twinkling glint, those shiny acrobatics. I watch my own reaching hand, watch it grasp and fumble, then swoop and grab again. I stare at the dagger in my fist—a delicate and deadly instrument, it shines like luxury.

I think on nothing else. Not the sudden turn of tiny fish, billowing away in large, clouded colonies, nor the growing darkness that overtakes me, and certainly not the slow and giant movement, the widening jaws of the mammoth beast lying in wait.

It all happens slow-mo, happens like in a trancey vision state; the thing opens up and up and there I am inside it all, and then the thing closes. Closes down, shut tight. Knifey and me swish darkly in the dank cavernous pit, the smelly inner tubing of the beast.

Loo: Happy Yellow

It looks strange, bobbing on the crest of gentle waves. The texture is all wrong, the color too garish for this endless green and gray. It's the color of something familiar. A thing from far away and long ago.

My head drops forward again into the water and I stretch to float, arms wide, legs dragging down, hair spiraling out. Little fishies swimmy up to me and their tiny mouths open like "oh-oh-oh." They nibble the ends of my long hair, suckle my fingertips. On my next big breath, I see that thing again. It burns into my mindcore, rememories me of somepod. It is the color of the liquid in our Sleep Now vials, the amber sparkle of hope. That same cheerful shade of a sleep mat. *Rafty!* I dare myself to keep it in my sights, to now kick with purpose and renewed strength, to move the heavy logs of my limbs toward it. *Happy yellow raft.*

An image of the golden planet once worshipped by the ancestors sends itself, unbidden: from before the New Revolution, before the Treason Times, and before the Great Planetary Collide.

The raft seems always a podlength or two away. It spins on a sudden current. I ride the crest of a wave, drop heavy from its singing tips.

I am Icarus, chasing the sun: a non-programmed thought from my infancy.

And when I finally come within arm's reach, I want to weep like a hatchling. There it is. With a lumpy blue core hanging on tight. *Shona.* Her eyes bulge, dart aimlessly, close shut. Her skin is a strange, hypothermic shade. Her chin trembles then falls; her mouth quivers open with exhaustion. Her head droops. She squashes her face into the last remaining tattered piece of our raft.

Shona, I send.

She's blanked. I try kicking her dangly legs a bit when I'm closer. I say, "Whafa Solomon?" Her eyes glaze over and her response is as bleak as I can bear.

"Nowhere now."

I rememory those spurting fountains of gushing red water. Guilt cramps my bellyparts.

"I swimmied down to find her," she says at last. "I saw her in the thing's mouth." Shona shudders and begins to rock back and forth. "I swimmied as good as I could and I grabbed her. Her hair and, like, her arm. Her mask strap was caught around its big tooth." I'm impressed Shona even figured that out. It must show on my face because she snaps, "Solomon texted she was caught, so I, like, tried to find the strap and I did, and it was down the gummy sides of the thing's tooth, so I pulled the strap out and, like, totally clawed the fleshcore." Shona opens her hands. The nails are broken and torn. There's even somepod's meat chunked underneath them still. "The strap came loose but I couldn't see a thing. It was all cloudy, blood everywhere."

I touch her icy flesh.

"I swimmied as hard as I could, and the big things were all around me. I think I saw Solomon later, floating away. I was trying to find the raft. Then I blanked. When I woke up, I was here. She was gone."

"Was she bleeding?" I ask. My voice is hoarse and the sounds croak out strangely.

She shrugs. "There was blood everywhere …"

I hold Shona's wrists; ask her to do the same with mine. We grip fiercely on either side of the raft.

Solomon, I coo-send.

"No!" Shona jerks away from me. "The beasties will come."

"Prolly." I actually hadn't thought of that. I am losing it, full-frontal. All my years of survival training, all draining out the rememory banks. We have to go way back to Level One basic training, where every element of a new world is potential danger, where we are prey. Where any kind or comfortable thing could give way to predators, to death, in a milli.

"Anyway, she's, like, prolly Deplugged?" says Shona bitterly. She bites her bottom lip.

Prolly, I think. But I can't allow that idea to take hold, just as I can't admit the same for Rustle.

"Shona," I say, "if we do not Pod-send, how will Solomon ever track us?"

Her eyes reflect my own, dully. She does not believe either, but we make pretend, if only for each other's sake. We coo pod-style and float on the small rolling waves toward what I hope is the still lightening line of the horizon.

There is one tiny dark spot above it.

Rustle: Guts

Blaat.

All around me big big black. Gurgle and drip, drip. The stench. *Unfit.*

Salty, stingy water swooshes around in the thing's awful mouth. I stumble back, lie prone on a pulsing textured carpet. Small circles of it suction onto my fleshcore. The carpet ripples, tickles, and tugs me along, rolls me back on its muscled floor. Beside me, a fishy twice my length grips and bucks. It sonic-sends a quiet **Blurp!** An almost silent protest of this terrible discovery. We are on the inside. Swallowed whole, this fishy and I, inside a giant beast. Strong acids in its saliva sting my fleshcore. I don't have much time.

Try to escape? Or try to reconfigure Loo's last battle?

I read death-wave on this tool; I know it found a recent kill.

Please not Loo, I Kronk-send. When I grip the knife tighter and concentrate, my mindcore begins to open. A warm and vibrant lifeforce sings the name *Loo.* It washes over me, strange and supple touchlings; her fingers, printed on the tool, push back up to my own; the heat of her handgrip echoes onto mine. The pulse of her blood thuds lightly, unevenly, and her tantalizing image swells up and into me, fills my core. Then more. Her panic-scent fills my nostrils, those now gratuitous holes in my face; her adrenaline surges through me. Her terror floods my veins. Then the last battle plays out inside my mindcore. I see the manimals charge and twist, attack again. I see fuddled pictures of Solomon dragged underwater, of Shona pulling her up and away, of blood spurting freely. I see Shona swimmy and drag Solomon's weight through the bloodstorms. Confusion, bubbling walls of water, then afterwards, I mostly see Loo's hand in front, holding the knife and stabbing it into the horrible gaping eye, over and over again. I see her swimmy away from the flowing blood, watch it billow and fill the seas, and watch the heated response of the other manimals. They catch the bloodscent and dive, ripping through waves and torrents and foaming rushes of sea. The feeding begins—a violent frenzy. Loo swimmies past it all as the knife makes its lazy descent, unnoticed by the feeding beasts.

So. I slow myself, feel the internal coil loosen. The trance stops. I return to the state of me, watery wet, shaky, and worn. Loo may dandystill be alive, although it's not entirely certain. She fought several large manimals, killed at least one, and swimmied past the others before she lost the knife. I trace the shiny length of it with my finger, rememory the sight of it strapped in her leg holster, ready to quick-draw, always ready to fight. My shoulders shudder. I quake. Rolling waves of podsickness heave through me. Even through this new underwater self I've grown into.

One Pod.

I fight the urge to lie back and let this monstrous beast devour me. I think of Loo, handy fused with me, think of her steely eyes and soft mouth. I lunge forward as the sad fishy next to me is suckled toward the tunnel at the back of this giant's slimy throat. I stab with all the fury I can muster. I slice my way to the big opening, roll forward along the bumpy tongue, drag the sharp edge along behind me, and cut my way out to the ocean again.

Back to the big big sea.

Loo: Black Blob

Retinal damage?

I blink and it stays. I look away but the spot doesn't follow. There is something out there behind Shona, far away and much higher in the silver sky. It is, no doubt, some large flying carrion cleaner, maybe more than one, coming to pick flesh from our soggy bones before we sink eternal to our watery last sleep. They like to eat the eyes first; those juicy fruitballs splurt in their beaks and render such despair and terror that most manimals tend not to fight back. Carrion cleaners will eat us alive, prolly without risking a single injury to themselves. Then we'll draw those wary scary beasts back over with the scent of our spilling blood. At least those big big fishies would Deplug us more quickly.

I decide to not mention it to Shona. She will panic, prolly, and suffer me more.

Instead, I say, "I've been ruthless, right?" I say it like that's a bad thing, although I know it's not. It's my ultimate weapon, really.

"You, like, never respected me as Leader," she says, quietly.

"No." Funny that saying this feels almost tender to me.

"Why not?" She looks steady on, and we pretend that these are not our last millis alive, ironically trapped for this great final passing with each other, and not with those we truly love. "Why don't you like me?" She sniffs.

I think hard on it. *Whafa text?* That she is the best petty manager ScanMans ever programmed? An adminimalice product built to spy and report against us, like Roku always said? Solomon and Roku would be kind, at the last. Rustle would crack a joke, prolly annoy her to death before any valkyrie gobbled up the last of her squirming organ parts. *And me?* Normally I'd claw her frontal, kill her fresh while I still had the chance, gain some more lifeforce for my next battle and increase my odds for survival.

Instead, I say, "You just try too hard, for all the wrong reasons. You believe in all the wrong things. We all did, I spoze."

Shona coughs. After a bite, she says, "It was never enough. You, like, have—had—Rustle. And Roku had all the mysteries of her head strength, and I—"

"Wanted Solomon," I say.

Her face crimples; her brow furrows. "I wish we'd fused. I know I'm not, like, wired for it?" she adds quickly, "but I wish I could have tried it with her. Like, once."

Clever ScanMans kept her sterile like us all, but shortwired to never podfuse. *Neutered.* Shortwired to never betray her duties for some heavy-synch romance. *And yet,* I think, *she did.* She did make her preference known in as many ways as possible. *Maybe there's still hope for her.* Her face is so wistful, yearning for that precious unbroken rule, that I feel a rush of shame. Now I get why Rustle was kind to her at times, even though it went against training or instinct. Even though Rustle was at least as annoyed with her as me.

I look again at the dark shape growing larger in the sky. The blob is flying fast. There's no way it won't spot us on our yellow raft. If I still had my dagger, I could finish us both off before the thing got close enough to start feeding.

"Do you have any weapons at all?" I ask.

She shakes her head, glum glum. "What do you, like, think it was all about?"

I don't hear Shona because I'm busy scanning the thrump in her neck, wondering if I have enough strength left in my wrinkled, peeled hands to seal off that air pipe forever. My first and last mercy kill.

"Hmm." I am imagining a mutual Deplugging: part strangulation, part double drowning.

After spitting out a wash of seawater and weeds, Shona says, "Loo, the least you can do in our last millis alive is, like, pretend to listen to me."

I want to laugh. Even on the verge of extinction, we still fight. "Why?"

I say, "Why whafa? Why are we out here? Why did we end up in Living Lab? Why did Roku take off?"

"No," she says. "Bigger whys than that."

"Oh." I don't think about the big questions. Neither does Shona. That's whafa Roku and Solomon are good at. "You mean, why did they make us the way they did?"

She nods.

I shrug. "They needed protection, so they Found us and they liked us, and they made us to be exactly whafa wanted: top military killing units. That's why."

Then I think, *Who did they need so much protection from?*

Shona says in a trembly wee voice, "I wasn't Found, you know. Not like you others. I don't know whafa am."

I rememory so many things that Roku used to say. She'd fire sudden comments or questions like from a camouflaged tank. Even Solomon would wonder out loud about our orders. *And Rustle refused to kill that mark.*

I say, "I guess I'd like to know whafa really going on in StarPod."

Shona and I look at each other in silence. I see the tired misery of a failed Leader. Someone who hungered for what little recognition ScanMans ever doled out. Just as I hungered medallions and pins, hunting trophies, and high scores on Mission. How Roku hungered truth stories, and Solomon harmony and healing. How Rustle hungered me. When I look at Shona, I see that we chose a poisoned meal, both of us, and that now we had to live out our last millis knowing our mistake.

"Honestly, Loo." She pants lightly. "You are so hard. A full-frontal Warrior."

"We are different species," I say. "But we are One Pod."

She smiles a vulnerable tilt of the mouth and says, "Thanks." She closes her eyes.

I hear the faint sounds of its arrival above the crash of waves—a furious, wet sound. The loud slapping beats are wings that bring the creature closer to us, racing at windspeed. They smack the air like wet flesh on fleshcore; the force is even more a rushing movement than a sound. It shakes my innards, rattles my rusty bowels. A cold breeze lifts bumps on the skin of my arms, on the back of my neck. A strange pull in my fleshcore causes a stirring deep inside. The fine pale hairs that cover the backs of my muscled arms and legs stand stiff. A niggling shockwave rides the length of my core.

The great black bird screeches. Its long feathers trail and slice the water's surface, sending whirlpool currents rippling out and away from the shadow of its immense body. Two strong legs would blend with its dark tail plumes, except for the golden talons that shine and reflect light from their razor-sharp points. The heavy wing beats slow, allowing the thing to hover directly above us. Its plump breast lies open to an easy shot; I could have felled it with my crossbow, a spear, even a long fighting stick, had I any with me. I stare into the large orange eyes with amazement. It sends a sonorous long note, a formal greeting and a grief knell rolled in one.

It cannot be. And yet I know her in my core. She sonic-sends, her Pod-waves quibble my ribsticks, rumble my bellyparts. She hovers above, impervious, powerful. So much a new creature that I feel awe. *She has feathers!* She has come for us.

Roku.

Take Shona, I send. **She won't last long.**

Roku nods, and with a great twist of her feathered neck, swoops in to grasp Shona's slumped shoulders. With massive wing beats, she hauls upward, taking her collapsed cargo. Within millis she is off, up and away into the great barren sky, growing smaller in the distance.

Will she return in time?

Another sonic-wave booms through my aching chest.

One Pod, sends Roku. **One Pod.**

Rustle: Flutter

Weeds tickle when I wriggle through their clumps. I swimmy fast. The silver I hold glints, leads, pulls me, almost. I swimmy gurgle in the deep. Hold the little dagger tight. It's in the way but there's no dropping it now, there isn't. There's no place to tuck it, hardly any clothes to hide it in. Just me and my cognizant hairlings, my fins, and my streamlined flesh. Knifey leads me back to where I first found it, to the site of Loo's last battle.

Visions flash: I scent the blood of a recent kill. I am on it; I am in the milli. *Carnage.* Wee fishies nibble up the chunky bits, the floating glue and the sinking bones of whatever Loo fought. My pulse quickens. My organs strain. *Whafa?*

I swimmy low and slow, scour the bottom and hidden craggy spots for any signs, any traces. Only big manimal bones, crushed and ground and torn apart, stripped almost clean of their meat, lie here. More than one, by the looks. But no pod trails, no Loo, no hints left behind.

I push upwards. I swimmy hard the whole long way, up and up, until I break the surface. I don't see her, not at first. But I feel her nearby, feel her pulling farther away with each milli. *There!* Loo—in the claws of a giant carrion feeder, flying high and fast. I scream, but no sounds come. Breath leaves me and I flutter. I flip. I dive down and suck back water through my gills. I rise up, leap the waves, and sonic-send, feel-send, any-send, but she's gone. She's a shrinking spot beneath the large black bird, soon to be devoured. Soon to disappear forever.

Book
2

Loo: Rifted

Roku drops me on the craggy rock. Blood runs from where her talons gripped my shoulders. My bellyparts lurch as though I am still dangling high over the hungry waters; there is a mad churning in my core. It was a long trek with Roku flapping hard, soaring high, swooping with more power than pod could ever imagine. She flew while I blanked; while I stared down over the unending waves; while I dozed; and while I woke with a fiery sun stabbing through the cracks of the mountain ahead. Not like the rock we crawled out of—a deeper, softer, reddish rock covered in greens and yellows, plant life of some kind.

I spit. I hawk and heave, but there's nothing left to spill. No feed mush inside and no more water drops. I am a dry sack of bones with scaly flesh stretched over them. Roku hovers above. Massive wings beat hot air over my face, my core. *Whush!* Her scent is all over me, the scent I buried my face in all this long while. Roku is Kronk strong. She is Beyond. I try to stand, but it is strange to bear my own weight again. *Me, weak!* My thighs quiver and each step hurts after being so long in the water, then so high in the air. When I get my balance, I unknot the crumpled bag from around my waist, the only thing I scavenged from

Shona's bag.

Shona hides in the greeny fluff, sends Roku. She points her beak. **She told me whafa happened back at StarPod. Loo, I'm sorry if it was my fault.**

"Take me to her," I say. And I don't even think about the rest.

She screeches a wildness that rakes my hearholes. **Rustle?**

"Drowned," I say. I want to weep.

Oh, Loo.

I blink. I stare at her glowing orange eyes, seeing them for the first time proper. They are so like the autotron image of our base mantra, burned by repetition into our mindcores.

Solomon is—

"Ate by sea manimals." I blank.

Not ate. Bit.

"Whafa?"

I found her first. Shona tends her now.

Solomon is not dead, then. *Thank Kronk!* Not ate and torn and blood-stumped to bone mash. Suddenly, it is all too much. I shiver shake. My core trembles. I coo pod-style. It doesn't come out quite right, but the sound warms me from the inside and, although Roku doesn't join in, it's some comfort to have her there, larger than Kronk and blacker than night.

Later, I scramble in the scratchy tall weeds, looking for sticklings and such. Roku is sightstrong but has no fingers any more. She hops about and lifts heavy branchlings in her powerful beak, but can't light a firestick from my salvaged bag to save her new-grown self. Together we make a small fire to help warm Solomon's ragged core. Yellow tongues crack at the pile and smoke puffs out. Soon, flames dance higher and the light brings us close, Pod-circle. Solomon is feverish. She has lost so much blood. Shona fusses over her like she's a wee hatchling and not a mighty Assassin Settlement Warrior. I fuse-wave Solomon to detract from her pain. The tourniquet on her left shoulder is stained red, but has helped stanch the blood flow.

"Does she know the arm is gone?" I say, quietly.

Shona glares.

Roku clucks. **I don't know.**

I say, "Whafa do without two of them?"

"Shut it, Loo," says Shona.

"Well, it's not like they blaaty grow back now, is it?"

"She might not have lost it if you'd, like, helped or something?" Shona mutters the terrible word under her breath: "Podtraitor."

It burns me right through.

I hunt now. Roku pushes off the ground and her strong wings extend. They pull her up. Flap, flap, and away.

I gather more twiglets from the hairy grass, from around the big plants. I sniffle a bit, nary much as I'm so dehydrated, but a teeny drop leaks out. Back at the fire, Shona mops sweat from Solomon's brow, drips precious water into her cracked lips: one, two. Fresh leaves cover her other wounds. A raw scent hangs over her. *So unfit.* She is delirious, and none of us are true Healers, only Solomon herself.

Shona mixes a bit of ground waterweed into a can of Rustle's Fizzy Drop, both from the bag I'd stashed from the raft. She trickles the mixture into Solomon's mouth, one bloop at a time. My stomach gurgles loudly. I look at our few soggy, mangled items: five more firesticks, all coated to stay waterproof, one small packet of ground waterweed that we will save for Solomon, and three sterilizing pills to treat water.

"Sure you don't have anything to add? Anything from your pockets or tucked in your boots?"

"As if," says Shona. She drips another feed drop.

I force myself to look at Solomon then. Her skin is the shade of cooked ash, not her usual rosy-brown hue. Her dreads hang limp;

her lips are dry and cracked. Her eyes roll restless underneath the thin skin of her lids. Yellow blaat crusts in the corners. I feel sick when I look to where her left arm should be, with its large healing hand, its mystical power center. Her spiritwind is very low.

Oh.

Roku flutters down with two squirming widgets in her bloodied claws. I quickly prepare the cooking sticks, peel the bark, and sharpen the tips with my fingers and teeth. I break the squirmers' necks, then pile them by the pit. *My blaaty knife,* I wish.

We will find our way, sends Roku. She looks me in the eye, fuse-sends warmth. Then she flaps and raises herself into the growing dark, leaving us alone again.

"Shona?" I tap her shoulder lightly. She's fully blanked. "Shona, not talking won't help Solomon get better. Pod must work together."

Her eyes snap open. "Together? You weren't *together* when Solomon needed you most. You even let your own Rustle go."

I grind my teeth to avoid tearing into her. "Not the same thing at all. But you're right. I failed Solomon. Now I want to help."

Shona growls.

"No matter whafa, we are—"

"Bramy shut it with the One Pod blaat!" Shona's chest heaves with emotion.

I back away in surprise.

"I'm, like, so sick of you, of everything. If that sky manimal is Roku, and that's a big big if, then she has, like, completely Declined, Deformed, and Disobeyed! We shouldn't be anywhere near her. Roku's the reason any of this ever happened to us."

"We don't know that, Shona. That life, StarPod training life, it's over now. We have to treat this like a serious Survival Op and be fit. Whafa Solomon would do."

Shona sniffs defiantly. "That's just your adaptability program talking. You've always been the best at enviro transplants."

I say, "You're still thinking of going back there, aren't you?"

Her chin juts up a notch.

"Are you blaaty convulsed?" I can't even believe her. "I knew we should have dropped you in Living Lab." The old anger flares up inside me. I throw another stick on our fire. "That's Roku. I can't explain, but in my wires, by Kronk, I know it's her. If Solomon wasn't hurt, she could handscan to find out."

I can't help but wonder. *Could Solomon even do that with one hand?*

Shona quivers with rage. "I don't want to know anything about that manimal. It's like wicked Deformed."

"So why did Roku save us?"

"We're not saved. That thing has flown away and left us. We're going to starve and die in this wary scary place. We have to go back."

Back where? To Living Lab? Roku appears as silently as she left, with only a warm rush of air from her beating wings. She has two more furries, bleeding in her claws.

Shona jumps in surprise. She turns her back in a huff. I take the wee things and snap them quick. Now I spear all four with the peeled and sharpened sticks. I rest the sticks at an angle to the fire and let the dripping juice sizzle in the pit.

Roku sends, **How? Pod can't fly or swimmy.**

I shrug. "She's got a point, Shona."

Roku hops about in the longer grass and returns pushing a strange stone, rounded on one side and hollowed somewhat on the other. I pick it up and place it near the fire where she points with her beak. Roku brushes it clean with her wing.

Shona is saying, "You could take us back. You could at least take Solomon back. It's the only way to save her," says Shona.

"How would that save Solomon?" I ask. I am wondering whafa Roku wants with this stone.

"You know she loves the tunnels. She loves the underground.

ScanMans could reanimate her, but they need her core to do it. She could start over, fresh, back where she wants to be. It's the only way."

"You mean in those corpse fakies?" I hiss. "Roku, you don't know whafa found, whafa saw in Living Lab. Blaaty unfit." I rememory walking through the rows of cots, all those blank mindcores and empty Pod shells.

Roku steps closer and mindsweeps me. I feel her powerful waves probe right through me, right through my sealed rememory bank. It knocks me back. She sifts through images: the cots, the faces, the blank cores waiting. She sees her own face, and mine with the eyes open, the mouth moving. She sees me destroy them all, all save mine. When she hops to a perch a few millis away, the sweep fades. She gently pulls out. I feel warm tingles where her mind fingers have been. *Wary weird.* It is hard to read Roku with all her new strangeness, but she seems agitated. She bristles and ruffles her feathers, shaking their very tips.

That would not be our Solomon, she sends. **ScanMans would reprogram her.**

Shona's lip quivers. "She'd have her arms, at least."

But not her own Spirit, Roku sends. **We need water.** And off she goes again, this time carrying our empty pack.

I stare at Solomon's furrowed brow. If only I could mindsweep her, whafa Roku did to me just now. I'd learn so much. I touch her hot skin. "She'd have some serious mindcore tuning. You know it, Shona. They'd delete all her rememories. Our Solomon would hate that." I wish Solomon had been snapped in two and never left to woffle so in pain.

Shona doesn't speak. The widgets are almost burning in some parts, still running raw in others. I turn them, then tend the snappy fire. Shona sits and broods.

Roku whooshes back to us, hovering with the pack in her

claws. The thing is so full of water it seems ready to burst. I take it from Roku and pour it carefully into the hot upturned stone.

Add your pill now. Shona does, but she keeps well away from Roku.

"All this feed will strengthen Solomon," I say. I turn the smaller sticks again to cook the furry things evenly. Fat drips into the fire. The smells water my mouth. It's strange to eat manimals, but sometimes on Mission we have to, like if we run out of powders, or if it is ScanMans' orders. Testing fleshcore from other species, whafa.

"See? We'll completely *not* starve to death," I say to Shona.

She glares from the other side of the fire. "Shut it!"

I thank the furries for giving over to us and, for a brief milli, I wonder where they are now. *Where are their spiritwinds?* Soon to be inside us, partly. The rest might go straight up to Kronk's garden, if pod dandystill believes in it. That's the autotron story ScanMans teach wee hatchlings to make them feel better when all their teeny mates start dropping like stones. I haven't rememoried Kronk's garden in a very long time. Maybe they're really all up there, laughing and lolling. Playing. Waiting. *Rustle, too.*

Roku senses my sad-wave and she clucks a tiny sound at me.

"So you can't mouth-speak anymore?" I ask.

Roku shakes no. **Throat changed. Sounds wary weird.**

"No kidding. But you dandystill understand us, right? Sent text and mouthspeach, too."

She nods.

"Whafa like, being so different?" I say. *Kronk, that sounds like Rustle, not me!*

This is really new. She fluffs her wings. **I still don't know how I work yet.**

Shona finally speaks. "So, like, whafa happened?"

I hand her a stick with one crispy widget. "Eat up, Shona," I say cheerfully. She growls.

I offer Roku one but she shakes her head. **I eat them fresh.**

"Blaah," I say. I sit close to the fire and start picking at my widget. The hot juices run down my chin when I crunch it. The fleshcore tastes so unlike protein powder, our main feed at StarPod. This is wild and textured, chewy and crisp. *Yum.* I slurp my greasy fingers and suck the dirty stick. I reach for another.

Roku nestles down comfy and starts sending us the story.

Roku: Fire Story

They crouch and quiver around the fire, little broken things. *Poor Solomon.* Splayed out like Kronk's daughter, bleeding into the ground. Dying. The others are too fully convulsed by me, by my changes, to nurture Solomon proper or to see how far gone she is. Loo is keen on my new powers and would love to have them podself. She is fascinated, scanning me whenever I turn my head. She doesn't know I can see, sense, know, almost all the way around me.

I hear every snapping twiglet, each puffing gust of wind that shakes the leafy plants and trees. I see so much more now. Color vibrates with song. Darkness only brings more depth to the world. It lights up the heat trails of other manimals, lights up their nitrate spills into a glowing path. Tiny flying and crawling things, earth-plowing worms call to me against their will, and down I swoop to suck them back, peppered with seeds and leaves and thin stalks of tender weeds. I eat almost constantly to feed this new hunger of mine, this new strength.

Shona and Loo make more of their tiny gestures, their goggling eyes and secret sends. Shona seethes with hate. She can't stop the low growl that rumbles her chest whenever I hop too near. She's guarding something, cradling a hidden lump under her uni. I watch as she pulls Solomon closer to block Loo from noticing. I make mental to find out her secret. For now, I struggle to stack words together, organize them Pod-style so they can get my meaning.

Things wary weird, I send, and they jump back, startled. **Have been for a long time.** I rotate my neck to look at Shona, then back around to Loo, who nods eagerly and says, "Go on."

Things change inside first, then sprout outside. It's impossible to describe the internal convulsions I'd been having for so long, impossible to find words that fit. Even many of the new ideas trapped in my mindcore and guarded by my new larynx are without words.

"Things changed, like, when?" says Shona. "Because we completely GeneScanned not too long ago. Why didn't you get caught?" She is full-frontal convulsed for not narking me, right at the start.

Maybe GeneScan didn't catch it. Or maybe ScanMans knew. Maybe they are testing new pod species. I still don't really know this part, if they planned it just so, or if this was all some freaky mishap. I hop back and forth, light in my new bones, strong in the clawing feet.

Loo says, "Either way, it would explain why nopod got rerouted or Deplugged."

I can almost hear her thinking through it all, fighting to make sense of things, armed with logic, reason. But, still, she's missing data, and I can feel the questions, the suspicions bubbling up.

Teeth were changing long long ago. Claws, inside my boots. Rememory, I started bathing with them on, even? Skin got thick. Arms grew wide.

"I thought you were big big pumping up on protein pals," says Loo.

Even now, I can feel the rippling muscles across the shoulders, along my wingspan.

"Wary scary, ya?" says Loo.

I nod. I hesitate before asking the next dicey question. **Nopod else changed?**

"I'm not blaaty Deformed, if that's whafa mean," says Shona.

"I'm the same, too." Loo laughs uncomfortably. She bites her lower lip and looks down. "Rustle?"

Prolly.

"But I would have noticed," she says.

Many other Scouts have been changing. That I learned.

"Rustle was Deforming, too?" Shona rips the head off her widget. She crunches down and sucks the brains right out. "Now, that's funny. Just as well we lost her."

"Rustle's blaaty gone, so just shut it, Shona," says Loo. Her voice tremors with warning.

"Sorry." She spits out a tiny bone.

"Roku, did you feel, like, over-emo? All meek and leaky?" Loo's mindcore churns and creaks.

Sometimes.

"I never noticed with you," says Loo. "But Rustle, she was full-frontal. Not half the Warrior she used to be."

I hid. Tried to find out whafa happening.

Shona sits up straighter. "Whafa mean?"

With my growing powers, I snooped, sneaked. Mindread ScanMans data, stole hard drives right out of the heads of others, planted hearing helpers, re-set monitors.

"Blaaty Kronk," says Loo. "Full-on Undercover Ops!" She smiles wide.

"Convulse much, Traitors?" says Shona.

I needed to know whafa happening, Shona. My changes became too drastic to hide, so I finally escaped.

Loo picks flesh from a third crunchy widget. "Rustle said something about you narking her just before you disappeared."

I tried texting her about all these things. She wouldn't respond. I wanted to take her with me before anypod else noticed. I tried to warn her.

"If Rustle was changing, why didn't I see any feathers?"

Shona says, "You, like, completely would have, if she had any. Always fusing and making kissy—"

Shh. Poor Loo. I send a warm glow, like a sonic coo, to buffer the sad waves that slurp up inside her. **Maybe she didn't grow feathers. Maybe she grew other things.**

"Maybe," says Loo. And her face crinkles as she thinks that over. "Well, we hadn't *really* fused in a long time. Like, not completely full-frontal like we used to, all bellyparts melting and gynos rupturing and big, deep kissy touchlings—"

"Ew!" says Shona.

"Relax, Neuter." Loo glares at her. "Not for quite a while, anyway. She always had some excuse; always wriggled her way out of it." Loo snaps her widget stick in two. "She was getting wary weird in the gynos," she adds suddenly.

"Loo, I'm trying to feed, for Kronk's sake," says Shona, rolling her googly eyes.

"No, really, it's important!" says Loo.

I chirp and hop closer. Solomon would be able to handscan her, if she wasn't dying, that is. Instead, I read her my way with all my new mindstrength. It knocks her to the ground. She clutches the sides of her violated head.

Sorry, Loo, I send. **Too strong, that.**

This time, I tap inside Loo's mindcore gently. She's all revved up, full-on emo. I scan her rememories of kissing Rustle in the cool water, and the strange tingling of their fusion. How Rustle touched her inside, pushing deep. My own parts tingle and clench. *Mmm.* Loo has that same stirring inside her even now, but also something utterly foreign: I read the microscopic beginnings of some new life-form planted inside. Loo, distracted with the fusion feel, smiles. *She's flowering!* And she is completely unaware of her new host status. I pull out carefully and think on all I've learned.

Okay? I send.

She shakes her head. "Mostly. Felt like you put two claws in my eye sockets and lifted my scalp from the inside out." She shakes her head again.

Solomon moans loudly and turns in her sleep. Shona drops her feed and leans over, checks Solomon's throat pulse, feels her forehead. When Shona leans forward, I can see the small packet clipped to her underthings.

Loo says, "Do you think Solomon is changing right now?"

Solomon is dying. Her spiritwind is so much weaker than when I first found her. **We have no tools to save her.**

Shona sniffs.

Loo says, "Oh."

Loo seems confused, which is strange, since she's always been the most adaptable of us all. Prolly in shock a wee bite. Loo pokes the fire with her greasy widget sticks.

"Do you think I'll change, too?" she asks suddenly. She would love to fly like me, racing, hunting—diving down to kill, flying away fast.

If only she knew the truth of it. The changes she'll be having soon enough. She'll be growing larger by each new moon, bloated, gassy, and nauseous. Pained to eventual collapse, bleeding and excreting on all fours, she'll deliver forth this new thing that grows inside her. She craves power and will get it, but of a completely different nature than she imagines.

Loo turns back to me. "Roku, how did you escape?"

On an Eighth Level shuttle. Unit was leaving on Mission.

"Huh. All the rest of those Kronk-kissers were busy locking us down," she says.

She's jealous, I think. A wave of regret clouds Loo's face. Even now, she is picturing herself dressed smartly, all in black, lined up with the other top warriors in Eighth.

I hop lightly to one side. **I hid in the weapons storage area. Grew feathers, my beak, while traveling. After landing, unit came to the back hatch and found me half-dead and shaky, mid-change.**

"Whafa do?" says Shona. "Report you to ScanMans, prolly."

Prolly. I hop from one foot to the other. ScanMans must know a wild manimal is out here somewhere, skyward. Though they might not know I'm Roku.

"Killed them all, didn't you? That's whafa I'd do. Then take the shuttle," says Loo. She cracks her swollen knuckles.

No, Loo. Too weak. I played dead. Unit dragged me off the shuttle. They went to get a long sword to finish me, but I flew away. Not far. Far enough to hide and finish changing.

"Oh." Loo seems disappointed.

Wary scary blaat.

Shona leans forward. "Is this unit still close by?"

"Think they'll give you a ride home, Shona?" Loo stretches out her long legs and crosses her arms.

"Why not? We could get Solomon back to Living Lab, at least."

"Solomon wouldn't want that." Loo leans forward and tosses some more twigs onto the fire.

"Like, how would you know, Loo?" Shona mutters under her breath. "Nopod would rather be completely dead."

"Well," Loo says, "ScanMans prolly dispatched an Assassin order to track and Deplug the whole lot of us. So maybe we'll all be dead in a milli."

"Maybe not, like, *all* of us?" says Shona. Her lip quivers a bite.

"Meaning?" snarls Loo.

"Meaning, like, not all of us wanted to be any part of the Traitorous Aberrant disaster our unit has become."

"Get over it, Shona. A lot of zlotan blaat has happened to everypod." Loo sits up taller and stifles a yawn. "I used to love assassin orders," she says dreamily.

Book 2

Listen. I hop closer to the fire so the light plays on my feathers and sparkles in my eyes. I need them to stop fighting, to pay attention. *Especially Loo.* **In the big sea, there are Volcano Islands. Eights are rating habitation levels and tracking electrolls there. Not far from the sea feeding.**

Shona holds Solomon closer.

My first flight, I followed sonic pod-sends right to the feeding. Much splashing and blood and big scaries—I scooped up the bleeding pod but didn't recognize Solomon's scent. Not until later. I had no clue our unit had already escaped.

"Then you came back for Shona and me," says Loo. "Must be big tired, Roku. You really are Kronk strong." She yawns again, loudly this time. She tidies the fire by flicking half-burned twiglets back into the center, into the hypnotic flame.

For the first time, I felt truly One Pod. It was like Kronk Herself gave us another chance. I fluff myself up, peck at a claw shyly.

Shona rolls her eyes, but Loo leans toward me, smiling. "Whafa odds?" she says, but I know she is thinking about Rustle far away, and Solomon trailing close behind.

We have this one chance to do everything different. I learned much in my snoops, I send. I wonder how much to tell them. How much to say in front of Shona. But more than that is my fear that we must keep moving, else bring the Assassins right to their new target: us.

"Like?" says Shona.

Like, there are others who live out here, above the ground. Whole colonies without ScanMans. Some live at the Red Soil Settlements.

Loo perks up. She shakes podself awake with these words.

Shona shouts, "Lies!"

ScanMans know of them and study them, but they do not live in units. They are not Warriors like us. It is only a few flying days from here.

"Blaaty blaat!" says Loo. She starts pacing around the fire.

There is a large parcel of burned-up earth on the other side of the hills—the deadlands. I stretch my wing away from the cliff edge, away from the crashing sea. **I saw it when I circled high above. It has been eaten by fire. I want to fly over that, past to where the faint red lines of earth begin again. Prolly there.**

Shona snorts. "If pod didn't learn this in training, it can't be true. Like, whafa species could live here without ScanMans, out here in the wide-open wilds? I've never heard a thing about it, like, nary a word in all my Leader programming," she says, mostly to Loo. "Prolly Roku got confused with Deforming and all?"

I watch Shona closely, staring right through her face, past her blueness and into the small suspicious lump inside her cranium. Something churns inside, something bad. Her hand falls to her lap, to resting above the secret purse. My impulse is to knock it from her, one flap of my great wing would do it easily. I decide to not use force, to still try and win her over through the power of mind-speach and logic.

"You two must be, like, so tired, especially Roku, after everything pod went through," Shona says. "I'll keep first watch first while you do Sleep."

No, Shona. I hop closer to her. I dare her to bring out the Drop kit.

Loo says, "It's okay, Roku. Sleep is good, right?"

No, I send. No time for Sleep now, Loo.

But Shona unclips her wee satchel and pulls out two Sleep Now vials. I swallow and chirp in spite of myself, and Loo lurches forward, across the snappy fire, to grab at it. Even though I know it can't lull my Kronk-size senses to dreaming the way it used to, I still rememory how much bliss it brought. All that rest and all those dreams.

Loo is practically right on top of Shona. "I didn't know we had Sleep," she says. She can't tear her eyes from the yellow liquid.

"Umm." Loo spits to clean a spot on her arm and the needle glints a happy shine the closer it gets.

Loo, I send. **Wait.**

Shona uncaps one barrel and Loo leans in close.

So much more story. Listen—I hop forward, my great wings spread wide. **Blaaty no, Loo!** I push Shona but it's already in. Loo's got the kit in her hands and she's smiling and shivering. She flops back to her spot and curls around the heated water bowl. Her features relax, her mind stops its constant whirling. Sleep Now, it sings through her veins, and she does. Oh, how she does.

Loo: Podless

When I wake, I am alone. I'm buried in green brush, lying in a shallow ditch dug by furious claws and a beak. *Ah, Roku.* The sky is bright, the fire long dead. Ashes stir in the breeze, and they blow softly into the leftover water from the upturned stone. Bugs and tiny pieces of bark float in there. I cup my hands and slurp up mouthfuls of it, swallow, and splash some on my dusty face. The ground still smells smoky but, when I put my hand in it, the pit is cold. The roasting sticks have been burnt, as have the tiny bones of our feed. The rumpled survival pack is gone. There is no scent trail for Solomon or Shona. I catch Roku faintly when I circle the pit. The wafts swell and fade, enough to drive me mad, but I can't find the source.

I yawn. My limbs are stiff. I am groggy from doing Sleep. When I rub my sore jaw, it relaxes and the chem trail drips down the back of my throat. I've been grinding my teeth again—I can tell from the hollow ache. I feel very still. *Podless.* The others are prolly building a new pit, a safer shelter elsewhere, I think. Roku has flown them away and will come back for me. *They could have left a message,* I think. I sit quietly beside the pit. I try some meditations to pass the time.

Or maybe Solomon died.

The thought comes suddenly and jumps me to my feet. They would do the letting here prolly, and then whafa? Bury her in the soft ground? Toss her to sea? Burn her flesh like the ancients did? I know plenty of pod whafa disappeared, dozens. And hundreds of Found hatchlings never even made it to Warrior training, nary the First Level. Whafa happened to their cores?

Some forbidden things creep my mindcore now that I think on this awful thing, death. Things Rustle sometimes spoke of—her rememories that stirred my own forgotten ones. Vague pictures, stories, haunt me from that other life before StarPod, from the long ago Treason Times. Cores piled high, riddled with disease, viol Deformed. Some covered in rough sheets, some hanging naked from the stacks of ugly limbs. Now *that* was death. I rememory being so small—a wee hungry thing, crying, running past all those stenchy piles of rotting flesh. Running past The Lighters. Scary blackened skin on them, The Lighters, with their wild eyes and singed hair. They lurched around, tall on stilts, dousing body piles with precious drops of that fuel, the stuff they'd fought wars over for two hundred years and more. How terrifying they were. And when they emptied the can of its pungent liquid, they would strike a match and set some stick alight—long sticks wrapped in oil-soaked rags. And they would do the lighting. Our villages went up in stinking smoke this way, in endless flames. All those pod we once knew. *People, not Pod.* Our whole human world.

"Stop it," I tell myself out loud. "Be fit!"

I sit down, shake off those awful thoughts. I think instead about the dreams I had while I dropped. I flex my toes, stretch my legs. My joints creak and pop from all that Sleep. Rustle was there in that secret land of dreams. I was cutting open her fleshcore with sharpies, pretty daggers, and she was saying, "Loo, no look, you're, like, completely missing that part," and she was pointing at some strange bloodied inner thing I'd never seen before. It pulsed and throbbed on its own, and Rustle sat up and stared into the open mess of her own bellyparts. "Zlota. That's blaaty convulsed, Loo. It's like a wee hatchling." In the dream, Rustle's face was perfect and I made kissy, climbed up onto her, even onto her open fleshcore on the table and wallowed right in there, fused right through the ribsticks and the blobbing, hot inside parts of her. Messy, but nary a bit bad about it. *Mmm.* Better than those other rememories, ya?

Everypod has her weakness, and mine is this: sitting, waiting, all alone. Not *doing* something. Brings me, like, complete convulsion. Rustle loved lying around, wondering things and imaging blaat. *Rejuvenating my mindcore.* That's whafa called it. But, especially now, it terrifies the nerve right out of me.

Rustle.

Not here, not anywhere. Not let and drained, nary laid and perfumed, nor splayed proper on the dust of Kronk's earth. *Oh, death again!* The stopped-up sadness, the rage, burns my innermost organs, heats me up and down my veins; it leaves my hands clammy and shaking. I rock back and forth, squatting on my heels. I sob for the first time in years, sure that nopod hears me, that nopod cares. Sobs turn to weepy, wailing howls. The voice that stretches my vocal chords is not my own, it is the wild manimal locked inside me someplace, some coded unknown beast that haunts my genestrands. I screech and choke, pummel the grassy ground with my fists 'til they bleed. I leak from the nose, from the eyes. The hot tears run into my hearholes, down my neck; they wet the pounded earth.

Then I am done.

The sky overhead is still brilliant blue but the heat is fading. I roll onto my back. I wipe my face. I look up and watch clouds blow across that miraculous sky. Already I can see faint twinklers up there. Still no sign of Roku flapping podward. I feel the wind on my wet cheeks. Grass wavers in the fragrant breeze. The air is cool and clear and smells pretty, right? Like from the greeny trees and bushes all around. I suck gulps of it into my bruised lungs. It's so different from the damp cavey tunnels we trained in with all that cold metal, all that rock and dirt. That dust.

Rustle would have loved to breathe this up, bright and warm. I pretend she is lying beside me. I talk to her out loud, tell her stories and dreamweaves, all the secrets she already knows. When my voice crackles rough and dry, I at last tell her: *Goodbye.* I empty myself. I purge all that is Rustle. I plant her there in the red ground, and the void inside sickens me. I suture that openness, seal it up for good. I am done with these organs, this love. *It is finished.* Drowned and burned and buried at last. Now I must move on.

I scan the greeny fluff, the rough rock edges of the cliff where Roku landed from our flight. There is one ridge near the cliff that is higher than the rest, so I run there. Blood pumps through me, stretches my muscles; movement makes me strong and competent once again. No more wally emo-wubbering. At the edge of this tall cliff, I catch my breath. The Kronk-size sea glints below. I scan for the Volcano Islands. For shuttles tearing up the sky. For vessels on the water. For a growing black speck on the horizon.

Nothing. I kick at a pile of dirt. Some stones bounce away and cascade over the edge. I hear them scatter and smash their way down, down. I could throw myself there, too, dive down and grit my teeth, and hope to smash my skull neatly on the jagged rock below. But I know I won't. I am a survivalist, after all, and I'm not programmed or trained or altered to self-destruct.

No can swimmy, no strong wings for flying, no shuttle or travelshaft awaits me. Only my own boots to carry me, and only one place comes to mind in this strange land: *The Red Soil Settlements.* Just the thought brings back my fakie and that song from the ancient times. A tingle grows in my scalp and travels down prickly. I walk back through the waving vegetation. Tufts of grass tickle my knees when I crush and crunch them. It is cooler when I reach the bushes. I slow, avoiding the thistles and scratchy thorn patches. I find the shadows. My long limbs blend with the slender trees.

I try chewing different plant stalks that grow here. *So hungry.* Most greens taste bitter and are hard to swallow. One brings water to my mouth, and the chalky drying insides of the plant cause my belly to knot instantly. *Poison, prolly.* I spit. I take a handful of long pieces and tuck them away carefully in my boot, just in case. I drink the rest of the water from the stone bowl to rid myself of the bad taste.

Night falls around the fire pit. Strange sounds peep and chirp out from the leafy darkness. The Sleep has left me jumpy. There are no firesticks, no tasty widget morsels, no protein powder packs. The water is all gone. I climb a tall tree that stands near the ashes of our fire. I clutch at its branches, bury my face in them, freak at every new click and whirl. Each creeping manimal that lurks beneath me, each winged beast that flits through the air, even the crawling bugs set my hair twitching. I watch and learn from them. I wait. But Roku never comes.

Roku: Promises

"You promised." Shona's voice is ragged. She rocks back and forth on her heels, arms wrapped around podself. "You said you'd take us to the shuttle." She is completely convulsed.

This is where it landed. See the marks on the rock and on those trees? The base camp is further along that path. I brought you here. I kept my promise.

"Where is this unit? Find them now!"

Find them podself. You need water, Shona. You're dehydrated.

It's like her tuning somehow went wrong during our flight to the Volcano Islands. Her hair is matted. Dried blood covers her shredded uni. She looks wild, like something they'd hunt down more than something they'd invite into their shuttle. Solomon lies quiet in a clump of tall grass. I peer closer. I can't believe her chest still rises, still falls. I carried them both the distance, while Loo lay crashed out, back by our fire pit.

Shona lunges at me. I hop away and flap to a higher perch. The sky is lightening to gray. Silver slices the horizon between the water and the big big sky. I am tired from carrying both their heavy cores. From listening to all of Shona's blaat. From everything. I feel hungry and dizzy and sick of it all. I need rest.

I send, **Scouts prolly tour the islands and come back here to camp. You have the survival pack. Make a fire. Feed Solomon. I must get back to Loo. She will wake soon and wonder whafa.**

"Take us back to StarPod. Do it!"

No. I'm too tired to cross the whole sea.

"Solomon will die if you wait," Shona whines.

We'll all die if I try crossing right now.

Shona paces wildly. "No. This is all gone wrong."

I brought you here. In fair exchange, you promised to let Loo and me make our own way in this new world. Now I must go before the Eights return. They'd Deplug me in a milli.

Shona spits at me. "Go back to that PodTraitor then, and await your own death beside her."

I hop away, into the darkest stretch of trees. The sky grows even lighter. Every instinct tells me to fly away: *now, now!* Instead, my ragged core drags me down with fatigue. I hop on the branch of a knobby, widespread tree. Leaves drift down with the weight of me. Sap oozes between my claws. I close my eyes most of the way and chortle into sleep.

Strange, I think. It is much later. I stretch my wings. The Eights are still not back. Hunger gnaws my bellyparts and makes me watchful. I blink. These new light bones tinkle inside the mawing yap of a bellybag that always gurgles. My feathers rustle and twitch. Blood pumps: chug chug. The heart patters strong, fast—a teeny jogging rhythm. *I am awake!* I am music now. I make it wherever I go.

I twist my neck to scan. I see everything, all in sharp detail. I have been resting a long time. Night is ready to fall again. Colors fade. Blue-gray mist settles on the grass, the trees, the bushes. My night vision is better than ever, better even than StarPod's training goggles, tracking infrared pools of warmth. Here, under a leaf, a widget trembles. There—a long thin strip inches along a quiet branch. *Snaky.* Phosphorescent trails stream every which way in dribbles and splashes. A stuttered trail peeks out from the long grass, over hard rock, in dirt. The sharp scent of urine leads these trails right to the manimals that made them, right to a squirming hot nest of wet furry hatchlings. The mother is prolly off hunting. She'd make more of a feed, but who'd raise the wee things? There are an odd number of them, mewling and squeaking, blinking and writhing in the nest. I take fewer than half. They squish in my claws. I stab the centers; slurp the hot wrigglies right up. Their jelly bones go down smooth. It's the furry patches that have me squawking and reeling to choke down. Just when I think it's all settled, up it comes. I cough out the raggy scraps of teeth and feathers. *Pellets.*

Next, I fly to Solomon and Shona. Neither has moved a milli. There is no fire. There is no water, no feed. Shona is slumped beside a rock. She is full-frontal wire-snapped. I must get back to Loo, but all that training and tuning, all those mantras shine through and I cannot leave them here, so unfit. So up comes the gooey mash, the regurgitated pulp, and I drip it into Shona's throat like she was one of the wee things I just devoured. Shona coughs and gags. I wait. Then I drip some more. Shona revives quickly. Solomon does not. Her fever keeps climbing. Her wounds are septic—the smell of rot is worse. She doesn't swallow whafa dripped into her mouth. It collects to one side and either pours out to her gray cheek or pools at the back, choking her.

I peck the ground, find a green worm. I crackle it in my beak.

"Do something!" Shona pulls at her strange hair. Tufts come right out. She thinks I don't care, that I don't ache with podlessness the way they all do. That I don't miss Rustle. That I don't hate whafa happening to our good Solomon.

Solomon has suffered enough, I send. **Let Kronk's spirit go before it is too poisoned in this dirty flesh.**

"There is no Kronk!" Shona yells. "There's no such thing as spirit, you stupid manimal!"

And that's it. I hop forward. I grasp Solomon's head between my sharp claws. I twist and jerk quickly. There is a snap. It is done.

I don't know why I waited so long. Shona looks stunned. She rushes, crying and hitting me with her dirty fists. She pummels me and I let her. I flap my wings wide for balance. She is so weak that the bruising will not be deep. I take it all, martyred good and strong, for everything that hasn't turned out the way she expected, the way that ScanMans instructed. All those lies: that we would always be together, training, following orders, moving up the military ranks, until we were good enough to pioneer our own colony someplace else.

I laugh an ugly squawk of a laugh. My noise scares Shona so she stops her assault. She wipes her face with her filthy arm. I am loud and raggy, screechy and wild. She thinks she's killing me, I realize, and that makes me laugh even more. *As blaaty if!* Later, after I collect podself and settle down for a huddle, I try to explain. She blanks me, but my waves are powerful and I push aside her little mental shield like so much fluff.

Shona, I send. We *are* following Pod Destiny. We are in true Survival mode, outliving our orders. We are pioneering in the now. We have become whafa were trained to be. Only for real, not on some invisible leash.

She looks at me guardedly. She understands. I think she even realizes that it is the truth, but pod completely does not like it. Not one bite.

Other units lost members; you know they have. On Mission, on Kill Ops, on tours. Did we also? I watch her so intently, I can hear her mindcore click.

Of course, she thinks. But out loud she says: "Don't be stupid paranoidal. You would rememory if one of us died."

Would I? I hop closer and she flinches. Or would I be reprogrammed and fitted with a new rememory card? Maybe I did Sleep through the whole thing. Maybe we all did. Tell me. Have I already been replaced, like Loo was saying?

Shona shrugs. She hunkers down in the dirt. There's no place for her to go. She can't climb down the stony cliffs. Can't climb up the burly trees. Can't fly. She can only wish herself back to the clearing where we left Loo, or wish herself all the way back to StarPod. She's trapped on this island with me, her biggest nightmare.

Pod gets mindtuned, over and over again. Stronger and more resilient and more full of Obeyance, right? I already know this much from my snoops in StarPod.

She looks away. I push right into her rigid mindcore. Shona says, "Solomon can't be replaced unless we take her back, you know. As far as I know, they still need part of her mindcore to transplant." She breathes deeply. "Please. I l-love her."

But did you love every single Solomon? Even after she made some mistake or started Deforming? Even when she Disobeyed? Did you still want her, even then?

Shona says, "You don't get the beauty of the whole thing.

Like, every time pod messes up too much, pod gets another chance. To be, like, completely perfect. ScanMans are getting better and better at the designs. And you all are getting easier to control."

I screech long and loud into the night. It echoes out over the cliff, over the rolling waves below. The hot wind from inside me blows into her face and she cringes. She shrivels her little body away from me. I knew she was informed, but not how deeply she had participated in our betrayal.

I collect my senses. I fluff my feathers down. **Maybe some of us are getting better at hiding from you.**

There's a flicker of doubt on Shona's face. "Shut it?" Shona stands up now. "Just shut it!"

Tell me everything you know. It doesn't matter anymore. I'll either fly away free or get shot trying. You'll either be saved by this other unit or taken prisoner, lugged back to StarPod, and given a royal Send Down.

Shona snorts. "You wish," she says. "You still believe pod can fight or fly or think a way out of this." She laughs meanly. "ScanMans hold the power lines and they, like, give those reigns to Leaders. We steer with them, not you-all. For instance, right now, Scouts are tracking us. They'll be all over this action and they'll find you, and you'll be Deplugged. But I'll go back and I will get to start all over again with a blaaty new bunch of you. This time, they might not even bother revising you, Roku. You've always been too much trouble, if you want to know the truth."

Funny that I can tell she isn't bluffing. I have always been too much trouble—suddenly, I know this like I know my own wingspan. **Whafa Rustle and Solomon?**

"I really don't know. Maybe they'll have to retouch the replacements with some other pod's mindcore." She looks worried for a milli but pushes away those nagging thoughts. "Frankly, I'm sick of Rustle. She's only getting, like, weirder with every incarnation. But Solomon—"

You know for sure that Scouts are tracking us right now?

Shona smiles. "Maybe." She looks strange. Dangerous, almost.

I leave as soon as we tend to Solomon.

"Maybe there are other things you want to know. Things I could tell you." Shona has edged away from me and set the second yellow vial down on the ground within reach. Still she bargains, trying to swap secrets for a way out of this unplanned ending.

Keep your poison. You might need it to dull your own pain.

She grimaces.

Maybe you will get another chance, Shona. Maybe you'll grow a whole new batch like us. But they won't *be* us. Sooner or later, ScanMans will find a better way to run things, and you and all the other Pod Leaders will get downsized, too. It makes sense. It's only a matter of time.

"Stop trying to trick me," says Shona.

I'm not the one tricking anypod. Go on, and do whafa will. But do it without more of my help.

"Ha," says Shona. "You've already helped plenty and you don't even know it."

Enough. Do the letting or die by my beak.

"There's no magic in letting," she says. "You know that, right?"

I squawk. I pull Solomon's arm and legs out. I splay her proper on the ground. I extend my sharpest claw and nudge Shona. She takes hold of my claw.

"It doesn't mean a thing, you know," she says. "ScanMans invented letting to keep your feeble minds occupied and to teach you the taste of your own blood. That's all."

I chirp in spite of myself. Everypod wants to believe in something.

Beautiful, strong Solomon.

Shona's hand shakes with my claw inside it. She presses my claw against the thin skin of Solomon's broken neck. Shona starts to cry.

Now you must drink, I send. **Pretend you are a believer. If you believe, then maybe Kronk will come for her.**

She cries and gags and she does not believe. But I blaaty make her drink. Completely.

Loo: Hunted

Before I see it, I hear it. Before I hear it, I sense its terrifying arrival. I feel the changed air pushing through me. Wind fills my open mouth, my noseholes. It rushes down my core and out through microscopic holes: tear ducts, sweat glands. Wind blows right out, leaving me unable to think, to send, to move. There is the noisy growl of metal, the tremendous thundering whirl of technology. I stare into the distance at the growing dark shadow. It speeds toward me on a dangerous wind. A sudden drop and it is gone from sight, although the sound grows steadily louder.

I blink.

The shuttle reappears and hangs above the cliff's edge like some evil planet blocking out my sun. It sucks up dust, dirt, branches. It sprays out fountains of red sand. I spin back into action, throw myself to the base of a large tree. The black shuttle rises up. It is an Eighth Level ScanMan issue, a newer model than ours. It passes low to the ground, dark and deadly. Lights scan the red earth and the fluttering green grass. Red-beamed lasers burn and slice. Branches crash in the wake of its passing. Sky manimals spring away in alarm; small furries ripple underfoot; panic-scent blooms and fills the air. Trees crash and shake the ground as the killing beams sweep forward. Smoke billows, flames lick.

Deep in my bones and my quivering guts, I know this is no regular Kill Op. My *blaaty weapons!* I have nothing—no mask, no dagger, not a gun to my name. Not even the wee slingshot, left behind in Living Lab. So I run. I scramble and slide through the crackling trees. Dust and smoke fill the air. Dirt clods plop all around me. Wood splits, bark rips, sap runs freely. I leap and duck in the thundering chaos. Bushes scratch my stinging face. I dart. I zigzag to try and hide the trail I must be leaving.

Focus.

Whatever tracks me is at least as cruel and skilled as I am. Were I the Leader, I'd drop Warriors on foot to wait in the undisturbed clearings. I'd level the forest from the shuttle above, let it flush out the prey. And when the poor mark raced ahead, I'd have her killed, just when she thought she'd beat the game, just when she'd stopped for a rest.

The sounds of the shuttle fade as it turns from where I crouch. The crushing forest booms and falls still. If I hide, they will find me ever in the end. But I am a Hunter, and so I have a chance. I will track their unit instead, killing pod for pod. I turn back into the fray; pick my way over uprooted trees. I find a place to set my trap. I purposefully spread my scent, pheromones and sweat. I mark my body heat all along the cool upper branches of a medium-sized tree. Then I jump down to the rough core of a fallen giant one just below. A family of small furries scuttles out their nest hole, a wee hatchling dangling from its mother's mouth. Out they go and in goes me, my core hidden, my scent buried in the rotten tree innards. I ball up inside the hollow tree, in the dried leaves and bits of nest. I breathe deep, slow my pulse, lower my body temperature to match the tree and leaves, and so make myself invisible to their masks and cams.

It's dark in the treecore. Speckles of light peep in from spy holes the furries have made here and there. Smells fill my noseholes: tree guts, molting nest, urine. Angered by the sudden bombing of their home, a horde of glistening red insects swarms me inside the tree. In their race to escape out the wee holes, they pour around me, over me—up my face, over my lips. They scurry over my quivering eyelids—I feel them marching the greasy planes of my scalp. I am full-on freaking but cannot even move, so I trance. I blank to this strange new invasion. Some race inside my noseholes and set my nerves aflame, until I blow them out with my own warm wind. *Steady, Loo,* I tell myself.

Later, after the wee things are gone, the press of my full bladder wakes me to my cramping limbs. Below comes a *crunch*. One and more—the slow, steady sound of measured footfalls. I rememory the marked manimal I stalked with Rustle, the one she refused to kill. Now I am hunted, dirty and matted. I twist the dented ring on my finger. Somepod is outside, scanning the slaughtered woods for me, pausing and listening beneath my very self.

The slender Eighth steps into my sightlines. She has knotted dark hair that spills over a thermal-cam mask. A sling of arrows and a small crossbow are strapped to her black uni. Her knife holster is empty: she's holding the blade in her ready hands. She tracks the scattered heat imprints from where my feet touched the cooler grass, from where I grasped stone or tree to climb and jump. My marks will glow red against the cooler background in thermal imaging. She moves gracefully, quietly turning, eventually facing the hollow tree. She is dark-eyed and stern-mouthed. Pretty. Well muscled. She wears a sparkling necklace of rounded rocks, unlike anything I've ever seen. My core is invisible to her mask, blending with the tree temperature perfectly. She creeps closer, her knife still out in front. The knife passes overhead and, right behind, her pale face looks up at the branches above me.

When I move, I am faster than sound. My hands find her neck. Before she can even cry out, I twist it, snapping the spinal connection. Her dead eyes stare.

I've killed my own kind.

I jump from the tree. I collect her weapons: strap the knife holster onto my own leg and hoist up the arrows and crossbow. I drag her corpse under some greenery. She is pale. Her limbs stretch long. I tell myself it could have been *me* now, silenced and cold on the ground. I score her thermal-cam mask—better than mine back at StarPod, even. I press her lids closed. I touch her pretty mouth. I take her strange necklace off and fasten it about my own neck. The stones sparkle and spiral when the sun hits them. *No sense wasting lovely jewels,* I think.

Then I use her knife to bring forth the lifespirit, the frothy dark blood from her throat. It is hot and spiced in some way I do not recognize. I gulp and swallow it down. She had much strength and power—now it is mine. I wipe my mouth, my face, on her uni. She has a water flask; I drink from it, then attach it to my wide belt.

The wind picks up. It is cooler now. I relieve my bladder in the long grass, shake myself dry. I look around. In this new Kill Op I am Leader, Hunter, and Scout, all in one. *Finally in charge of something!* On this Mission, I tally the score: one down, one steers the shuttle, three more Scouts to stalk and slice.

Rustle: Sugar

It is dark under the coral ledge. Mossy treacle flits in the cracks like thick hair wafting. Fishies swim past in their brightly colored troupes, first one way, then the next. I am their hidden audience; they are the parade. Fishies shoot forward and tight-turn on some unspoken command. Just like our Warrior Scout formation back in the training hall. I laugh: *Rrak rrak rahh.* The other fishies, they don't laugh.

It seems forever since my underwater change, and I am only now starting to balance my new Fishness with my old Warrior self. Here I swimmy, bubble and blurp my way around these rocks, these strange underwater plants. I watch things crawl and sway and float by. If I'm hungry, I feed. Scoop up nibbly stones and choke down long, hairy weeds. I slurp speckles of lifeforce from the clouded water. Shadows zoom and I hide, wary scary since the big mass of manimal swallowed me up that time and, happily, happily, spit me out. Sometimes I fear too much to move, full-on paranoidal that each wee stone is a hydrophone, an underwater cam or hearing helper, projecting my feckless wanderings on a large screen in Controls, a room full of ScanMans idly standing by. Then I huddle, just as I am now, under the coral ledge, and hide.

A movement to my right sets my heart thrumping. The coral branch I'm hovering beside disengages itself and swivels. *Tricked again!* I gasp. The stick-shaped fishy—not a hydrocam after all—swims past and that's it, I think, that's my last good nerve gone!

I swear on Kronk's daughter there must be some reason for this. Why take a perfectly trained Warrior Scout, a finely tuned Assassin, and let her become some floppy, soggy underwater monster? There must be some bigger purpose than to scare me pissless and deprive me of all companionship—and not just to be devoured in some vague future by an unknown manimal in this ferocious sea! I nudge the heavy rock I keep on top of Loo's pretty dagger. It's all I have left from the old life. Once in a long long milli, I allow myself a peek. The flashing glint of silver is too dangerous down here and could draw the carnivorous likes of any imaginable creature straight to me, slobbering for a feed. I must hide it in the elsetimes.

All those precious blocks of dreamtime, curled up on my cot in the dank underground cavern where we trained and lived and loved and fought. I miss it so. Loo hated lounging about, trancing. *Fiddle and frack.* I found it rejuvenating. Now it's drowning me, there's so much to be had.

Loo.

And I'm back to one of my favorite rememories: the first time Loo nuzzled me full fusion. We had just finished a tricky mission, a routine scout and report that turned full-on aggro. Some strange species ambushed us: three trained beasts, the likes we'd never seen. Their stink was horrible! It preceded them by many miles, and they trudged loudly, haltingly, down a stony path. They didn't seem afraid of us, though they should have been, as maybe they'd have lived longer. Hair they had, down the fronts of their faces as well as the backs and tops of their heads. They barked sounds from no mouths, but when I finally caught one, the littlest, it turned out it did have an opening. Only, the hair covered it. Except for when it screamed, like. Hair covered them, their large, veiny arms, their fuzzy legs, and when we cut away the hide covering, we saw strange wee dangling bits in another dark nest.

Solomon and Roku studied them closely. Shona was nervous, twitching and chirping on her Pod monitor, trying to get clear access to ScanMan personnel. Something about these things set her off. Prolly thought they were hatchling electrolls. Well, they could have been. After we killed them, we argued about whether or not we should drag one back to the shuttle for ScanMans to categorize. In the end, we left the corpses piled there. Loo wanted to blood-let them, but nopod wanted to drink their lifeforce. Would have tasted as bad as they smelled, ya? We were filthy and tired and hungry, and by the time we got back, the shuttle and all of us stank as badly as those beasts. We bathed in the water room, and the others hustled off to Canteena Time for whatever was left of the nightly feed by then. I stayed on my cot, wanting some time alone. It was rare enough.

I rememory it like it was last night. Like I can still feel the bruises on my thighs and feel the fullness of my softened lips.

Loo.

She hung her crossbow and sling of arrows up in their spot. She walked to the end of my cot and smiled. Her silver eyes shone, her sharp teeth were gleaming in the blue light. She tossed her pink hair, sent whiffs of her pretty perfumed braids over to me. She bent to remove her slippers. I could see more of her through the top of her unzipped uni. Two scoops of soft skin. Water pooled in my mouth. She looked up then, caught me staring and laughed. Loo sat down. Right beside me on my blaaty cot, right on my crumpled foamy. Her arm grazed mine when she tossed the balled-up slippers over to the bilge bag. I wiped my sweaty palms on the crumpled cover. Loo lowered her zipper the rest of the way. She snaked out of it and kicked it into a pile on the floor. She had nothing else on. Just her muscled, pale fleshcore. When she crawled toward me onto my surprised lap, I could see the wee prickles along her skin, the tiny white hairs sticking up.

I said, "Uh, aren't you going to feed?"

She shook her head, no.

"The others went," I said. My voice crackled.

She said, "I know." She moved against me slowly.

Not hungry? I sent it telepathically because I couldn't trust my voice to work any more.

She shook her head again, laughing.

Cold? I traced the bumps on her shoulder with my finger.

"Uh hmm." She said this into my hearhole. Her breath tickled and, when she leaned forward, her naked podbumps swung against mine.

I coughed.

She straddled me and pushed me back onto my foamie, tugged the tips of my purple dreads.

"Rustle," she sing-songed my name. She was so far away. The view was terrifying and also gorgeous. From down where I lay, there seemed to be miles of naked fleshcore, miles of beautiful Loo, and all of it crushing into me. All of it waiting expectantly. After all that time wishing and wanting, now that it was actually happening, I froze like a blaaty twig. I didn't know whafa do, no more than I knew whafa had ambushed us earlier in the day.

Loo tilted her head. She looked right at me. She traced my lip with her finger—lightly first, then with more pressure. She smooshed my lips and then stuck two fingers inside my mouth, moved them in and out slowly, made me suck. My teeth scraped them a wee bite. Next, she pulled them out and replaced them with her mouth, her tongue. Loo kissed me, blaaty well kissed me through and through, tingled my spinecore, fused my mind, melded it, set my wires aflame. *Twitchy fit.* She leaned back and sucked her own fingers a bit more, then brought them down low. She touched podself. She closed her eyes and arched her back and moved slowly. I touched her bare skin, all those places usually hidden by our crusty unis. After a milli, she took my hand and brought it down to where hers was. She showed me. I tried so hard to get it right.

When I rememory that first time with Loo, it takes me all kinds of other places. Like right back into StarPod, into the scent of our lair, our unis, the filthy overcoats we wore on Mission. The smells of our weapons and the gun rags we used to oil and dry them after each operation. Then the sounds—voices, autotrons, sirens wailing. The constant crackling of monitors in every chamber, in every corridor. And the next layer of sounds: the whirling ticks of cameras, mics, the hearing helpers randomly resetting themselves. The never knowing for certain when or if pod was being watched. Beyond all that was Loo: her scent, her voice, her shifting eyes, the way she touched me. I tuck my dreams of Loo away with all my most precious rememories.

Like when I was first captured, barely more than a hatchling. The Settlement Scout whafa found me thought I was some filthy manimal and was about to Deplug me, like, completely. Pod says I rolled over from my dirty hiding spot in the rubble and yawned a big pink stretch, my tongue almost touching the tip of her heat-seeking rifle. It shocked her right out of pulling the trigger. She picked me up. For lack of any other feed, she gave me a hard pink candy wrapped in crinkly foil, while the rest of them decided whafa do with me. I had never seen anything like it before. I didn't know how to open the wee thing. She gestured to put that strange pebble into my mouth. I had no words for it, no concept of it, even. The outside hard color and, when it softened, the different shades inside. *Sugar.* The taste, the smell, the idea will never leave me.

Like this thing with Loo, this first time fusing with her, I knew I was changed and that nothing would ever be the same. Even before she flipped me on the cot, tugging away at my filthy boots. I let her do it, let her do it all, whatever she wanted. I knew and she knew, so that it never had to be texted or mouthspeached or scribbled in lead. I was hers now. Now and for always.

Kronk, I miss candy.

Loo: Killing Game

The second goes down easy. *Some Warrior!* I drop on her from the leafy tree above, slicing through the back of her neck with her Podmate's knife before even touching ground. She doesn't unsheathe her sword. Pod rears up, eyes wide, and shrieky screams a deathcall that echoes around the clearing. My newly harvested mask tracks the heat of her shooting blood. *Red.* Her core temp fades quickly. *Pink.* I shake her to silence. Instead of fighting, instead of choking me or striking or stabbing my unprotected torso, she grabs the pretty stones I have about my neck. She hangs onto them even as she falls to her knees.

"Nooo." A sob catches her throat. **Jemma,** she wave-sends, and the grief rolls over me, tingling the wee hairs at the back of my neck. She pulls me down.

At the last, I worry she'll strangle me with her final twitchy spasms. I can hardly knife her again without cutting myself at this close range, so I push her skull back with one hand and stab her heartcenter with the other. She gurgles. I pry her cooling fist from the jewels. *Blue.* She is even more muscular than the last—more than a match for me in my underfed, exhausted state.

I harvest her razor-sharp throwing stars, clip them to my utility belt next to the flask, and lift the glinting sword in its fitted case. I can't wear it *and* the crossbow at the same time, although I try. At last, I ditch the sling of arrows and the bow. The sword, I worry, is almost too heavy to carry, but I want it so. It has a beautiful inlaid handle. I pull it out, exhale with delight. It is perfectly balanced with a long, gleaming blade. I lift and slice the air with it, I dance and thrust, hear it sing in the wind. *Whafa sword!* I drag the corpse to the base of a large tree. Then I buckle the sturdy sword casing around my core. I can hardly stand to sheathe it; the metal sings to me so. But away it goes and off I trot, into the glooming shadows before I rememory her lifeforce. Poor trapped spiritwind, suffocating inside that stony core! I run back to the spot and make quiet amends.

Forgive me, Kronk.

I take more millis to fix this one's meaty core. I fluff her tangled green hair and splay her arms and legs to send the spirit forth proper. I clean my goopy blade on the grass before I take her throat. I choke down the hot, red rush, then lean back on my heels.

Mmm.

Pod tastes like some dark berry, some rare treat from a long ago Survival Op, back in Fifth. Rememories me to that time, sharp and sweet, how Rustle and I got lost from the rest to make kissy while on Mission. In the heat of deep touchling fusion, we galloped and rolled blindly in the greeny bush, stopping only for Rustle to disentangle from the thorny, scratching twigs. There, stuck to her uni and ripping it more with every blaaty move, was a wee branchling, dark-leafed and tender, with several tiny, deeply hued fruits. I picked one slow and careful. I brought it to my lips. Rustle cried, "No, whafa poison?" but I crushed it on my tongue and slurped the tingly juice right up. Next I fed Rustle. We shared the rest between us, kissing and smiling, and tasting this secret new thing.

Snap!

A broken twig—and my mindcore shuts off. Instinct and years of training shoot me fast fast up the tree. I climb hand to boot, racing up the leafy boughs as fast as my bruised core can. I gain momentum. I bend the branchling low, feel it swoop, and I leap with the power, up into the air and into the next standing tree. I climb and swing, swoop and glide, never stopping to look, and only sometimes cursing the added weight of my trophy weapons. Swift and rough, I fly my way until the felled forest trail looms wide ahead. I scan the next tree over for a good place to stay the fight. Ever behind me are the crackling sounds of the third Warrior on my heels.

I jump and spin, grasp the slippery bark, and swing myself up so I'm sitting on it, straddling the branch and peering down below. The wee Hunter is pale. Her braided yellow hair streaks behind in the blur of leafy gloom. Three shakes and up she goes, into the higher branch at my left. Her feet tuck up and away, and the tree shakes with the weight of her bounding jumps.

Blaat.

I swivel around to somersault backwards, forgetting the long sword is there and will not let me curl my spine. *Whump!* She is on me, dropped hard from above, and I am pinned dangerously by my own limbs, my knees drawn up to my shoulders. She perches upon me, crushing the air from my surprised lungs. She slaps my face hard and screams into my face, splitting my hearholes. I can only blink in shock. Next, she grabs the stone necklace and slams the back of my head against the tree—once, twice, more times. Then she leaps down, pulling me by the stones, and I fall heavy, awkward, tumbling through the shady mess and smashing painfully through smaller branches all the way down. At the end, she lets go to land stealthy on her feet like some savage manimal, while I go solidly crashing to the hard dirt ground, wind pummeled from my core.

I lie stunned for the milli. Pod drags me across the lumpy earth by the hair, my arms bound in front. I'm burning raw and rubbed sore. Every part of me hurts, from the roots of my ripping hair to the shivering nails of my clenched feet, deep in my dirty boots. I try to relax so it hurts less, and also to save whafa energy I still might have for the fight to come. Pod is taking me to the brushy green to do the letting, prolly. *Or taking me prisoner?* She breathes deep with me, her heavy haul, and sometimes snorts loudly as she wrenches harder. Funny that she is smaller than the others and, so I thought, would be more fluff.

When she pauses to get her bearings, I fast fast draw up my legs and push off the ground to send my weight tumbling backward into her, knocking her face forward. She loosens her grip on my hair, so I strike the back of her head with the only thing I have— my bumpy skull. She rolls forward. I fall with her, twisting as we go. I knee her in the low back while trying to wriggle my numb fingers around my utility belt. My legs wrap around her middle and my knees clench. I bury my boot heels into her gynos and grit my achy teeth. She reels and screeches, bucking to toss me off. There's no way I can reach the newly holstered knife at my calf. Instead, my fingers grasp one of the throwing stars from my belt. I core-check her hard so she falls back to the ground, and I pounce on top, straddling her chest. My tied arms cannot bend at the elbow, but I press the throwing star under her dirty chin. If I'm not careful, her neck will split whether I want it to or not.

"Don't move," I say.

She snarls but stops struggling.

How am I marked? I send because I have no breath to spare.

"PodTraitor," she says. "Ultimate Deformed Disobeyance: hostage taking, podicide, you name it. High alert for extreme violence."

"Orders?" I gasp.

"Capture and return," she says, "or Deplug."

And the others?

Pod frowns slightly. She hesitates, and I know in that milli that she doesn't even *have* orders for them. Not Shona, not Roku bird, not Solomon. Prolly thinks I killed them all.

Why didn't you kill me? I send. I would have, were I in her boots.

"Should have," she snarls. There's movement in her eye, a thought billowing through her mindcore so clearly that even I can read it.

Oh. Saving me for the big Send Down?

She doesn't blink.

Believer. I sneer. I can only imagine. GeneScan trussed out with the entire StarPod military fleet to each take a turn at the ripping of my requisitioned fleshcore. There hadn't been a sacrificing Send Down in a long time. Not since just after we were brought onside for training. Wee hatchings, us: lined up to watch and learn from the outset exactly whafa happens to a Traitor.

Pod stares me hard, like she's daring me to get it over with. She's furious. The throwing star has already indented her skin, has already opened a hair's width line that must sting sharp. Blood rushes and brightens when it hits the cool air, but the pressure I'm putting on her neck keeps it in check for the milli. It's wary weird to send with somepod I know I'll have to kill. *A Hunter like me!* It makes my insides lurch, and I start wondering if there's another way around it. Like, if only we could both just walk away from it all.

Like Rustle, for Kronk's sake.

"Untie me and I won't kill you." I don't know why I say this.

I don't even know if I mean it. I just want to be untied before the fourth appears out of nowhere. Her eyes say I'm a liar. They say I am capable of no mercy, no ethics, of keeping no promises. I play that to my advantage. "Untie me, Spietchka," I say, "Or I'll blaaty bleed you dry and leave your spirit to rot." It's easier for her to believe the worst. Her face contorts as she reaches for the ropes. She can't fully see whafa doing, but she feels her way around the knots and begins to undo them. "Faster," I say. The fourth must be nearby; I sense somepod. My arms start to shake from being held at such an awkward angle.

Her panic-scent blooms. She tugs at the rope. It loosens in one area and feeling starts to return to my wrists, but the skin burns. Sweat trickles down her forehead. I feel her core strain underneath me when she crunches forward to reach up the length of the knots. If she leans any closer, her neck will be sliced right through.

"ARRUGH!" The low bellow startles us both.

"Blaat," I say.

The gruff voice yells again from behind me. There is crashing in the brush and the crackling sound of something rolling over dry branches and twigs. She and I do not move, nary a winkle, while the huffing puffs of this new thing come closer. I hold my breath. I cannot see who it is, though she can. I watch her stony face, trying to read her reaction. The yellow-haired Hunter doesn't look relieved. In fact, she seems more terrified than when I was sawing at her throat. She holds her face perfectly still, but she continues to slide the last of the restricting ropes through a loop to release it. She mouths the word to me, sends it into my mindcore, too: **Electroll.**

Then this is not her fourth.

The blaaty spietchka needs me free now, to help her fight whafa beast has got us cornered. *Full-frontal ironical!*

It's me staring into Hunter's frightened eyes. They are blue like the big big sky, with violet swirls in them and tiny dots for pupils. The long pale lashes clump in wet triangles: eye juice leaking. Me, still perched on top of her, for so long that now it seems we breathe as one. We are a new beast, conjoined by fear.

The electroll breathes loudly. It smells strong. It grunts—a sound that accessorizes effort—and the loud crack I hear matches the sharp pain in my skull. I slump forward. I fall into those blue eyes. I fall into them and past them, into darkness.

Again, I think. Again, not dead. My skull will not survive many more hits like this. Inside, whafa brains I have left bang around in their bony bed. Like an axe has severed the center part and that sharp metallic pain burrows down and through me, unlike any I've ever known. Light blinds me. I close my eyes and the pain lessens. I am lifted, carried, and thrown onto something hard. In a milli, I hear the thing return and grunt. Hunter is tossed half on top of me, half beside me. She stays where she lands. Then there is more grunting and a creaking, and whatever we're on is lifted and pulled over the rough ground. My teeth rattle in my swollen head. Every bone cries in protest. My spine slaps and bounces against the pallet such that it just might snap. *Whafa now?*

We are hostage, she and I. Her yellow hair flies in my face. Her small core bounces against mine and also against the hard wood. With each trotting mile that passes, her scent, her skin and long hair, her bones, and the very meat of her imprints itself into me, dents its way into my being, into the great unconscious vault of my Podless self.

Roku: Fanfare

It grows dark inside this clump of trees. Shona's breath leaves a tiny fog in the cool air when she sniffs and puffs. She crouches beside what's left of Solomon's corpse. As sick as it made me, I had to sever that beautiful neck and be rid of the entire mindcore, not knowing exactly whafa uses in the reanimation program. Though Loo destroyed the fakies in Living Lab, ScanMans can prolly create more. I could never leave her to be renovated into some mindless freakshow.

Shona is tired from wheedling and threatening, and is no longer speaching me. Rustle, Kronk rest her, would find that hilarious. I hop my way to the outer ring of ragged stones at the utmost craggy tip of our perch. Shona cries out, wary scared to be left alone on the island.

Be Podless, I send. **Like us all.**

I flap my strong wings. I am skyward. The air cools me, helps blow the stink off me. Let Shona go back, then, to the old world, to that place of deceit. Things are simple when I flap and fly, when I twist and soar, when I track wee movements and glimmers of feed down below, soon to be caught unawares. All this other business, this grating emo clash, takes away from the pure sadness I have for Solomon. How unholy this new game. How ugly, the deep layers.

I twirl on the winds, ever higher. *Loo will be wondering where I am,* I think. Blaaty convulsed she'll be, to be left alone so long. But she will turn about and have her Hunter's mind racing with new possibilities, with strategies and plans. I can finally speach plainly about all that I have learned in my snoops. All the fetid truths about our StarPod colony, about our militia training program, and the way ScanMans have been using us all—stealing us from our biological nests, deleting our human and ancestral rememories, training and tuning and modifying us into their own perfect, elite bodyguards. Using us up, one generation of brainwashed Warriors at a time.

We will think things through. We will have each other. *We'll go to the Red Soil Settlements!* I chirp out loud. A place full of

Deformed, rabbling, escaped pods, all in chronic Disobeyance. I rememory how frightened I was when I first learned of them. Later, when I thought on this colony, it was hope that pulsed inside me, keeping me alive and sharp-eyed. Hope kept me quiet through my painful change and hope kept me busy, picking at the mindtrails and rememory glitches of my mates. I had wanted them to learn for podselves.

Loo will shimmy split to know this. I laugh out loud and the buoyant bubble grows inside my feathered chest. But when I round the bend toward our fire pit, all the goodness I am building, all the scrappy bits of plans plummet to my bowels. I lose them— *whush!*—like that, into the night sky.

I take in the severed outlines of the razed woods. Smoke lifts from place to place. The strong smell of earth fills me; uprooted trees and torn-up grassy plots expose dirt to the palest trail of blinking stars. I can see where the shuttle must have grazed the grassy clearing, where it knocked about on rock piles, leaving scratchy scars and chem-trail stains. I circle up above. I scan for a warm body mass or carrion, spilling beneath the toppled trees.

Oh, Loo. I send but don't expect a reply. No wonder the Eights didn't return to the island base. A flaw in that ill-conceived plan. I left Loo crashed and alone, without a word. Alone except for the mysterious millipod that grows inside her! It seemed more likely that they'd track Shona, Solomon, and me, not flit about this forest for one lone scout.

I swoop lower and catch a glinty stream that leads to a wee puddle—Podsize, indeed. I speed toward it. There is a corpse beside the puddle. She has been let, the ground soaked with her powerful blood-feed. I peck at her, straighten her limbs and scan her uni. I sigh. She is not Loo. She is a decorated Eighth. Her death came clean and fast. Her weapons were harvested. Her jewels, if she had any, were stolen for trophies. It's Loo's kill, without a doubt, and Loo's pisspond right beside her.

It's all gone wrong!

A sudden rushing in the air alerts me. There is movement, even before sound. Up I hop to the nearest pile of blackened tree stump. I bury my beak in my chest, bury my claws in the sooty rubble. I hide my colors with ash. I blank myself invisible, camouflaged in the smoking ruins, and I wait to see who comes.

Loo: Hostage

The blond Hunter moans. I am strangely relieved to know she is not dead after all, that I am not alone. Our legs tangle and hang over the edge of this stupid crate. We bump and rattle our brittle bones along, forever, it seems, stopping only when the thing wants a feed of dried paste from its pack or wants to piss from the tube it otherwise keeps hidden under its hide skirt. The electroll does not rest. It does not speak to us. Neither does it send. It only grunts if we move around too much in the pallet. And when I try to throw myself over the edge, or when I succeed and start to lunge away, it comes. It always comes and crushes its massive hands around my bruised ribs and throws me back down again. Harder each time than the last, until I fear there may be nothing left to keep me in Kronk's stay.

When I have the strength, I lift my head from the wooden pallet and scan this creature. It looks like the electroll pictures that filled our screens in StarPod, only uglier. It is tall—taller even than Solomon—and three times her width. It must have more than a hundred stones on me. It is hairy, filthy, and stinks. Its head is round and pushed forward on a thick, veiny neck. The hearholes stick out with sunburnt flaps, stick out even past the mass of dirty hair that falls to its scarred and muscled shoulders. It has a large, cobbled club. No gun, but it does have my flask by its side and my shiny sword. That pretty thing I harvested is strapped around its thick core. The too-short straps push up its chest-meat like podbumps in heat. My stolen knife glints about its massive waist when it lumbers forward heavily into the dirt. The throwing stars are gone, nowhere to be seen.

Why doesn't it kill us? I send because my mouth is so dry, and also because I'm afraid the electroll can understand me.

It's programmed. A trained electroll manimal, mixed gene species, she sends. She looks bleak.

I hate being so bruised and broken, so hungry and weak. I hate not understanding this thing.

Like our dronebeet, she continues. **My unit observed many on our last Mission. Before your security breach.** She seethes with the painful rememory. Anger revives her, brings some heat to her cheeks.

I almost laugh. I had actually forgotten that we were in the middle of exterminating each other before this thing came along! Before I killed her kronking podmates. *Oops.*

"I'm Loo," I say. I try to smile, but a lurch of the cart snaps my teeth together hard. "And you are—?"

"Blaaty stuff it," she hisses out loud.

So she doesn't want to be friends. *So whafa?*

"Are you going to try and kill me again?" I say this calmly, because I know she won't. If I was in her position, though, I would smash my bruised skull open, right in the pallet, and avenge my podmates' deaths. Still, she doesn't move. Nary does she hide her hate flow. I stare back at her. I wonder if she was there at GeneScan; if her unit helped to lock us down; if they were the ones to freeze us solid.

"Marta," she mumbles at last. "My name is Marta."

I nod. Then I point to the electroll. "Whafa know about this thing?"

She says, "They're designed for hard labor and ultimate

Obeyance. They don't send or receive, prolly don't understand our mouthspeach, even. They've been Pod-hunting us some time."

"On ScanMans' command?" I ask.

She shakes her head. "Not ScanMans', and not just for you and me. For *any* of us." She trembles. "You'll wish yourself Sent Down once you meet its master. It lives at the edge of this dried land. It feeds on our fleshcore." The waves of her terror fill the air between us.

Whafa mean? What could be worse than the PodTraitor Send Down?

In a flat voice she says, "They will make us into dronebeets of their own. Into fusion slaves. For growing hatchlings they plant inside us."

I pull her blanking face to mine and shake her. Acid rises in my throat. Never in my training have I heard of this, imagined such a vile demise.

"We'll escape," I whisper. "We'll fight. We'll travel by night to the Red Soil Settlements. We'll hide there. We'll live," I say. But she's not listening. She's, like, completely blanked.

I prop her upright as best I can and settle in beside her, so as to get a better view of this strange land we cross. I scan the drying sandsoil, the thirsty earth, the small, scrubby grass that tufts along the flattened path. I search for things above, behind, anywhere in the big big sky. Nothing casts its shadow down, only the occasional wisp of cloud. Nothing rises up from this parcel of land, nothing to run to or hide in. No trees or bushes, no forests like whafa felled to hie me hither. Only burnt-out stumps of blackened trunks from time to time, like the shuttle left behind, and toppled piles of stone, and broken beams where somepod used to live. More than once we pass a bleached and fragile sculpt of somepod's bones, neatly curled at the side of the path, marking out the miles of this desolate place.

It will take us nearer to the Red Soil Settlements, I hope. But I do not know for certain, and I am too weak to risk more broken bones with the stinking thing. I cannot fight my way out alone. *Where is Roku now, when I need her so?*

I push away that sad note and lie in wait. Let the hairy beast tire itself carrying us. Let me stay wary watchful for any helpful thing. And let Marta snap from her dreary woe and pull her weight, else be left for flowering; she can incubate a milli bug-eyed beets for all I care. Kronk knows I'll not be fusing to any pod's command.

Roku: Four Winds

My ever-hollow belly gurgles. *Time to feed again.* There are ghastly grubs under the stump on which I perch. They look juicy, but I've had them before and they taste bitter. They'd bring the bile up my mangled throat. I hear sweet, long pullworms turning deeper in the baking ground. Some are crisp where fire sizzled down the roots of burning grass and weedlings. Some still inch to the cooler moist earth below. Flying gnats are everywhere, and tiny prickflies buzz around the abandoned scout corpse. The furries are slowly coming back to sniff what's left of their nests, but they will be too filled with panic to taste friendly in my beak.

I blank myself in tight, freeze on my burned-out roost. An Eighth Level Healer creeps quiet quiet, her dark uni blending with the sooty trunks and the blackened brush. She is stealthy slow and oh, so careful, picking her way among rubblestalks and smoking staff, that even I almost miss her clever movements. She carries a dead Scout over her strong shoulders. Slight she is, and so like me—like the me I *used* to be—I catch my birdy self yearning to chirp. Her dark hair hangs fine; her eyes shine like beetles in the red earth of her skin. She circles close; she has come for her other fallen mate.

All the while I sit and watch her, I pine for my former self: my agile bones, my supple limbs and delicate fingers, my face, the skin I used to never think on. For the first time since the change, I am glum glum, envious of this unknown Healer. She fills the air with little coos. She lays the corpses side by side and splays their limbs Kronk-style. She rocks back and forth on her heels. She wave-sends grief and, finally, she touches a pulled hem from one bloodied uni with her trembling fingers. She loosens a clump of mud from the other Scout's knotted hair. She kisses their cold foreheads. She leaks eye juice, I realize with a start. Something I rarely did before and now am completely unable to. Finally, the Healer stands. She opens a small pouch at her waist and takes a small handful of glistening salt rocks. She surprises me by tossing it to the four winds. She burns a small pile of dried herbs, also taken from her pouch. She rubs the soft ashes on the five podpoints: feet for running swift, hands for fighting should they need to, mindcores for shrewdly thinking their way into Kronk's garden. It's a death-maul ritual from before the Treason Times, one I've heard about and read about but never witnessed. It, like other ancient arts, is passed only in secret from one like-minded Healer to another.

ScanMans would dandystill freak on this!

Interesting, I send, accidentally. **Hmm.**

Her back stiffens. She dives into the bush ahead and rolls cleanly through to hide behind some large, mossy rock. Now she'll scan until she picks me out of the dirty landscape.

Blaat. I frizzle in my mindcore to think up some way to form Allegiance with her. And since I can't undo it, I send some more.

One Pod. I wave Kronk-size so the tiny, drying leaves shiver on the fallen trees. I stand up on my claw feet and extend my wings. I make myself big, knowing she watches from her hiding place. **I guard the Four Winds for your rite, Healer.** I turn slowly, all the way around on my perch, showing her I am unarmed, allowing her plenty of chances to fell me.

"Who are you?" she shouts.

Roku of Seventh Level StarPod. Formerly. I wavel a wing.

"Not killed, then, by the PodTraitor?" She straightens herself up. Her hands hang lightly at her side, only a twitch away from her weapons.

No. Am I also marked?

She doesn't respond. Her mind is well sealed, but I tap my way inside, sweep through its blueprint of ordered corridors. **Oh, I send. You have been instructed to kill a feathered imposter who may *claim* to be Roku Pod.** I wait a long milli. **You have false orders. I am no imposter.**

She stares at me, and I open myself. **Sweep me, mindcore and all,** I send.

But she can't. I forget these wee things cannot do this at will, that they only rarely grow fusion-close enough to catch a glimpse inside somepod's other workings.

Healer, you must know there are many troubled things about our StarPod Colony. Don't be fooled by these commands.

She cocks her head to one side, and although her face is hard, her eyes glinting, I know my send reaches some part of her. Surely anypod practicing the Ancient Rites must on some level dispute ScanMans' heavy-handed dominion.

Listen. I seek Loo to travel onward. We have no future in StarPod. I cannot live underground with my new skybound self. They will Deplug me for certain. Prolly you, too, if you return. ScanMans would snap her in two. I gesture to her fallen podmates. **Whafa Pod Leader?**

"She's on her way here with another unit." She hesitates. "Our Hunter is still missing."

I will help find her.

"An easy trap," she says. Her voice is low and measured.

I have nothing to gain from your death or hers. I stand quietly, wings tucked in to seem smaller now. **I need nothing from you. It's you who will need me if you want to survive.** I pull her spiritwind toward me and guide it inside. **Scan whafa will. My outer core is changed, yes. But Pod will find nothing Deformed on the inside.**

She penetrates my mindcore with her cold, impartial wave. She is cautious, but she sorts through the rememories she finds. She clings to some more than to others: the old me in uni—so like her now— my unit laughing together at CanteenaTime long ago, our training, our Kill Ops. Then, my more recent changes, my fears and my snoops about StarPod, right up to my quiet escape inside her unit's shuttle. She sifts through the rememories of my actual change, the painful transformation I survived alone. Her suspicions shift. I feel a lightness inside her. A clarity.

She believes me.

"You were so frightened," she says quietly. "We only felt our own fear."

I nod. **I must leave before the shuttle and the next Scout unit arrives. Come with me.**

She doesn't say a thing. She's thinking it all over, and the mistrust is plain to see in her eyes. Now more than ever, I hate that ScanMans have scaled a full battle, pitting us one against the next. We'll do all the dirty work for them at this rate. We'll be lined up, all dead and cold on the ground, while they stay safe in the Lab, in their underground lair.

I must find Loo, I send.

"She killed my podmates. She blaaty killed yours! Why would we want to find her breathing?" The Healer flares in anger.

Loo did not kill my mates. They live, some. She is full-frontal skilled. She could live rough in these lands, hiding and hunting.

"Perhaps. But there are other dangers here," she says, with her chin jutting forward. "Electrolls who trap Warriors for slaves.

Marta, our Hunter, could be captured. They can prolly scent this dead flesh, even through this smoke." She hiccups a quiet sob at that.

So burn them as they did in the ancient days. I think of Solomon and how difficult it was to do that to her beloved core. But also how necessary.

She looks at me, mouth wide, then down at her mates, choking back emo. She grips her fists tight at her sides.

Elsewise, ScanMans will reanimate them back in Living Lab, making them less themselves and more slavey. I wait for this to sink into her mindcore. **My unit discovered their own empty cores, waiting to be reprogrammed.** She raises her eyebrow. I wonder if she would believe me were I to tell her all that I've learned. All the ugly truths.

The sun climbs higher and heats the wounded earth. Flies and buzzers and stinging beetles multiply endlessly. Their nests have been disturbed, their routines destroyed, their feed hidden, and now the only source of their blood lust remains the warrior, the corpses, and me. They love the corpses as much as me, since neither of us bites back.

At last, she comes to some decision. She says, "This is the last death rite I will perform."

I tilt my head. I think: *I doubt that, Healer. I somehow sadly doubt it.*

We drag the corpses to the forest's fiery edge. I carry them, one at a time, and drop them from above, into the heart of the flames. The Healer nervously checks about at every turn. I wave-send her some comfort.

We did the right thing.

"We should leave," she says, although she seems uncertain. "My Leader will come back in the shuttle. She'll find the clearing. I need to find Marta before your Loo does." Her face sets tight again and, before her mind closes, I glimpse a picture of her

Hunter, a wee wiry thing with bright yellow hair. Only, in my mind, I see her crushed in Loo's violent embrace. *Wary weird.*

Loo will listen to me. I hop sideways and flick my feathers. *At least, I blaaty hope so.* If she hasn't gone into complete convulsions, that is. A complete cidal spree.

"Marta has taken the tracking stone from Jemma's neck. As long as it stays intact, we can follow her."

Whafa stone? I chirp. I wonder: *Did it shine? Was it pretty?* For Loo was never one to pass on a sparkling bit stripped from a steaming fresh kill.

"It's pink, and cleverly hides a tracking unit. It looked well on her." Pod grows quiet now in rememory.

How track it?

She removes a decoder from her waist purse. "With this," she says. "It's not precise, though. It leads through an area of baked ground, toward some settled lands beyond."

The Red Soil Settlements? I chirp.

"Is that whafa called? Electrolls take the stolen scouts to their leader's compound near there." She clears a code on the small machine and puts it away. "So, she could be their hostage."

She could be blaaty dead, if Loo had anything to say about it, I think.

"We must hurry. ScanMans will give my unit some time to clean this up, but they will send another unit if they don't hear back."

I hop toward her. **Come. I will fly us there.** I snuffle up a pullworm, gnash it in my pointed beak, and swallow it down in lumps. Then I lean toward her. She smells so good. **Pod never name shared,** I send, and wait quietly.

"I'm Nadya," she says.

Nadya. I like this pod, this strong warrior, so much the way I used to be. I fear her fate, should she return. Maybe I'm just lonely, podless, feeling affection for anything on two legs. Missing my Warriors. I peck up a large beetle—crunchy outside, juicy on the in.

She watches me, not with disgust like Shona, but like she wants to learn how I do things. How I work. *She's curious,* I think. I'd smile if I could.

She climbs aboard my back and holds me around the neck. I stretch my full wingspan and flap. I bounce on shining claws and lift us skyward. I fly slow and silent in the smoke-filled, windless air, over the carnage—whafa left of the bleeding forest.

Oh. Her send is a cold tickle, a surprise to us both.

Your shuttle did this.

I feel her sadness, her shock at the damage.

I send, **Those trees are homes and food to the furries, the sky manimals, the wee crawlers. They are all Pod.**

Not according to ScanMans' doctrine, but this is the bigger truth I am learning on my own out here in the wilds. The creatures slink back in streams and trickles. They climb over fallen trees, scratch into the charred earth. Large manimals snort through the bush for their hatchlings. Here and there we see a tiny furred thing alone; we feel their terrified waves, their hunger.

All this to capture Loo, when we only needed to be let alone.

She says nothing. She is soaking up the images, the smells and sounds of the ravaged forest. Her spiritwind is very low. She will dandystill think on it, I know. This pod is cavy: many paths run inside her. They twist and turn, not dangerously, but with careful intent. She will sort it through in good time, I think.

I will show you something pretty, too, I send. Something you can never see from the inside of a shuttle. I swoop higher. I take her from this place, shaking it off and setting her mind free, reeling in the open air. Wind rushes. We are into the clouds.

Whafa soft puffs, she sends.

The clouds mask us from StarPod shuttles and from other predators, too. I don't bother to tell her that. She shivers from the cold, thin air, and my feathers fluff up to warm her. My wings stretch wide and strong: I have more power now than ever before. This pod, Nadya, soars high with me, not fighting or hating me, not fearing the skies we find ourselves in. She has mighty power like Loo, careful calming like Solomon, watchful thinking the way I do, or the way I used to be. I just dip and soar, trailing her through it all 'til she laughs out loud in awe of the newness, the bigness of the blue-filled sky.

Rustle: Currents

A warm current has all the little pretties swarming in it: bright colored flashes, wee flicking tailfins, bubbles. They rub and shimmy against each other. They frisk and swish ahead, dart in and out, playing as they suckle up the tiny specks of feed that billow through the tidal stream.

On whim, I grab Loo's dagger from its hiding place. *I want to go with them.* Maybe it's some unknown call to nature. Or maybe I'm just tired of this dark, cold shelf, this gloomy murk, and the feel of certain doom. Even if I should be sucked up or speared by something monstrous, killed by some stinging jelly or other unimagined beast, I decide to follow the flock. At the very least, I will be warm and in the company of flitty little jewels. They ignore me for some millis but, as I relax and lose my nagging fears, they come to me in ones and twos. They nudge me, and the delicate press of their mouths leaves O-shaped kisses along my fleshy core. I shiver and wriggle, and they push away, tiny sounds rippling with them. Then they scoot right back. They call to me and chase each other toward me, fluttering fast like bats, tickling my lonely skin. I am their newest game!

The islands, they gurgle. *Let's swimmy to the islands!*

Some scout ahead, some go way above the rest, up near the surface. The others wriggle with excitement for the delicacies they will find in the coral reef around the islands. They come this way every moon cycle and love it dandystill. Their excitement is contagious, and soon I shimmy with my supple length. My limbs are strong and winsome, my hair tingling and alive. I open my mouth and laugh along with them. *Rrak rrak rrah!*

The water comes, shallow and clear. Fishies make chase then spin back, flutter slow to the sandy bottom. They root for wee grains to roll in their mouths. I float up to the surface. The closest I've been since—well, since dropping down deep. My hair fans out, snaking through the gentle waves. I see the topside world again, and it is so different from when I submerged. Now, the water is calm and warm, and the big big sky is blue, not black. The clouds drift in white puffy stacks, so unreal to me. So completely unreal.

I pop up. Air rushes the top of my head and the wee bits of skin that breach the surface. My eyes are up, now the bridge of my nose. I blow large bubbles into the water. I'm afraid to try and breathe the old way. I shrug my shoulders up, the tips of my fingers, the length of my arms; the warm sun feels like love on them, like fusion, such soft touchlings. I float on my belly parts with my limbs splayed out, the bottoms of my feet turned up, my buggy eyes face down. The pruney wrinkles of my toes shiver with a passing breeze. I roll onto my back. Water streams out my nose-holes. I sputter and spray it all out. My chest tightens; my core seizes up. I hold my breath. I'm stuck in the middle of two worlds, panicked, with no rememory of how I used to work. How lungs—those sagging inner flaps—filled themselves with air and squeezed it back out again. Pain knifes through and through, my vision blurs. Things go dark.

And, suddenly, it's there again—a gasping, raging tear inside. I cough. I gag and snort. Fishies zip away I'm so loud, splashing and choking. *Be Fit,* I tell myself. And soon it comes more easily. I float backside, paddle my feet gently, swerve and steer with my webbed hands. I relax and stare up at the big big. It's all above and below me: sky and water, water and sky. And then, ahead, in between those two things and framed by my pointed toes, are the black rocky piles of sheer cliffs, and the greenery fluffing way up high—the islands shimmer in the strong gold light.

I shield myself, one hand up to make shade on my squinting face. I always loved when our unit landed in big-treed forests on Mission. I loved climbing, scraping my knees on the rough bark, nibbling fresh leaves and spying out from up on high. I stare up at those pretty fluffs and rememory galloping about in the green with Loo, one time. I rememory such kissing, rolling in perfumed long grass.

Oh.

My chin wibbles. My bellyparts twist, lovesick. I drop my hand. But the shade remains, grows even, to cloud over me and the fishy flock. The wee things flit and hide away from the dark shape that moves overhead. I bend backward. I scrinch my neck to gaze in awe: the shiny blackness of a large shuttle churns its slow motors, grinds to a hovering halt. It's larger than ours was. It's longer, with more powerful whirling engines. Newer, with weapons docking on the base and outports for lasers and missiles. The blaaty shuttle scrapes a rock pile, sparking a fountain of fire, then parks itself on a nest of falling greens.

Whoever's inside must have seen me, might be out hunting me, even. *I'm, like, completely dead already,* I warble. I can barely breathe on my own, let alone fight off a StarPod militia with my soggy flesh-core and one shiny knife. Hardly fair, ya? I submerge myself and blow bubbles under the water in defeat. I sit on the sandy bottom and hold my breath. I watch a watercrawler inch past, rolling a small shell with its claws. I run out of breath but am suddenly scared to suck up water through my gills, now that I've been inhaling air up my noseholes for a few millis. It's all confused. I panic.

I bob up out of the water and gasp loudly. I swimmy to the shallows, close to the black rocks. The shuttle has definitely landed, and the frumping bouts of dust no longer puff over the cliff edge in violent bursts; it is quiet now. I'm not sure if it's hair and water in my eyes, or if there was a quick, darting movement up high, a pod shadow flitting about the top of the cliff. I rub my face, shake the droplets clear. Nothing up there now.

Maybe they've come to rescue me? My own private rescue shuttle, full of brave Pods who dandystill have news of the others. Prolly even have them aboard, ya? Might even have Loo in there, come to save me from the sea. Come to warm me through and fuse me well again, cure me of all that ails.

Rustle Pod?

They know me! The send is cautious but clear. It snaps me from these hopeful wonderings and pulls me to the water's edge. It is so strange to bear my full weight, to feel my feet bury into the sand with each wobbly step. I look up to the tip of the cliff—I can't climb it, not with my water-soaked limbs. Maybe some mobile travelshaft will come to lift me up. I see her then, a wilting shape up high among the rocks.

"Rustle," she yells in her unmistakable voice, "Get, like, your Deformed self up here. In the now?"

Mothering blaaty Kronk!

Shona? I send in complete disbelief. She's back from the dead to torment my fishy incarnation. She'll never leave me in peace, whafa! Serious, my first impulse is to dive down and swimmy far away, back to the boring old scary land of the miserable.

Loo needs you. She sends with just the right amount of annoyance that I know it must be true.

Loo. Even the name song fills me warm and happy, fires me quick, so that I am able to do anything, anything at all. *Of course I can! Anything for Loo.* I throw myself farther inland, limp to the nearest pile of rocks, and begin my perilous climb.

Loo: Imprint

The cart lurches and bangs onto the red ground. My eyes pop open. Everything that is mine hurts. The electroll grunts and shakes foul-smelling sweat from its dirty core. It snuffles and spits, blows gloop out its noseholes into the hard-packed mud. A loud sound honks from beneath the skirt. It staggers away some distance and lifts the flask to its hairy mouth.

Water.

Marta raises her head. She looks rough—gray skin, dull eyes. Her chin wobbles and down goes her head—*smack!*—against the wooden ledge. I lean forward slowly, shrink from the sharp pain in my ribsticks. I reach for her. I clear my throat. I fuse-send her a cooing. Her anger flares up, but she doesn't say a thing. I think of Solomon, think how good it was to have her wave-send warmth, while all that hurt built up and overflowed, all that time after Rustle sank in the sea. Still, it is wary weird to do this with pod from some other unit. I pretend it is Solomon now and not this stranger. That I am sending all these things to her while I had the chance. Marta's face relaxes, her energy levels rise. Finally, she joins in and the coo-send builds our strength, speeds our healing. It feeds our spiritwind a wee feast.

When the electroll comes back, I gesture to the flask it carries, whafa stole from me. *And I from that other luckless Scout.* The electroll sniffs my face, presses a blackened meaty finger to my mouth, splits my dried lip to blood. It licks that hot drop from its finger, growling. Then it tosses the almost empty flask to me. I slurp up the warm wet. I offer Marta some, but she is blanked again, healing podself, no doubt. I suck up the last of the water. I'm on the verge of swallowing, when something moves me. I lean forward and let fall the mouthful between her teeth. She swallows it down gently and licks her bruised lips. Mine tingle as though they've been kissed, as though more than just a drop passed between us.

Whafa doing? I think with disgust. *Feeding the enemy!* Sharing water lowers my own chances for survival. *Complete tingly emo blaat!*

The beast roars and grabs the flask. It shakes the last few drops onto the thirsty ground and tosses the container back at us. It heaves ho and picks up the wooden handles again. And I can tell by the lightness of its step, the renewed energy and the set of its massive shoulders, that wherever it is bringing us, we are nearly arrived.

Screechy creak and halt. *We're here.* The thing dumps us over the edge. *Splat, ow.* We land in the dust. We're still in the deadlands— the ground is dry and hard—but not too far off, I can see the blurry outline of greeny fluffs: treeshapes and bushlings. Grass, maybe. We have crossed the wide expanse of the burned-out plain.

"Marta," I say. "Be fit."

She nods and opens one eye.

There is a wee hut leaning to one side, looking like the wind could prolly gust it flat in a milli. It's even smaller than the travelshaft back at StarPod. The beast kicks us in that direction, into the wary darkness of this blaaty diseased collapse. It smells as though a hundred furries died in there, as though the rotting sticks that hold it in place are the lardy bones of poisoned manimals. As though Kronk herself had piled her waste and forgotten it in this small circle on the edge of these damaged lands. Marta, she's stuffed inside first. I hear her gag, hear her scratching into the cold ground. I try to crawl away, but the electroll kicks me back to the cobwebby opening of the hut. I retch as it stuffs me in, limb by limb, right onto Marta's pile of brittle bones. My face is the last bit of flesh to feel the air and fading sun on it, the last part to be planted by those sweaty hands. The electroll stands in front, blocking the opening with its massive hairy backside.

"Rrawk." Marta heaves and the sound completely makes me start into it, right? She tremors underneath me, in a panic.

"Shh," I say. My mouth is too dry to speak more. I coo. I coo to calm myself, to stop her from this contagious heaving, to blank from the unfit shack we find ourselves in. I pull her up, facing me, cover her mouth, lean her forehead against my own. I grip her shoulder with my other hand and send for her to do the same. The sparkly pink stone crushes between us. Our faces smooshed, I hope-send Kronkwards, something I've been doing a lot of lately.

Give us strength, I send, **Help us heal.**

Solomon's face shines inside me, her voice fills me when I coo. I feel her spiritwind pouring through us and filling our broken selves with her powerful light. We suckle it up and breathe it in, let it radiate through and between us, let the magic happen.

In time, I feel Marta's strength pick up, hear her cooing along with me. Her scent is in me, in my head, and when I breathe, so does she. When I exhale down to the last bruised bottom of my lungs, she does, too. We are in step, almost synch-fuse, building our core strength and our mind power, learning each other in this rushed weirdness.

Pod building.

Later, we lie on our backs side by side in the dark. It's the only way we can both stretch out inside this hut. If either wants to move, we both have to wiggle and turn together or else clobber podselves with boots and curses, plonks on the head, whimpers. It is dire, but we still feel the shyness of being forced together too soon, so much closeness with an unknown pod. It's like in fusion, when pod can read another's thoughts, even feel her sensations. I can tell that Marta is thinking about the pink necklace. She wants it. I am thinking about my bladder. *Where will I pee?*

The electroll breathes loudly, deeply, but once in a milli, it snorts and jerks itself upright. It is struggling, finally, to stay awake.

"Give me Jemma's stones," says Marta. "It's all I have left from my unit." She turns her head toward me. It's dark, but I can see the fuzzy grays of her features, the pale glimmer of her eyes, the shine of her teeth. "Please?"

My kill, my trophy. Rustle knew how much I hate sharing. But I nod. It's the least I can do, what with killing half her unit and all. I touch the stones with my filthy, swollen thumbs. I exhale. I give it to her, and she quickly snaps it around her own neck.

Shall we escape now? I send. I slowly work my joints. I breathe the stabby knots out of all my battered muscles.

"How? We can't get out without waking it."

I scan the frail boards that somehow hang together to make our shelter. We could easily kick or smash our way out, but not without making a Kronkload of noise. Plus there's nothing nearby to hide in. Not that I even had a full milli between being dumped on the hard ground and being kicked into this room of bilious whiffery. *We need a shuttle,* I think. *A machine of sorts. A big black bird to fly us away from here.*

I shake my head. "We need to out-race this guard," I say. "Or stop it solid."

"I feel a bite stronger," she says. "Not completely fit, though." She rubs the swollen knuckles on her right hand. The same ones whafa shined my eye, no doubt. "If only we had some weapons. Some chemblasts or poison."

"Ahah!" I whisper out loud, then clutch my sore side. *Ow.*

She rolls her eyes. I can tell by the whitey shine of them.

"Poison!" I lean forward but can't reach. The hurts stab too much. My hip creaks when I lift my boot over toward her. "In there, stashed." I send an image of the grassy weeds, folded and dried, and tucked in at my calf, near where my holster hangs empty.

Oh, knifey.

She pushes her fingers into the tops of my thermal barbarian boots, wiggles them around. "Ugh." She grunts when she leans forward. I feel her fingers dance and poke around the circumference of my calf.

"Hee hee," I say and clutch my battered side. "Hee hee hee"— **stop it! No ticklies,** but it's no use.

"Get it yourself, then," she says. She drops my leg in a huff.

"Don't have to be snarkly about it," I say, "It's tickly." *It's not like I want her touching me.*

Not like I want to touch you, either, she sends.

Blaat. She is completely reading me, even without me sending, prolly due to the intense cooing we did earlier. *Blaaty blaat!*

Marta grabs my left boot again. She rams her fingers into the top and pinches around for the weedlings. I grit my teeth in silence. She finally finds them, squashed flatter than the bitey ticks we lay on top of. She tugs. She cups them in her hands, dry and crumbling. "Sure this is poison?" she says. She sniffs it cautiously.

I shrug. I don't want to talk or send. *Or think.*

"How will we get it to feed?" She tries to sit up, but that means rolling practically on me and such, practically killing me with her core planted in my line of bruised organparts; and it also means she clomps around and kicks the wood slats of our confinement.

"Rroawr," yells the electroll. It thrusts its top half into the wee opening and snatches Marta's face with one large fist and her outstretched hand with the other. Panicked, Marta tries to stuff the wee grass into her mouth but the electroll snatches that up, too. It sniffs the stuff, pulls the one strand from her lips and stuffs it all into its own mouth, slobbering and chewing it loudly, swallowing and licking its dirty face. It sniffs some more, sniffs right down my long legs, so its straggling hairs wriggle my bare skin. Satisfied that there's nothing else edible, it pulls back and garumphs a wee bite, then settles back down to block the port.

"Well, that solves one problem," I say. It's all so redundant, since she can sense my thoughts and texts before I ever deliver them.

Now we wait and see.

Rustle: Wary Stupid

Stupid.

That's whafa was, that's whafa am, that's whafa always will be.

Two trim black-clad Eights finish tying the knots. They don't send or speak, just turn and go back into their shiny awful shuffle. Shona gloats at my lump of trussed-up, roped-around fury. She wipes her drippy nosehole with the back of her filthy sleeve.

"Whafa say now, Rustle? Huh?"

She looks wild, caked in dirt and dried blood, her hair broken off in clumps, her uni a completely ragged mess. When she breezes past me, a rank stink billows around her. Her breath withers me. If I didn't know better, I'd say *she* was the Deformant. I can hardly believe that it's her. That she somehow survived the big wet waters and that we're here face to face again. It's too awful to be true.

Kronk knows whafa happened to the rest of them.

My skin flakes with the dry heat on land. My feet bleed where the sharp rocks cut into them during the long climb up the cliff. Of course Loo wasn't here, didn't need me. Of course I'm just, like, completely stupid.

She might soil herself, she is so smug. "You even *voted* to not kill me. That's, like, the really funny part?" She tromps around, spreading her terrible smell. "That's why fusion is a waste of time, you see. Clouds the mindcore. *Fusion folly foils the hunt,*" she sings. "Rememory that from the First Level training manual?"

Her voice is more shrill than I can bear. I'd gladly swim into the mouth of any waterbeast, just to be rid of her. I don't say a word. Seems so long ago that I knew how to move my mouth and make those funny throat sounds, anyways. *Pointless.*

"Like, fine." She hates that I won't speak. She heads away from this small clearing, over to the open door of the shuttle. Dust rises from her stomping feet.

The same two Scouts come out of the shuttle. They stand to one side, texting privately. The tallest and darkest of the two is a Healer. She has that grounded sense about her, the powerful hands and wide shoulders so typical of them all. The other is a Leader, although, judging from the color of her pins, she's from some other unit. She is in good shape, clean clean and wary strong. Her short red hair shines neatly; her green eyes scan carefully. She has far fewer badges than Loo did, fewer even than me, but Leaders rarely leave the shuttle on Mission. So it's not like they're out tracking manimals or rescuing hatchlings or dousing forest flames, that sort of thing. They don't take the same risks and, therefore, don't reap the prizes the way we Warriors do. *Did.* Funny how tidbits like this float back to me, small rememories of that long ago life in StarPod; Rules and Regs whafa used to be the only way to live and to think.

Suddenly, I'm panicked. *Oh no,* I think. *I can't go back there. Not anymore. Not ever.* I picture the slimy deep of the ocean floor and wish myself there.

Leader walks briskly toward me, carrying her mobile handset. She takes pictures of me and zips them off to ScanMans in Controls, prolly. I make a rude gesture with my webbed fingers. *That one's for you, Almighty.*

Healer watches from a distance, and I think I see a smile flit over her wide face. She covers it with her big hand, which is otherwise never more than a flick from her long sword. Leader inspects me at all angles, taking photos of it all. She nudges me with her beautiful unruined boot, grabs a handful of my hair, and saws at it with a rough blade. I wince but am tied too tightly to fight. She puts it away in a sterile specimen jar. Like I'm some convulsing freak show she found on another planet, and not Pod-kind. She pulls on the drying fins that crackle up and down the backs of my legs and along the backs of my powerful arms.

No, I think, *she wouldn't!*

But she does. She grabs a fistful from my leg and rips them from my fleshcore. I grind my teeth but still cry out. Scream, really, like a dronebeet does when you pull off leggies and watch the claw dance around on its own.

The ground tremors beneath me. My noseholes winkle with her smell. Shona's face grows larger. *She's rushing over to stop this,* I think.

"Make sure you take some from the arms, too," she says. Shona sneers at me, so tall, now that my face is in the dirt. She holds something silver in her hand. She puts it up to her mouth. She slurps. *It can't be.* She licks her wide blue lips. *It is!* My core reels with shock and need, an instant greedy desire it had learned to forget. *Fizzy Drop!* She swallows loudly. Pink foam covers her top lip. She shakes the can and slurps back most of it in long, torturous swallows.

"Ahhh," she says. She belches loudly.

I groan and lick my lips.

She crunches the can and drops it right in front of my face. Just below my noseholes. The scent stirs up a world of lost rememories: sugary berries and fizzy droplets, and all those electrolytes rushing your blood. Amphetamines coursing through to jittery, twitchy trigger-fingers. Analgesics to dull the pain. Saliva pools in my mouth. I rock forward a wee bite. Waterweeds and algae are feed dandystill, but Fizzy Drop sets my nerves afire. Fizzy Drop tingles my mouth and swirls my teeth, and stimulates every wee bud on my aching tongue. It is candy and feed all in one completely mind-core-altering juice. Nothing else tastes like this, nary a protein bar nor feed sample in the whole of Canteena Time. Nothing!

I wait for Shona to look away, to become distracted with some other thing, but she won't, and I can't do it, can't stand it, can't help but stick out my long tongue to poke at the bubbling rim of the can, squirming in my ropes, desperate for a wee lick. Shona snatches the can tight to her bosomy self. She flicks the last drop to the dirt beside me. I hear it crackle and hiss. Those tiny bubbles of chemical goodness sputter and die on the ungrateful earth.

I could weep.

"You see," she says to Leader. "You have to kick them right where they live. Rustle here, Deformed or not, lives in, like, the greedy bellycenter, far from the intellizone. Gets her every time."

Healer frowns at this performance, this awful meanness.

"I will prepare the Sleep vials," says Leader. "Prolly you should take some rest while we travel, Shona. The other unit has agreed to carry us onward." It's an order, softened with the pretense of manners, with the respect due Pod who shares the same title.

Shona says, "We need to go directly back to StarPod."

I can tell by the way she stands, shoulders hunched, flank tensed, and her claws slightly distended, that she doesn't like the Sleep plan. She doesn't like being told whafa do; doesn't like to lose the upper hand, not even for a milli.

"The Scout corpses are destroyed, but I'm still missing my Hunter and Healer. I can't waste time delivering you back right now."

Corpses!

"Your unit is in shambles, too. You will want to look to them." Her voice is low and even. "I have a report of a black-winged sky manimal who claims to be one of yours. And Kronk knows where your Hunter is, lost on a blood tide," she says thickly. "I'll need you well rested to identify the other Deformants and to code in."

Mother of Kronk, whafa happening!

Shona crosses her arms in front. "I still don't see why you don't, like, let me text ScanMans directly? I need to message them privately."

"I'm happy to relay any of your concerns," Leader says, and I notice her hand falls lightly at her side beside her knife holster. Healer steps in close. Shona's cheek tremors. I can hear her light growl from here. She is edgy and twitched, revved on chems, with no outlet for them but her bickering mindcore.

Waste of a good Fizzy Drop, is whafa I'd say if I felt like speaching right now. But I don't. I am too dread sickly from this death talk. Too worried for any words at all.

Roku: Deadlands

Nadya's tracker helps keep our course, but it works better on the ground than up here, so high in the clouds. Mainly I follow my own internal devices. We don't send. I'm busy navigating and she's busy flying. *Being flown.* She's blanked, or close to it. Prolly sick from altitude and exposure. Cloud cover is sparse now; we're a moving target, a black smudge in the clear blue. I chronic scan the skies for shuttles, for the heavy chem trails they leak. *Nothing.* I scan the ground for podsized nitrate spills, for thermal imaging patterns, for any signs of movement in the flattened expanse of deadlands. *No Loo. No yellow-haired Hunter.* There are slight rumblings in the blackened earth, far below. A trail, maybe. It's very like our own flight path.

I have the sudden urge to speach again, mouthwise, with this Healer. There are things I want to know and that I want Nadya to learn. I hold those wants in my beak. Later, I shimmy my feathers and rouse her. I send, **Whafa like, your Pod Leader?**

She snaps to. She sends a picture of her red-haired, green-eyed Leader. **Quiet,** she sends. **Efficient. Watchful, not fusey.**

Ours, too. I wait a milli before adding, **Ours betrayed us. She wants our whole unit replaced.**

By other Scouts? She sends a shockshiver with that question. Everypod knows that once a unit fuses, we are never torn asunder, never reshuffled. *Unfit.*

No. By reanimated fakies. My unit discovered them in Living Lab before their escape. Rows and rows of beds filled with replacement Scout cores. They found their own empty Selves among them. I let that information soak into her mindcore before continuing. There is a mass extermination order on us, Nadya. Pod changes like mine are sprouting up all over. ScanMans use regular units to track and kill the Deformed Pods and to return the corpse cores. Then ScanMans replace that Pod with a mindtuned replica. An altered version, reprogrammed to higher Obeyance.

Nadya is silent. I sense her mind churning, working through these new thoughts. If that's true, why weren't you our primary target? she sends. Is Loo also Deformed?

I flap and soar, tilt my wings, and circle a small descent. There is something down below, a small shack maybe, and a large flesh mound resting outside. The trail I've been reading across the Dead Lands leads right to this shelter.

I don't think Loo Deformed. And I *was* the primary target until the rest of my unit escaped from Living Lab. Our Healer is dead of a manimal attack, our other Scout drowned in the big big sea. Pod Leader wants Loo Sent Down for revenge. She lied, Nadya.

"Oh." She chokes out an angry cough, a mourning cry that shivers my core. My Podmates were slaughtered over lies.

I'm sorry, I send. And I am, truly, for all this pain. All the unnecessary killing. Pods, trained and vigilant, turned against our own. We're nothing but puppets entertaining ScanMans back at Central. Even now, I imagine us filling a large screen while Controller Almighty sits and laughs, sips a drink, crunches snack feed.

I am, too, she sends.

She wave-sends grief and I suck up the great aching rolls. I inhale it from her tired core and— *whush!* —blow it out into the vast sky. She feels lighter now, and the warming winds dry her tears. They blow the badness from us, those strong gusts. We fly free and slow, circling wide but ever lower to the ground. I squint, honing in on the rough terrain, scanning for any signs of life. There's a large fleshmass below.

Electroll? I'm not sure from this height. I feel Nadya's hackles rise the closer we get. She squirms when I duck down, when we're so close we can see the greasy hair on its large round head.

I think so. Prolly a trap, she sends.

No lifeforce sings to me. The thing is dead. No bloodstreams rush its system; no rise and fall of its massive chest. Its tree-trunk legs stretch out in front, two great logs covered not in barkly moss, but in hair and dirt. Stink clouds hover, retch-worthy. Beetles and bugs crawl about the putrid flesh. Nadya gags when I drop her lightly to the dusty ground. She wobbles a milli, covers her mouth and staggers farther away. She crawls upwind and sits quietly to get her earthbound bearings again. She sips water from her flask. Then she sets her tracker down and adjusts some of the fine tuners on it. She has a reading.

"It should be right here," she says frowning.

I stretch and hop. I flex my cramping claws and shake the weariness from my neck and wings. Foaming drool hangs from the creature's open mouth. Blood and bile stain the front of its hide covering.

I send, **Chemical agent?**

Nadya nods *yes.* The bloated face is blue-gray, the eyes yellow with crust. Ants crawl there, feeding. The smells from the dead thing compete with the horrific stench coming from the inside shelter. Poor Nadya heaves again.

The shack is kicked apart on one side. Flimsy dried wood panels lie on the ground. I peer inside; it's dark and small and stenchy. Even so, I can see the sparkling pile of jewels inside.

"That's it," says Nadya. "Jemma's crystal tracker." She crawls in and picks it up. "Marta would have kept it with her, if she could. She would want to be rescued."

But Loo wouldn't, I think. Not if she knew this was a tracking device.

Tussle marks layer the hard ground; small piles of sand and dirt hold fleshcore imprints still. Somepod was cowering inside here, waiting. I try to scent trail, but there's too much else to sift through: layers of rotten flesh, decomposing organics, stale sweat. Nothing to track whosoever may have lain there. Whosoever may have killed this hairy beast.

"Scouts will come for it," she says, fingering the pretty bobbles.

Then let them find it here, I send. I take it from her in my beak. I stuff it all inside the electroll's awful mouth, in between its broken teeth, its rotting blue lips. Terrible liquid pools at the mouth corners and drips darkly down the hairy beast's face. Nadya gags again. I steel my woffling nerves, my queasy bile ducts. I hop away from the mess, over to where Nadya waits. I rub my beak in the loose sand to get rid of the smell. Then I flap strong and lift off, try to scan from a short distance above the whole mess.

"No, Roku," she cries. "Don't leave me."

One Pod, I send on a fusion wave. **Not leaving, only trying to see Beyond.**

As if I could leave her, I think. A warm lump rises in my feathered chest. *As blaaty if.* I spy a darker patch of earth not far off. I land beside it, plant my beaky in the dirt, ruffle it around and plant it into the darkened circle. *Bladder drops.*

"What is it?" she runs toward me, still holding her nose and mouth.

Pisspond, I send. **It's Loo. She was here, perhaps with Marta.**

"Then they were hostage to the electroll." Nadya's eyes shine dangerously. "That's the species we were tracking, Roku. Either they escaped or they were collected by the electroll's master. Either way, we've got to find them."

I cock my head at her. **I cannot be here when your shuttle lands.**

"I know." Nadya is quiet for a milli. "How will we find them?"

Red Soil Settlements. Loo will ever make her way there, if she

can. And we can at least learn more about these trappers—where they live and hold the podmates prisoner, if they have them.

Nadya looks so glum glum. I wavel a wing and brush her sweaty hair back from her brow. I chirp. She smiles.

"Then take me, Roku." She hops back onto my broad shoulders.

I flap my wings and we are skyward, far away from the stink. Away from our last known clue, too, and off on a new adventure. Inside, I fear for Loo—up ahead somewhere, hiding and scheming, desperate and dangerous. She is hunted by many, podless, and unaware of the life that grows inside her. I swear on Kronk's daughter to find her first, before any other thing does.

Rustle: Eights on Board

Hah! Not so stupid on the shuttle, me. I drool when the red-haired Leader takes out her shiny needle and the big big dose. *Sleep Now.* I rememory when it used to make me quiver inside, when just the waggly suggestion could relax me and rev me up in the same milli, send me bonkers in anticipation. Not now, but they'd never guess. I even whimper and coo when she slides it into my drying skin. I shake a wee bite then collapse. I'm still tied, curled down on one side. I lie still. I breathe deep: in and out. I drop solid into fakie dreamland. I open my hearholes and suck it all in, every sent thought, every mouth murmur.

The Eights move things, rearrange things. They prepare for take-off. Leader speaks curtly to Shona. Something about the corpses—two of them. How they were ruined in the fire, but how *I'm not*. How I can be studied, at least, and examined full-frontal back in the Lab. Then a different voice—the Healer, I think—says something about how was I here, *anyway,* since I was spozly murdered by my own Hunter Podmate. *Loo?* Shona sputters something, but I'm still stuck on that other part: *spozly murdered by Loo!*

There's a scuffle, raised voices. Shona screeches something about

Living Lab. I want so much to turn my head and stare my buggy eyes over at whafa happening, but I don't. *Thump.* Leader exhales deeply. Healer sighs. Then there's the sound of somepod being dragged across the floor. I smell it and think, *Kronk, not over here!*—but too bad for me. Healer checks my ropes—blaaty nice of her—and actually loosens them around my wrists. The odd color of my drying skin must worry her. She clangs a few cubby doors. She drops a soft foamie over my core. I'd forgotten about nudeness, about clothing and unclothing. Now I almost blush with shame. But she's away, over to lock the shuttle door, not looking or thinking on me further. She goes up to the front where the Leaders of both units are already buckled into place, firing the engine. The Scouts are ready to go.

The floor shakes. I let my eyes move around in slow circles. Shona is a big, filthy dropped pile on my left. I don't see my knife—*Loo's knife*—anyplace. Leader must have it and I want it back. I look hard at everything in the hold compartment. Shiny clean clean. Lots of storage cubbies. I notice every Pod has her own pullout trunk, stacked high and secured to one wall. Each is labeled with pretty curling letters: Leader, Hunter, Healer, Scout One, and Scout Two. Way nicer than our old shuttle, ya? The rusting carriages for our blaat are half the size and nary a name tag anywhere.

I scoot away from Shona by inching my bound ankles down the floor and pulling the rest of me along behind. *Bump, drag. Bump, drag.* I wriggle my wrists around, fiddle and frak with the big rope between my fingers. I work at the knot, and the whole time, the floor rumbles underneath me, the engine whines. Before I can grab hold of something, the shuttle shakes its sleek self into the air. There's a sudden burst and another; my organparts wiggle and lurch, my whole core flops and slides around the hold. It feels like forever since I've been on shuttle. After a steady incline, it levels out and we chug along at a good clip. I sit upright, lean against the shiny wall. I get the last bit of the wrist knots to come clean. I untangle the ropes and loop them carefully into a pile. Then I untie my ankles.

I can barely hear the Eights over the engine roar. I figure they won't hear me much either, but still, I open the cubbies quietly. The first has a bilge bag full of dirty unis, all balled up and stinky. I haul those out and tuck them and the pile of ropes under the soft blanket where they left me snoring. *Ha ha, the oldest hidey trick in the book.* The next cubby has an extra uni, clean and black, which I pull on. The stretchy fabric scratches my dried skin. All it wants is warm water and the flowing weeds to tickle it. *And Loo.* Loo would be so jealous to see me standing tall in this black uni. I wipe the thermal scanning mask out carefully, then pop it over my head. It covers my eyes and nose. The back strap pulls at my long, sentient hairs. Now when I look at Shona, she is a large, hot, red spot lumped on the cool shuttle floor. My pink footprints glow where the heat still holds. The bilge-bag lump under the blanket is an even cool blueness, like the rest of this space. Except for where small motors churn inside the electronics, where pipes carry warm water, and where flickering lights heat their rounded bulbs. The refrigeration cupboards glow, too.

For shame, Rustle.

But there is no honor in me, only the next thing obsessing my mindcore. Not a shuttle takeover; not hauling Shona's carcass overboard; not searching for the corpses, or spying and infiltrating the System. *Find the Fizzy Drop.* And I do. A cooling cabin filled with protein shakes, sprout trays, and finely powdered weeds almost hide the sparkly seductive can at the very back. *The last one—take that, Shona.* I pop the tab and guzzle it back. *Merciful Kronk.* It tingles my mouth and swirls my teeth. It shivers me. *It's been so long!* Nothing like the frothy cold pinkness of Fizzy Drop!

Now I am indestructible. Power surges through me; the sugar

and speed rushes. Synapses fire and I move like liquid, like weeds in the ocean current. I scale the wall, slither along the ceiling, grasp and release, crawl quickly toward controls. The Scouts are all strapped into their seats. Both Leaders are at the controls. The red-haired one speaks clearly into her mic.

"I'm getting a weak reading for Jemma's tracker."

"Could be damaged from the fire. From anything," says the other Leader.

The first says, "Prepare to land, units."

The big Healer says, "I can't believe Jemma's dead."

"Slaughtered by their Podocidal Hunter." The redhead spits it out like poison.

By Loo? Then she's still alive! I almost yelp with relief. Then I swallow my joy. *Oh yeah, the blaaty corpses.*

I slither back along the ceiling, scan for a large enough storage space. Most cabinets are clearly marked for some purpose or other, but there's a big one in the back and I feel it straight off. I pull the handle and the drawer creaks loudly. It jams for a milli, but I jerk hard and out it comes. They are zipped up tight in see-through bags. They smell like charcoal. Like the burn piles during the Treason Times. Like *The Lighters,* those enormous, terrifying martyrs, all left to rot back in the old world. The Warriors' crushed heads lean toward one another, and their formerly pretty faces are smashed now, vacant. More of these beauties wasted. *But not Loo,* I think. *At least it's not Loo.* Still, I can't help but cry. I'm leaking for Pod I never even met. Little dead girls like the mangled dolls we had once upon a time, back before it all began. Back when wee things played games and sang songs, and never had to hunt or track or kill for a meal. Back when we slept in blankets made by our mothers, not ones sterilized, numbered, and issued by machines.

The shuttle engines grind more slowly, the landing gear is activated. I've got to move now. I push the drawer back in. When the heavy thing clicks in place, the drawer beneath it pops open and bumps against my shin. *Ow.* I try to kick it shut but it pops open again, and I have to back up to give enough room and bend right over, and that's when I see the other plastic baggy. That's when the third zipped bag reveals itself to me. The drawer barely holds the leftovers of her mauled core. So big. So strong and beautiful, before. *Oh, Solomon.* Solomon's parts, some of them, laid out final and cold, the blood still crusted to her battered core. *No head, whafa? Only one arm! Kronk save us.*

Then I'm not thinking, not scheming; I'm just a physical being in motion. I close it up, click that cubby shut, and I am a blur of parts scaling the walls, around the corner closets, until I find the excrete chamber and the micro bathing unit. In I go, and up the side of it. I pry open the water tank and stuff myself in. They're just like the trial tanks from training so long ago—a suspended column filled with water, minus the glass walls—where I can hide and blurble my sadness out to nopod. And nopod can blurble back.

"Blaaty Kronk."

The red-haired Leader grinds her teeth and swears again. Healer passes those large hands over the stinking pile of decomposing flesh. Flies cover it, burrow their eggs in the skin. In some places, the maggots writhe, making lumps of flesh look animated. *Reanimated.* They're standing by a stinking excrete hut guarded by the remains of a decaying electroll. The red-haired Leader gags and hurls, shoots a stream of green bile out her mouth.

Waterweeds, that.

I am peeking out the open shuttle door at the horrific scene on land. Shona lies in the hold, still doing Sleep. Hers was a big vial, twice whafa used to. They never stopped a milli to peek under my blanket and discover my trick, so here I am, spying.

"It's been dead a while," says Healer at last. "Hard to say in this dry heat. Kronk knows whafa killed it. Kronk knows if our Warriors were even here. It could have stolen the tracker from the forest."

"Pull it out." Leader is dark clouded. She huffs away to text ScanMans.

Healer shrugs. She pulls a stick from the hut's framework and uses it to hook the tracker out from the beast's mouth. Even I look away. *Too nasty, that.*

I scan the horizon. No water in sight. I couldn't live here, not without some big water pond. Not in all this stinging hot sand. I'd never make it. I tuck myself farther back inside the shaded hold.

Leader puts her handset away. She gargles water from her flask and spits it out loudly. "Double bag the tracker and toss it in the hold," she says. "We're heading back." She marches back toward the shuttle.

I scurry back to the water closet, plonk back into the cold tank. Splat! Splat! Water slurps over the edges. I slow my breathing and listen hard while they all climb back into place and get the engine running. The shuttle door slams shut; the locking system clicks. The engine churns louder and we are up again, the floor rumbling, the walls humming, the throttle popping, and me more miserable than ever, on my way back to StarPod. I plunge my head under water. Bubbles rush to the top. My skin tingles back to life.

"Hey!"

My neck in a vice. My hair pulled up by two tight fists.

The inevitable discovery comes swift and without warning. Of course, somepod would blaaty use the closet. Of course, she'd try to release the water from the tank and then find it stuck. *Clogged.* Then she'd turn and have a good look. Prolly find the splooshy puddles I spilled on the tile floor. Prolly notice the tank lid ajar. Prolly have a quiet peek and see me down in the back of it, submerged and blanked, meditating in time with the rumbling shuttle.

And then—*blam!*—it's over for me. No chance of giving them the slip in Shuttle Dock; no chance of blending invisible back into the underworld of StarPod. I'm captured and tied up and sat upon 'til landing. I'm full-frontal back to blaaty Living Lab, no holds barred.

Loo: Dojo Styling

We're piled up outside the entrance gate of a thick stone wall that runs the length of a small compound. I can see the tops of the buildings over the edge of the wall—there are towers on either end, and sentries posted in the windows of each. They're waving a gold flag. At our captors, I spoze, though Kronk knows whafa means. The three ironclad electrolls that guard us now are larger than that first one, hairier, too, and they all carry large poles with sharp choppers at the top.

Kill me, Marta sends. **Before they touch me, you must kill me. I'll not be their slave.**

"Kill yourself," I say between clenched teeth. "I'll be too busy fighting." I elbow her in the kidney. *How did she live long enough to get to Eighth, I wonder?*

Marta growls—she dandystill reads me, right.

The gate opens up. The electrolls gather us up with no fuss and carry us into the compound. The gate slams shut behind us and a heavy metal bolt slides into place. They take us into the large main hall and drop us solid in the center of the large circular room. There are three sets of doors: the way we just entered, another directly across from it that leads to a courtyard of sorts. Kronk knows where the third one goes, but prolly into the main sections of the fortress. Each electroll stands in front of a door, weapon at the ready. Hanging high on the smooth walls between two of the doors are two brightly colored tapestries. There are small round windows, prolly three or four podlengths high, scarcely wider than my waist. Pale light comes in these; the day is drawing to a close.

Now the third door opens and ten manimals march into the room. They encircle us. They are smaller and less hairy than the electrolls. Not as stinky. They're like the three beasts we caught on Mission one time, way back in Third Level. Their flesh runs the colors of the earth: beige sands, gray rocks, red earth. Mud, dark and cool. Black ore. Gold. Some have long flowing hair, and some have short curly hair piled up on top, sprouting out from their round heads like wild bushlings. Some have hair on their faces, around their mouths, growing right off their chins. Some do not. Most wear only short hide skirts and some kind of covering on the feet. They don't have podbumps.

The tallest, wearing more clothes and more jewelry, comes toward me. It seems to be in charge. It reaches out to touch me. Now it bleeds. Four lines from my sharp claws, right down the face. This one looks so surprised. It barks a sound from its red mouth, wipes blood from its cheekbone, and sucks it from thick fingers. It smiles at me: full, sensuous lips over clean white teeth.

"Nice," it says in a deep voice.

It likes pain, I send to Marta. She quivers behind me. I hear her slap out at something. She strikes again.

"Whafa want?" I say. "Like to bleed more?"

It laughs, eyes a twinkle, throat bobbing with a hard, round nut inside. I don't like this, not when I could snap it like a twig in two. I could kill them all on a good day. They're larger than me, many of them, but so whafa? If I had my kronking weapons, right?

So I kick to its gut, hard and fast, right for the inner organs, and when it bends forward quick quick, I punch the noseholes, the bobbing throat, that mocking mouth. I kick to the skirt for good measure. It spins back and falls to the floor. The others all shriek and yell. Two run toward me and I dispatch them almost as fast.

Fight, Marta! And so she does. *Finally.*

The next has a long knife at the waist, and I pull that out, stab it through, stab a second, climb up its front, and leap off the face. I dive into a third and sever its head completely. Now the electrolls race over with those deadly poles. Marta screams and head-butts one beast. She runs it backward with her head in its core, her hand on its big face, cracking the skull open on the flat wall when it hits. Two of the little beasts run away, right out the door we came in; they leave it wide open. One electroll blocks the exit, its chopper held across the open space. It dances nervously, looks from the open door to the bodies fighting.

I roll across the ground, away from one big-handed beast, leap away from the falling chopper of the nearest electroll. Marta shrieks into the face of the big-handed one, punches deep into its eye socket. Rips the flesh right out, and I think for a milliflash on the water beast I killed just so. I scurry away from the electroll, who struggles to lift the heavy chopper from the stone floor. I leap and grasp one of the tapestries. I climb the strong fabric fast fast and leap again to the closest small round window.

Marta, follow me, I send, as I burrow my way out. My head is out, so are my shoulders; the waist is no problem; my hips hang tight; and then the stinging sensation of a needle in my buttock has me squealing. The burn rages up and down my thigh; the tingling grows until there is no feeling at all in that area, and I've no control. There is a struggling behind me, a flopping of the tapestries, and a large hand around my calf pulls me down roughly. I fall. I hit the ground heavy.

Kronk.

The tall one, the laughing one, isn't laughing now. It stands above me, foot in my gut, hand on my neck. Blood drips from its broken nose. Everywhere, there are cores twisting in agony, bodies oozing fluids. Things are dying.

"Lock her up," it barks at somepod. "Before she kills any more of my men."

Just before I pass into prickling Sleep, I see Marta hauled over an electroll's shoulder. I see another coming for me. And I see the angry beast staring down, hungry for revenge.

Rustle: Back to Living Lab

The first time they give me The Tool, I wet myself. It is shiny, black, heavy. It weighs on me, crushing. Wires run from it to different core pressure points. When ScanMan flips a switch, fire streaks along under my skin, above the muscled layers, above the meat. My nerves sing with pain everywhere all at once: a chorus of tiny deaths, harmonic cellular disintegration.

I am a quick study. Now I scream whenever I see it.

"The mystery of any *new* form of torture," says the tallest ScanMan to three trainees, "Is simply that the subject has no idea how much worse it can possibly get. Your role is to demonstrate that precisely."

I hang suspended from some metal frame. Tubes run in me, tubes run out. Light burns my retinas. Voices blend. They murmur back and forth. ScanMans are back in the Lab. Their tall shadows dance against the wall. Their robes glide across the polished stone floor. Their large eyes shine when they look right through me. I see the long, thin needle coming closer, closer, getting larger. I see the spindly fingers on the hand that holds it. The needle penetrates my face coldly.

Horrors. I cannot move a winkle. I cannot, have *never* closed my own eyes. Here I hang, frozen, seeing all, feeling all, unable to make a whimper or twitch a finger.

No! I send, but nothing happens. The word and the feeling does not well up and spill over the way it usually does. There's nothing on the inside to project, nothing inside me that I can deliver mindfully.

HELP ME, I scream-send. I tunnel-text them, wave-hone my complete terror, but nothing happens. They cannot hear me, cannot feel me, and I cannot make myself known. Elsewise, they just don't care. The ScanMan closest to me picks up The Tool.

Oh, Kronk, no! My mouth can't stretch. Soundless. My throat is dry. I cannot blank. I cannot bear this.

Now it is quiet and dark. Cold. My bones rattle on the hard floor of this cage, tucked away in a darkened corner of the Lab. No brightly lit cot for me, not with all my wounds, my bruises and welts. When I move, the scabs pull away from older spots. Fresh blood drips. With a wrenching heave, my sides contract and out flows my own stinking mess all around me. I cry softly on the inside.

I argue with myself to pass the time. *Whafa worse?* Tied up and tortured for their amusement in the main Lab where the others also writhe in pain, or left alone, podless, to rot in this cage. Here, there are no songs, no sends. No fear smells from the other Scouts. No pheromones filling the room. At least in the main locked lab there are sometimes others like me being wheeled about in chairs or on cots, lined up for pain pills, laid out for cell samples. Wordless always, but sometimes with a shadowy movement in the eye, poor saps. Sometimes there is a pale halo of consciousness, a hint of Self left. If there is hope, it is hidden deep in there, buried alive for safekeeping.

Today, they plunge me back and forth, into the water tank, out to the air. In for a milli, then out again. The sharp metal hooks dig into my flesh with each wrenching haul. Water pours from me, burns my throat and nose, stings my eyes. It eats off the top layer of skin. Not treated properly, ya? Not clean.

"See?" says ScanMan. It's the tallest again, whafa carries a wee stick for pointing.

Ah, say the three that follow.

"See, the lungs collapse and along *here*—oh, and *here*—the hybrid respiratory system overrides."

Ahah.

"These external fibuloids," it says, tugging on the back of my leg, "these are possibly *sentient* when submerged."

Hmm.

"And most surprising of all," it presses my lower bellyparts, pokes at the angry lump between my thighs, "is this mutant genital transformation."

Three frowny brows, three electronic pads: furious note taking. I am fascinating.

Later, alone again, I think of Loo. I want to rememory my favorite fusion stories. I want to conjure her curled up and playing with my hair—though now it's brittle and falling out from all the medipacs they inject in me. I try to smell her, try to rememory the essence that is Loo, but I can't. The only smells I have are my own excrete, my own rejected soup, and the dank must of this underground lair. ScanMans have their own smells: chemclouds, antiseptic, burning flesh, and plastic gloves. All mixed with the taste of my own blood.

I roll over, stare at the other cell wall. I count the cracks that waver up and out until my vision blurs. I blank. At least I can still do that.

Book

3

Loo: Morning

I wake alone and in chains. They clang at my wrists and join to the tall stone wall above me. I shake them but they do not loosen. There is a window way up high, full of strong morning light that pools on me now. This is a new chamber I'm in. Not the dirty, damp cellar where they kept us all night and every day since our arrival. Marta is not here. I try to climb up the wall using the chains as levers, but I'm too weak. I fall back. I'm on a bed, a solid extravagant thing covered in soft sheets, covers, pillows. Never in my life have I seen such a one. I'm wearing some silken dress that hangs about my scabby knees. My flesh has been scrubbed clean. *I don't rememory bathing.* I smell like candy and green grasslings. My hair is washed; it's softly pink with silvery sparkles and no more itchy bites to the scalp. Deep piled carpets cover parts of the stone floor. Beside me is a table with a tall, water-filled container. I pull the flowerweeds out, throw them to the ground. I drink loudly, holding the thing with both my battered hands.

That laugh again. I gulp. It's the Leader of these beasts standing in the open door, watching me and laughing.

"Zlotan spietchka," I yell, but it laughs louder. I throw the container and it crashes on the floor. Water splashes up its legs.

It picks up the thing, puts the flowerweeds back inside, and sets it on the wee table. Then it claps its veiny hands and in comes a small parade of servants, all broken-looking pods with their round heads shaved smooth. *No sign of Marta.* Some I rememory from the cellar, some must be kept some other place. The first holds a smaller vessel that is the color of iron, which is filled with a sweetened liquid, cold and clear. I sniff and lick, but I'm too thirsty to care now about poisons. I drink it up. Somepod refills it for me. The next servant has a tray with bowls and utensils. The third one removes a lid from the bowl, and the air fills with intoxicating steam. There are wild greens brightly seasoned with tiny specks of spice, with slivered nuts and a yellow fruit that, on its own, makes a mouth pucker. Leader squeezes the yellow and drips it on the weeds. It dangles a long piece in front of my lips, but I decline. My stomach growls loudly. It laughs again.

Everything's so blaaty funny.

Since our arrival, I've eaten nothing but a handful of dry grain each day. I'm starving; I must be. I snatch the weed from its hand and stuff it in my mouth. The green stems crunch lightly between my teeth. The yellow juice and the wee crackles of spice tingle my poor tongue. *Mmm.* Then comes a bowl of long warm strands of ... of feed. Strings that dissolve gently on the teeth, that sing with hints of flavors I cannot describe. I feed furiously. The servants leave without making a sound. This Leader watches me devour it all. Finally, my belly bloated, my lips still greased, it gives me one last tiny cup. Inside, there is a round lump of cold, white ice. It melts on my tongue and the sweetness streams down my throat. Even in the cup it melts, so that if I don't scoop it up fast fast, it turns to soup. *Better than Fizzy Drop, this!*

Now I eye the beast nervously. I burp and burp again. I blink. I can kill it still—wrap its neck with my chains and it will be so.

"No need to attack," it says, as though it can read me. "No

one—no pod—will harm you now." It strides confidently around the room, keeping just out of my range. Its face is healed somewhat, but faint bruising about the eyes reminds me of our tussle.

How long have I been here in this place?

"You are our great hope just now, and so we'll tend to your every need."

I say, "Where's Marta, the blond Hunter?" I hate to speach with this beast, hate to even wonder how it learned our mouth language.

"The yellow-haired one is not so lucky."

I stare down its darkly pooled eyes. The feed sits heavy in my gut.

"We bathed you both, tended your wounds while you rested. Our experts ran tests. She's not fertile," it says with a grim smile. "And not full in the bellyparts like you."

I swallow the rising bile in my throat. My lips flatten themselves against my aching teeth, and I swear I will not show my deep fear, my ignorance.

Whafa means this? Whafa done to me, this ugly beast?

It says, "You will not be shared around and will not have to work. You are my match and will be mine alone." His wide mouth savors this.

Ha, I think. *I'm more than a match for this weakly beast. I'd have torn him in two myself.*

It says, "And even *I'll* not touch you while you're with child."

Whafa means this? Am I flowering after all?

The words terrify but seem truthful. My mindcore trips, fast fast and sharp to this new world, to my new predicament. How to fight when I'm broken and exhausted? How to blend in when I'm so different to this alien race? The Leader stands closer now, and the emo mix on its strange face shakes me to my bones. There's power and control. There's ownership and anger. There's contempt. There's awe. And there's that glimmer of something familiar: lust.

Book 3

I'd seen lust tempered by fusion-love in Rustle's eyes from our first meeting, every day of our training, forever, world without end. I'd seen flickers of lustful interest in other pods' eyes. In other species, too. Even ScanMans were not immune to this pull. I rememory with great nausea those early training days when ScanMans liked me specially well and used me as a plaything— the long nights of dreadful waiting and hiding. Of crying, sometimes, and, finally, of trying to do whafa wanted fast fast and wary well, so it'd all be over sooner. Then the feed prizes or wee jewelry trinkets they gave in exchange for their own pleasures. I rememory the dead eyes of those other wee hatchlings, the ones whafa also wore those guilt charms about their wrists, their fingers, and their necks. *Blahh.*

I shake off those nasty rememories and put my Hunter's mind to work. The beast stares at me from the other end of the bed. It watches every beat, trying to figure me out, I spoze. Just like I am also doing with it.

And so I decide: fusion-waves transcend species. This is the softness I might stretch, and so make up my new weapon, seeing as I have no other in the milli. If this spiny thing is the Leader of this place, and it will keep me pretty and well fed, not sharing me with the rest of its bungling crew, then I could have it dancing on its knees with want of me, and so make up my own way out of here. So make up my own new way, climbing to the top of the strange pile I've landed in.

I wave-send to see if it can receive. It does, although poorly. I'd just as well beat it over the bruised skull with a long stick to get my meaning made clear.

"Thank you for the feed. For all these pretty things and for the caretaking," I say. I stand up tall and set my strong shoulders. "I am sorry for those unfriendly beatings. Did I kill many of your friends?"

It blushes, shamed to be rememoried of my power. I lower my lashes and it stammers a bite. It says, "My surviving men are fine. No doubt you were trained to do as much."

As much and more, you low-grade, I think, meanly. *Human.*

I wave-send something warm and moist to target its emo center and to tug at its feeble core. The beast swallows and its blackened eyes grow darker. I see its tongue move behind those teeth nervously. My fuse-send hits deep. This befuddles the beast—its curiosity grows. Its pupils dilate. It groans with pleasure. It is a tingly, fusey mess.

Pink cheeks.

I use a husky voice. "Bring me my poor friend. She can tend to me as only our species know best, and, therefore, save your—men from filling all my tiresome needs. I wouldn't insult them further." The gown slips from my shoulder when I move slowly toward the Leader, my chained arms outstretched before me. Although it does not speach, I know I'm winning this battle. It sidles closer, hypnotized by my silver eyes, by my slowly snaking movements, by the smooth feel of my alien skin.

"What do you call podself?"

"Volchok," it says. And it says very little else for some time.

Roku: Red Soil

"Red indeed."

Nadya toes the soft earth. She looks down into the valley. It is longer, wider than we expected. Rocky cliffs protect the far side. They stack themselves into jagged points that tower above the green. Water pours steadily from a hidden mountain source. It pounds the rocky base and sprays back up. It runs into the wide blue river that cuts through the length of the settlement. On either side run red-tinged banks, framed by lush greeny fluffs and willowy trees. From our perch, we can see two small bridges.

Farther back and on each side of the river, small huts dot the fertile, cultivated soil. Figures move slowly among the rows of plants. Some ride machines that hover above the blowing stalks. Smoke drifts from the wee cabins into the blue sky: delicate lace, like dresses the Ancients wore.

"Pretty," she says softly.

Shy? I send.

She nods.

Poor wee thing. We'd never been invited anywhere. Only commanded places on Mission, to spy or track or kill.

"Should we walk right in? I could leave my weapons." She looks around for a place to hide them.

Too late. They've seen us, I send.

Nadya stiffens.

One guard trailed us the last bit of our journey. Two more hide carefully in the surrounding trees. *She's tired,* I think. *Losing her focus.*

Nadya tightens the grip on her weapon. Now she moves her head slowly, scanning on high alert. She sees one at last.

Set the weapons down, I send. **Show your empty hands.**

I fluff my feathers and call out to them. I send that I see them, that I'm waiting. That I see their net and don't mind. I don't know if they understand me.

They rush forward, yelling, spinning their long bos. Leaves rattle in the tree branches. The net strung up in the tree above us drops heavily. Nadya struggles and flails, but I fuse-send calm.

Shh, I send. **Rest. Let them carry us into their village. Be limp and unafraid,** I send. **Be fit.** I almost choke on my own beak when that programmed prop comes flying out.

These pod look different, one to the next. One is very tall with dark skin and nubs of gold hair sprouting on her head. She is strong. She slides a long stick through the netting. With a sharp movement, she flips us backside and hoists us up. Another one, not so tall but thicker and full-on hairy, picks up the other end of the stick and hauls it onto her shoulder. They lurch down a soft red path that cuts through the grassy hillside. Nadya and I jiggle as one, a pile of parts twisted inside the net. Guards march alongside us, holding spears a milli from our flesh. I try to not struggle, but we're crushed together and I worry for my wings. Nadya rolls onto my feathered chest to keep her weight off my wings. She clings to me, and I tuck my beak behind her neck so it won't snap if they trip or drop us. I breathe her scent.

A bell rings. It echoes across the valley. The carriers speed up and our bumping ride gets worse. The closer we get, the louder the pealing bell, until we find ourselves dropped and deafened on a hard, dirt-packed floor. Above us and attached to a towering pole, the heavy bell swings. Its vibrations hum in all our parts. Nadya holds my left claw in her wee hand. She's nervous. We're floundering in the cruel netting as the guards hover around, wary watchful. I smell their sweat and hear their heavy breathing. At least we've tired them out a bite. Meanwhile, all around us, the creatures gather. More run, hop, and lurch with each passing milli. The buzz is loud. The tongues they speach are not all known to me. I look from one outraged and unfamiliar face to the next. For the first time in ages, I feel afraid.

"Inside to the great hall," yells somepod. And the chaotic mass pushes forward toward the large wooden place nearby. We are hauled like so many sacks of dirt and deposited roughly on a wooden platform at the front of a large room. The main exit is blocked by guards. The only windows are at the far end of the hall, several podlengths high.

Somepod steps onto the platform with us. She is tall and muscley, like Solomon was. Her flame-colored hair falls to her waist. The others call her Red. She quiets them. A shout from the back of the room shatters the silence with a kill-cheer. Others join in. Red scrambles to quiet them again, this time using a large hammer to pound the hard floor.

"When did we begin to kill without question?" Red says in a commanding voice. "That is not our way. The Assassin Scout must explain herself, her reasons for being here. Let the winged creature stand freely." The guards step back immediately and pull the netting away from us. I shake myself free from it, ruffle my feathers. Some broken ones fall, soft and quiet as black tears. Some are still attached at the quill but bend out at odd angles. I nod to this speaker, this tall fiery-haired alien.

"We don't take kindly to ScanMans or their Assassins, as I'm sure you'll understand." Her eyes glint in the fading light. When she sends, it knocks me back a bite. Her mindcore is tuned powerfully, her wave-song honed hardcore. **Deformed Scout?** she sends.

Reformed, I send. **Not Deformed.**

She smiles.

I use my power well but not to its fullest. **I am Roku. I chose to leave StarPod. I'll not go back. This Settlement is my one hope, my new homeland.** I nod toward Nadya. **Nadya is a powerful Healer. She practices the Ancient Rites. She will be a great asset to the Settlement.**

"Perhaps," says Red. "But that is for the Settlement to decide. If we agree to keep you, then pod must learn how we operate and also unlearn many of ScanMans' teachings."

Red turns from us and opens the debate with a lift of her pale arm. Nadya bravely endures questions firing away from all corners. She speaks clearly, thinks carefully before doing so, and scans slowly, as though she's rememorizing each of their faces. The tall one watches her closely, hones her wave, and radiates into her.

"You all know my village was slaughtered by Assassin Scouts," says a voice. It's a small creature at the back. The one who began the kill-chant. "Deformed or not, they're still dangerous and should be locked up. At least 'til we program them proper."

"Always with the programming," says some other pod in disgust. "We'd be just as bad as ScanMans."

"Run her off and let her survive in the deadlands," says another. It spits into the dust at Nadya's feet. "The sky manimal can stay."

And so on. And so on. After some time, the focus is less on Nadya or me and more on the internal bickering of Settlement members. They have a hard time making decisions. They have no real Leader, only powerful speakers and less convincing ones, but each one takes a turn to speach. Even Nadya starts to fade after long millis of interrogation and input from almost every crawling creature in the settlement. "They hate us so much," she whispers. "They don't understand."

Perhaps they do, Nadya. It's all I can possibly muster. I really thought we'd be welcome—celebrated even, for our desire to join their rabbling ranks.

"What is our verdict?" says Red, at long last.

A scurry in the front draws my eye. A dronebeet clicks forward and says in a clear but quiet tone: "Set them both to work-camp detail. Let them learn this Settlement from the bottom-side up." It comes closer to the platform we're still standing on and says, "Defer podselves to every other creature you find already living here, for they have earned their place. Bite by bite, pod might, too. Elsewise, it's dismemberment and then death for Settlement Traitors."

A general chorus of agreement flies up and settles in the dust. Thus begins our new training. Nadya is given a shovel; I am thrown a bucket. We are led to a lately neglected hut some many dozen paces away from where we'd been. The smell gives itself away long before we arrive. She looks at me, eyebrows raised, and I can feel her pinchy send, though I'm trying to blank.

Great, Roku, she sends. **Blaaty great idea, coming here.**

"This dung heap needs clearing," says the dronebeet. Its feelers twitch. *It's laughing!* "I'm sure there'll be some feed left when you're done. Won't be as nice as Canteena Time, though, so I'd hurry if I were you."

Rustle: Frontal Lobe

Today, they leave me hanging from the metal stand a good long while. ScanMans are too busy with some other problem, plotting for some other unlucky pod. I'm in the main Lab, where our unit was caged and where we saw the fakies on their cots. Where we out-tricked the Eights and where we discovered our wee escape path. I roll my sorry head up and see the metal reinforcements that cover the grate. *No second chance for me,* I think.

Finally, one of the trainees comes to release me. It drops me in a chair. I pull my knees up to hide my face. When last did I ever sit? The cushioned chair moves—wheels. It pushes me through the double set of doors, down the long white hallway, and into a small room. It's quieter here. The muffled sounds of machines and cauterizing tools are comforting. No more whimpers, no more tears. ScanMan leaves me; something big big and important must be happening some other place. The door is open. I don't even dream of escape. I doze.

Much later, loud shrieks wake me: an awful voice, a struggle, another terrible smell.

"I am Leader. Let me do it right this time," she sobs, and I know who it is, come to join us broken playthings.

It's Shona—ravaged and then some. I recognize her swollen face when the helmeted Eights drag her past, her head shaved down to the scalp. I see her but she does not see me. She's fighting and screaming. *But it's too late for that sort of thing, I think.*

ScanMans slowly glide behind her, inscrutable to the last. One—the one that set me here in the chair—breaks away from the small group and enters my room, shuts the door. I shudder. It stands before me, leaning over me. When I lift my head, we are face to face. I haven't been this close to one since I was wee. In the beginning, they used to always be there: instructing us, correcting us, disciplining. Us, tucked in our tiny seats, row upon row, and one big ScanMan trolling the aisles, presiding over us all.

"Rustle." Its voice has that familiar hint of a metallic hiss.

I stare.

"Tell me about Roku." ScanMan leans back, long sinewy fingers interlaced. The large shining eyes pull me in.

Dead, I think. How does my mouth work?

"Dead," I say.

How does that one word text itself from the shrunken bit of my bellyparts up the raw tube that links to my stinking mouth. Past my dry lips. My loose teeth. Into the air. And more important, *nevermindthemouth,* I am trying to rememory *whafamouth?*— how that other thing worked—*mouth.* How we were first brought here to this place. I rememory the pod whafa Found me, rememory the candy in her palm—*sheputitinmymouth.* Then the shuttle, the long lines of crying dirty hatchlings. The terrifying first shower in the wide-open bathing room. The delousing.

"That's not what I want to hear," it says.

They were everywhere then, their long robes swishing on the polished floor of the reprogramming center. *We had to be quiet,* they said. We mostly were. We could hear their skirts rub against whatever they had underneath the fabric. *Whafa do they have down there?* I never saw. No flesh, no skin. No limbs, although they are so very tall.

"Rustle."

So cruel.

"I'm waiting."

Loo, however, may have known a bite about the netherworlds of ScanMans, ya? *Maybe.* She said things sometime. It made me wonder.

Ugh.

There is a scrape and a slide and then—*surprise*—there it is. The Tool.

"Dead," I say. "Roku's gone and dead, and so that's that." I'm babbling in a broken voice, not my own. "Roku narked me hardcore, so don't ask me." Sweat trickles down my scalp. I'm staring at The Tool. So sinister and deadly.

"What did Roku tell you the night she disappeared?"

"Nothing," I squeak. "Blaaty Kronk-all!"

"We have the footage. We saw you speaching. She told you something. *Sent* you something. What was it?"

That was a million years ago. A lifetime ago. There is a click. The black sound and the movement travel to my hearholes. The button is pushed. *Oh no.*

"Maybe too much this time."

"Nonsense."

"... frontal lobe damage ... Notice the distressed brain tissue *here* and *here*. See? It may be irreparable."

"Oh."

"Basic trials should tell us either way."

"Notice this section *here* is sealed off, almost a complete download of some sort. Not our issue, clearly. Not regulation, certainly. We'll take a closer look at that. Dig it right out. Lights?"

Something foul is pushed into my mouth. I gag. I'm loaded onto a cot. I'm wheeled someplace. I don't know where. I'm there for a long time. Forever, maybe.

Loo: Brittle Bones

"Loo, you look well. So rosy and so well fed." Marta's snarl would bite if it touched my flesh. Her eyes ravage my swollen bellyparts, whafa grown large beneath my pale blue gown these past weeks, while I've lived upstairs here in Volchok's chambers, and she, still down below with the other prisoners.

"Marta." *I've missed her.* I try to send but it doesn't come easily, now that I'm not used to sharing with my own kind. Marta wears a mostly clean dress. It's plain, though, not elegant like mine. It stops above the knee, showing her bruised legs. She has thick, protective foot coverings. Her head is shaved. I find that I miss her long yellow hair. I reach out to her, but she turns away.

PodTraitor, she sends, and I feel the sting.

I get closer, close enough to feel the heat from her skin. Her scent is there, whafa filled me and kept me sane during our long trek through the deadlands. "Don't fight me," I say. She steps farther back. "We're both prisoners here, you know."

"I don't see any chains on you, Loo." She is unforgiving.

I settle back on the luxurious bed, leaning against a pile of all those soft pillows. My large belly rises noticeably. I motion for her to come closer. She doesn't. "Yes, I've worked my way out of the chains that first held me. Now I am mistress of this small wing." I point to the far door that leads to more chambers. "I'll give you a tour in a milli. I suspect you agree that living up here in this palace is better than groveling down on your knees in the cellar. They're quite banged up, aren't they?"

She growls.

My patience is gone. "I have no time for petty grievances," I say. "Let's just get a few things straight, right? You're here only because I wanted you. Because I lobbied for your release. You can go back to servicing those beasts any milli, if you prefer."

I take a purple fruit from the bowl on my table. I bite into the juicy goodness and slurp it up quick. I feed not out of hunger anymore, but from fascination with all these new tastes. Such delights as we never had in StarPod.

Marta stares about the grand room in disbelief. "You would

have me live *here?*"

I say as softly as I can, "Will you stay here and act as my handmaid? Live with me and feed on such lovelies with me?" I toss a fruit. It rolls to the end of the bed. When I turn away to brush my hair, I catch a quick movement and, when I turn back, the fruit is gone. "I thought so."

Her ragged voice startles me. "I've heard all about how you fuse with that thing and let him use you as a pet. His stink is all over you, all over this place." She walks toward me, touching the pretty fabrics that dress the large bed. "You have the choice to fight, but instead, you sell yourself, a meal for a man. It's just better feed than the rest of us are getting."

I throw my comb down. "I never sold myself, spietchka. I was stolen for a prize and I'll not die for nothing. I am fighting ever, but in a new way: under the surface. I'm making room for myself and now for you. I'm learning their rules, as I mean to bend them to breaking."

Marta says, "What about the other Scouts? If I stay with you, will you help plan their escape? Or will we grow old and fat and die here, feeding in exchange for our very Selves?"

"How many others?"

"A dozen, easily," says Marta. "Who do you think bakes your bread and cleans your dishes and scrubs your pretty clothes?"

I'd seen lots of servants, surely, but to be honest, I'd stopped thinking of them as Pod Kind. They weren't like any Warriors I ever knew.

"Where's this fight you talk of?" Marta's suspicions are painted on her face.

"Listen," I say, eagerly. "I'm learning how these men run the compound, and soon I'll be leading their very Leader."

Marta crosses her arms and stares at me glittery hard. "What about your Red Soil Settlement plan?"

I swallow. *What did happen to that idea?* With all the changes in my own core and in my fortune—tumbled from the filthy prison up to the pretty tower on top—whafa learning all these new rules, new words, new gestures, new beasts, had I forgotten this goal? *Had I lost sight of the plan that Roku had placed inside my hopeful heart?*

Marta laughs, short and harsh. "I've been trying to make some escape plan for all of us to get there, while you nest with the enemy!"

I grab her throat and drag her bony self up the cushioned bed. "Don't you speach of will. My will to fuse died when Rustle did, and it'll never bloom so deep. Whafa left here is nary a twinkle of that. This here," I hiss, grabbing one enlarged podbump, "is a wee bite of magic, a poisoned candy in its mouth that tastes sweeter to him with every passing moon. And one day soon, once this parasitic demon stops leeching the lifeforce from within my own belly, I shall rise up and choke him with it."

Marta stares at the fleshy mound of my breast.

"I'm flowering, don't you see?"

"Mother of Kronk," she says. Her eyes widen. She puts her hand out, and I press it against my swollen parts. The inside thing kicks and she feels it—I can tell by the way her face suddenly contorts.

"It's why they keep me apart. They want the seed they planted. Whafa grows inside me, making me weak and whiney and fat." I can't stand it, but there they go again; the salty drops betray me.

"Oh, Loo," she says. She misreads my tears.

Hah. She's hard and small next to my hugeness. And though I feel weak in so many ways, I know I'm healthy and strong as a fuel can by her side. I am cold and smart and adaptable. I could learn to run this entire compound myself or burn it to the ground.

I am Beyond.

Marta sniffles, and blaaty Kronk if she doesn't start to cry as well. "It seems like I've been down there for so long," she says. "It's so cold at night."

The days are shorter. Leaves fall brittle from the branchlings outside my windows. They crunch in piles upon the ground. Weeks have passed since our first arrival at the compound.

"Many of the other Scout prisoners," she says, "are rewired to higher Obeyance. Some have the fight completely reprogrammed out of them; some can't even send anymore. I hate it. But at least I'm not alone down there."

I hug her to my core, my huge, hot, heaving core.

"Who would do that to us?" sniffs Marta. "Can you find that out from Volchok? Find out how they do that. So unfit." She buries her wet face in my neck. "Pod even self-destructed the other day," she whispers. "Ripped open her own core and hanged herself by her rotting wires." She sobs noisily.

To kill or to die. Pod never had that choice before. For me, I always want to maim. I imagine stabbing, slicing, punching, kicking. The letting—*all that blood.* Marta, I suspect, might rather choose the latter.

She sighs and I pull her gently by the hair. I kiss her. She gasps, more surprised than me. I pull her to me and kiss again, less gently. And again. Sharp angry bites, touches that turn rough.

"Stay with me," I whisper. "Don't leave me all alone up here." I don't wait for her reply. I already know I'll get my own way.

I am the contradiction: dreaming death but carrying life. Tasting the kill-pulse while coaxing the fleshcore to soften from her brittle bones. I tear her plain slave dress right off. I am vast. I hold her down. The prize and the prisoner—we are both. She sighs and moans, and I force the pleasure from her. We tumble and wrestle, not unlike how we fought so many weeks ago. This time, I am large and strong and healthy. *Well fed.* I am unforgiving, and this time I easily win. I am myself and so much more.

I am motherhood, the one archaic institution we thought for sure had gone extinct.

Roku: Evensong

Nadya and I sit on the steps outside the main hall, watching the red sun sink into another evening sky. She slurps her soup. It is evening feed for daytime workers—those who clear the land or repair huts, who reinforce the riverbanks, and those who harvest feed. I stretch my wings and yawn. Soon I'll begin the long night shift assigned to me. I scratch the familiar wooden plank of the top step with my shining claw. We'd had to scrub it every day for weeks after our arrival, until we'd earned enough trust to be given other duties at the Settlement.

"Don't spoil my mop job," says Nadya. She smiles at me and I chirp back to her. She looks tired but happy. We sit in silence, content to have a few millis together out of the busy day.

The earth workers, sunburnt and dust-covered, file past on their way to the main kitchen where others sling feed and wash pots. Nadya waves to some and I nod hello. They have been up long hours, bringing in feed from the late harvest. Some dig up the last large field roots. They sort and pack them into underground storage. Others pick fruit from the short, gnarled trees along the edge of the valley and pile them into large barrels. Nadya loves to eat them fresh but also baked in the fire or mashed into sauce. Some slice and dry them, storing them up for the icy weeks to come.

Solomon would have approved of sharing all this invisible dirty work. But how would Loo like living here without dronebeets or low-grade servants, without our former elite high-ranking status? I wonder if she is thinking about us, if she is dreaming about making her way to this Settlement.

"Healers were testing water again today," says Nadya. "We sampled toxicity levels all along the riverbank."

Whafa? I send.

"ScanMans dropped chemloads downstream in the river some

seasons past," she says, scraping her bowl clean. "Dozens from the next Settlement were poisoned by their own soup. The whole valley became sick with toxins. This is the first strong harvest Red Soil has had since then. The tox screens were all good." She shakes her head slowly. "No wonder they hate us."

Feed raid, I send. *Loo's specialty.* Every Scout knew it was one of the best ways to destroy an entire colony. I flap my wings and preen.

Nadya's eyebrow shoots up. She looks around nervously, as though the others might hear. "Roku," she whispers, "did your unit attack that Settlement?"

No, I send. **Many others, though.** We'd never done an open-source poisoning, but we'd targeted plenty of wells and feed storage areas. We'd always done whafa commanded, no questions asked.

"All that training, all those Missions," says Nadya softly. "All we knew was they were the enemy."

Every Kill another spill, another Drop for patriots. That'd been one of our most rousing cheersong slogans of all.

Nadya looks sick. "I hate to think on it, Roku. How mindtuned we were. I never wondered at the whys of it. Only followed orders."

Yet you still learned the Ancient Rites in secret. I chirp. **And I still asked questions, snooped around to find out the answers they wouldn't give me.**

"Is that enough to fight the whole StarPod colony?" Her brow wrinkles.

Prolly not. I peck at the ground. It's almost certain defeat for us all. Nopod knows that better than those of us who trained as Warriors. We know firsthand the growing power of that underground army.

Nadya says, "Funny how vital we are to Red Soil—as important to their defense plans as we are hated and feared." She shrugs.

I think on Rustle and her warpy sense of humor. I laugh and send it for her: *Full-frontal ironical!*

"The dronebeets say an attack is imminent. They hear things, you know. They say they can communicate with their sistren back at StarPod. They say a great war is coming." She shivers when she says this, and I hop closer.

Do you trust them?

She hesitates. "Yes. Though they are prone to exaggeration and have more to avenge than most."

Each night I fly the perimeter, scouring the horizon for shuttles, for spyware, for any unfriendly activity. Talk of ScanMan retaliation is terse; the other guards are jumpy and high-strung. Nopod wants to admit it, but we are all walking a nervy thin line. **Some expect an ambush to come at any milli.**

"Is that why we can't send a search team for our mates?" Nadya asks this quietly. "I hate knowing they are held as slaves but not doing anything to free them. Why can't we just go?"

I peck at a tiny glistening beetle in the sand. We both know how heated discussions get in the main hall, how many times our request had been denied or had set off other arguments, everypod discussing each detail. Meetings waged on longer than battles on some of the smaller planets we'd patrolled in the past.

They fear a ScanMan attack in our absence. But if we find Marta and Loo, if we break them free, they fear the slaver compound's army will retaliate.

I feel Nadya's frustrations as keenly as my own. But her comfort in the daily routines at Red Soil grows. Her confidence in this village and her hopes to really be accepted by the others is stronger with every passing milli. When I close my eyes, I am high above this place; I am far away from it all.

She says, "It doesn't seem right to be liking this new life so much. Not without Marta."

I nod. Loo weighs heavy in my heart. For that matter, so do Solomon, Rustle, and even Shona: my long-lost unit.

I will speach with Red again tonight, I send. **I'll tell her we must go.**

Nadya curls against my feathered chest, and the scent from her skin and her hair fills my beak. "Thank you, Roku," she says at last. We sit and contemplate the burning red sky until it extinguishes itself in cold twilight.

Loo: Bubbles

Marta wrings out the cloth. Warm water streams over my shoulders. *Mmm.* She sponges my neck and back while I soak in the perfumed tub.

"Loo," she says, "Volchok is away again tonight. Come with me to the servant quarters and hear our plan. You must."

"Must I?" I push myself deeper under the water. My huge belly protrudes up and makes a fleshy island surrounded by a soapy moat. My swollen feet glare at me from the other end of the bath.

"Yes, Loo." Marta sighs impatiently. "You haven't come even once to meet the others."

"I wouldn't want to draw attention to your activities, would I?"

Marta ever speaches of this current, this widening riot that threatens to split the compound in two, but I've never seen any evidence to support it. *Why should I risk my place near the head of the table for a few promised crumbs?* I flick my foot in the water and wriggle my toes at her. "Could you—please?"

Marta sighs again.

"You know I can't reach them anymore," I say, smiling prettily.

Marta walks to the other end of the tub and kneels down again. She takes my feet in her hands and rubs them with the wee soap.

"Thank you," I murmur and sink my lips below water. She starts speaching again and I completely submerge my head.

Closer to the truth, if I could bear to admit it, would be that I am not certain whafa want anymore. The thing that grows inside me rolls and jabs at my organparts, wrenches my guts and fills me with fear. I roll, lethargic and ungainly, sending tidal waves over the tub's edge. Even underwater I can hear Marta squawk as she gets soaked. In this compound, I sit as though at a game board; I try to make my smartest moves alone, while at the same time maintain my friendly gestures to all the other players. *Whafa must do to land on my own feet—such as they are—and win this game?*

When I resurface, Marta is still speaching. "It's coming, Loo. A great war is rumored, and we can't sit and wait for pod to rescue us. We must leave this place!"

I'm hardly listening.

"The others are undecided—most want to return to StarPod. A few like the sounds of this Settlement you spoke of. Either way, we've heard that your Volchok has a new device to alter our programming. There's talk that we'll be re-wired as soldiers, not just servants, for the Compound." Marta's face is gray, her skin drawn tight with worry. "We'll have to fight once more, but this time, on his command. Don't you see?"

I don't feel in league with them. *Never should these so-called Scouts have allowed themselves to be so demeaned,* I think, rather crossly. At least with Volchok, I have a direct line to the power plays of the compound. When I stand, water pours off my fleshcore and back into the cooling tub. Marta throws a towel to me and I wrap myself in it. Besides, I'd heard about this Settlement from Volchok and didn't like the sounds of it at all. I'm not escaping from the compound just to shovel excrete or play at being some *farmer*. How bored I'd be tilling that dirt, slurping stew, and singing songs at twilight.

Marta busies herself with the tub plug. The water begins to drain. "Loo," she says again, and this time I face her. "You think you don't need us. You don't feel the prisoners' suffering. You think you can stay here and rule this roost in time. I think you have serious mind-poisoning." Her hands are fists against her hips. Her lip quivers.

I say, "I come and go throughout the day. I walk the compound grounds every morning. Whafa want, I get. You think I'm mind-wasting away for nothing, but I am ever learning about this place. Besides, where would you have me run in this fattened state?" I find that when I remind them of my belly, I usually win.

Her face darkens. "You use me as your own pet while he treats you as his. I hate it and I'll not stay beside you much longer."

This outburst surprises me so much that I cannot even speach.

She's flushed with anger, spiced with venom. "You think you're so free, then test it yourself. Do something you're not meant to. Travel farther than your own pretty chambers and see. You're no queen here, only a spoiled and insulated manimal." She drops the soap dish with a clatter and leaves in a snarkly huff.

Well done, Marta, I think, impressed by her passion. *But blaaty bad move for you, right?*

Rustle: Cozy Corners

I'm wheeled someplace else: a cozier corner of some faraway part of the Lab. Others stagger around or stay collapsed on their cots, like me. This room is brightly lit, painted a happy yellow—*likeraftylikesleepdrops*—and filled with the stench of our own insides. That, and the powerful cleansers they use to cover it up. There are large monitors in each corner. Autotrons flash a special program full of prop and promise. The volume is unbearably loud, squelching me.

Kill me, I beg anypod in the room. Naturally, nopod does.

Blue light flickers and an important autotron update interrupts the show. Somepods sit up taller, and somepods start to clap or drool or make some kind of noise. It's Controller Almighty!

It's been so long, I think, *since we've had a good talk with Controller Almighty.* I was under the misguided belief that we would meet in person. That perhaps I'd behaved so badly, I'd get a front-row ticket and a personalized can-kicking from the Great One, but no. *No.*

The volume is loud and Controller's mouthpiece moves in time, but I cannot comprehend. Kronking meds rot my mindcore solid. ScanMans stand on either side of Controller, a chorus in unison to this mysterious pronouncement. Tall as they are, ScanMans look tiny by comparison. There is a solid barrier between ScanMans and all the Warriors who fill the rest of the hall outside Living Lab, a world and a half away. Scouts of all levels crowd on either side of a stone walkway leading up the center. They chant and sway, full-frontal zonked, like they got free vials of Dreamy Drops and a fusion blast, to boot.

There is movement on the monitors. Photos go up. It's our unit, all of us. Autotext captions scroll across the screen. *Electroll Alert: PodMartyrs from Seventh Level devoured by beasts!*

Solomon's photo zooms large. Mine is right beside it, and techno spirals radiate around our mugs. They blink on the screen. Scouts sway and sing our sad, proud cheersong, the one we save for heroes and other Pod slain on duty. I sway, too, in spite of myself. Voices swell, and they stamp the floor with their heavy boots, hundreds of them, in time. I sniffle. *Poor us!* The chant at the end of the song whips the frenetic gathering up a notch. It's patriotism—I can taste it from here. When the noises stop, when the music ends, all that sadness is perched on the edge of a mad mad cliff. There's power in that milli. There's anger and fear all bottled in one raised fist.

Be Fit. Be Vigilant. One Pod!

The next photos zoom large. Roku Pod—those dark eyes burning through space, her hair shining and long, her quiet mouth smiling. Then it's too much. I cough. I lean forward. It's Loo. *Loo.* Alive and gorgeous: her eyebrow arched, the silvery eyes slicing through me, her pink hair filling the monitor. *Oh. Oh.*

PodTraitors, screams the text. And the uproar is too much for ScanMans to control. Hissing, booing jeers fill the speakers. Even in our reject room, they start banging on the walls. Some throw their slippers at the monitor; some rip out their IV tubes.

Spy Alerts: Seventh Level Traitors remain at large!

Controller Almighty waves long arms at the front, but nopod listens. Nopod can stop the wailing hate pouring out her own mouth. Scouts at the back push forward, and dozens get knocked to the ground, get trampled as the raging Warriors push toward the front. Controller Almighty slaps the closest ScanMan—they all seem frozen in awe at the spectacle—who then activates the barrier reinforcements, keeping them safely apart from the Warriors' chaos. ScanMans blast a sonar squelcher into the masses through the speakers, and Scouts stumble, covering their hear-holes. After they quiet down, Controller Almighty gives some kind of stern pep talk and leads them in another song, to not dampen the mood too much. ScanMans release vapor blasts on the other side of the barricade, and soon the fervor mounts once more: *Ampheta-chem clouds, yum.*

Scouts are wary weird, full-on freaking, like they chugged major doses of Dreamy Drops. In the reject room, we are also transfixed. Even we are perking up. Autotrons load the next full photo op and there she is—former Pod Leader, failed and reviled, blue and buggy-eyed as ever. It's the first Send Down in ages.

The crowd is wild, literally ripping into each other and screaming, crying, gyrating in total emo frenzy. A small figure lumps up the bottom of the monitor. She stumbles up the path, crawling at points, clinging to the center part. Warriors on either side leap toward her, all on the kill-pulse, all programmed to tear her flesh from those doomed bones. Mainly they bounce back against invisible shields on either side of the path, but some slip through. Some reach past and grab a handful of flesh, of shredded clothing from her. She weeps and curls into a ball. The cams zoom close and her face fills the monitor screen. She bleeds and shrieks and hardly looks Podful. She's not anymore. She is hunted and stripped and hated Beyond. Somewhere, somepod pushes a button. The invisible barrier lifts itself. Scouts rush in. The cams move closer. Blood clots and flesh clumps fly.

Ugh.

Poor poor Shona. I wonder: would Loo be happy to know her fate? I roll away. I push my cot into a corner. I cannot bear to watch.

Later, alone in the dark, I speach to Kronk—she who never reveals Podself, in whom I place my wary skeptic's heart. Kronk bless Pod Leader—*raving blaaty Traitor, all ripped to shreds*—and Kronk bless Solomon—*dead dead and hero severed*—and Kronk bless Roku—*Traitored now, and maybe dead*—and Kronk bless Loo. *Loo.* I only just saw her photo fill the large monitor, and still her face won't come to me, only a blank round thing with pink hair on top.

Oh. Oh. And Kronk bless me.

Loo: Placenta

"Breathe, Loo, breathe."

Marta sits behind me, shushing my cries. She pets my sweat-soaked hair. I grunt. I rock on my swollen feet, squatting in a puddle of my own making. My insides twist and knife me; I clench and cramp and scream. Something inside me tears. Marta puts an old soup bone in my mouth and I bite down.

Volchok paces back and forth on the other side of the partition. He's here for once, not off galloping the deadlands on his top-secret meetings, not traveling about and meeting with his peers. He himself helped to prepare my chambers for this wretched day,

Book 3

fussing about with towels and bowls. Demanding soft blankets to cover my hateful lap, wee gifts to cheer me on. I'd strangle him bare-fisted were he any closer, so he keeps his place. Instead, he rings a quiet bell. Podslaves scurry in and out of the dimly lit chamber, all to his bidding. Marta knows them each by name, though none look familiar to me. None calls up the old glories of StarPod training. But who'd wonder, since they're all so skinny now, so bruised and wasted away, shorn heads and short skirts dulling them into one anonymous blur. *Their new unis.* These are the soldiers of Marta's revolution? I snort to think on it.

One kneels beside me, wetting a clean cloth in the basin she carried in. She wrings it out. She wipes my forehead. I turn toward her and she gasps. She drops the cloth quick, so fearful to be so near me. I read her in the old way, the StarPod rhetoric flying clear from her mind to us all: *decline, deform, disobey.*

So. They fear the feverish disease I own, whichever it may be. When the pain doesn't double me over, I spy them wary watchful. They breathe small, shallow puffs away from me, they avoid touching me. They do as Volchok commands, but nary a pod looks me in the eye. Nary a pod would come to my side on her own. All save Marta. And she, I note, holds rank with them all.

"Breathe, Loo," she says. "Expel this thing from you."

Her scent mingles with mine and with the other strange ones, now filling the room: blood, excrete, and some manimal pheromones. Marta presses into me, holds me from behind, and when I faint, she bears my weight in her wiry arms. Her hair, finally growing back, hangs in her face, knots with my own. It's no longer the happy yellow it used to be, but a dull ash. Malnutrition, likely, and stress. She talks to me, mouthspeaches and mind-sends and never stops, the whole time my core rips, the whole time this monster claws its way out of my belly.

"Push, Loo. Do it."

Now the pains come more quickly. No more silent gaps that let me prepare for the next bout. It is constant, this building terror, and I no longer recognize the sounds coming from my own throat.

"Now!" shouts Marta. "Blaaty now!"

And the thin man, this special man friend of Volchok's, comes into the room. I see his long robes and, in my fever, I panic. *ScanMans coming!* He holds shining things in his small, gloved hands and rushes to me, to my spread thighs and the battered, bleeding spot between them.

Marta squeezes me to her tiny chest. "It's the medicine man, Loo," she says, "The medicine man."

Without so much as a greeting, he slips his alien fingers into me. He tugs at this awful lump. He pulls the tumor out.

"Oh!"

Hunter leans forward, snapping my spine as she bends toward this newest bloody pile. "Mother of Kronk," she says, staring.

Medical man wipes off the thing, wipes at it with a wet cloth, then pulls the cord that strangely connects us—this choking, snorting handful and me. His knife blade shines and I think, *no, no more stabbing,* but he simply cuts that living wire and fusses with the thing's end of it. He ties it in a knot. He cleans the thing in a fresh basin of warm water, then wraps it in a soft blanket. He takes measurements, makes notes, speaks harshly to Volchok on the other side of the screen. He lays the thing back down and tidies his things, and sometime later, he leaves the room.

My insides heave again and the cramping continues. I fall back to the cot and grit my teeth once more. More spills from me, more and ever more. Marta finally pulls herself away from the soft bundle, sees me writhe in agony. "What now?" she says, and I think, *Blaaty don't ask me!* The hot wet parcel slides out from my center. It stares back at me like some hunted prey's innards.

It is some organpart, I think. And now I die.

I think back on these many weeks in captivity, back to the tree fire and the Eights' ambush. Back to the campfire, to Roku and her blackest wings. To the big big sky and the icy waters. Back before that, to StarPod, its musty underground lairs and dark tunnels—the drills and training, all my missions. To Rustle. And then a glimmer of that time long long ago, even before we were hatchlings, when we were orphaned and wild, living that other life among the rubble. *Was there something earlier?* Was there some kind and friendly touch before all that violence? Was there a scented skirt, a tender hand, a powdered cheek to kiss?

Marta wipes my face clean. She pulls away the bloody mess, wipes gently at my filthy legs. She quickly bathes me, changing the water often. She pulls the stained dress from me, settles something clean around my shoulders. Carries me to the wide bed. Wraps me in blankets, tucks the ends in tight. And then she does the strangest thing possible. She hands me the bundle. The squirming mass of monster presses to my chest. Incredibly, I look at it and it at me.

The rememory comes swift like another stabbing bolt. A single slice of yellow light from the ancient times—that worshipped star up in the darkened sky. The soft voice. The curling hair tickling my small face. Me looking up at the moon, at the huge pale contours of her orb. What was her name? Her mouth smiling, opening, closing, kissing. Singing. Singing a song for bedtime, humming the parts without words. *The song I rememoried when I saw my own fakie.* Singing her love for my very Self, my hopeful spirit. Delivering me up to the unknown world: to the bleakest, most unimaginable, hostile future. What was her name?

It cries, pulling me back to the present. There it is, small and weak and red-faced. Its wee fists wavel the air. Its eyes scrinch shut against the awful truth. It is hatched into a world of sorrow and pain, of awful lies, of evil. I stare. I pull back the blanket and hold it up, naked, for us both to see. Its soft fuzzy head fur—there is no doubt at all—is purple. The tiny hairs stand up to nuzzle my skin when I draw near. Along the backs of the wee arms and legs, they grow more solidly and in different colors. There, between the tiny toes, I see some webbing. The strong translucent skin I'd ever seen only once before. I bring them closer, closer, and exhale. *Whooo.* The wee things wriggle and twitch, curl up, and the feet kick. *It tickles, Loo, stop!* Always saying that, she was. Always chiding me, so shy of those weirdly shaped feet.

"Rustle?" I choke. From beyond her watery grave she haunts me. It was she who planted this seed. Not the small fighting men who guard us now. The wee thing opens its mouth and there inside its gummy pink hole, a tiny tongue flicks out at me. It shapes an O; it winkles its lips. It yawns.

I wrap it carefully, afraid to drop it or break off some flailing part. Marta bites her bottom lip, watching. I smooth the fabric, stick an arm back inside the bundle, pull the wriggling lump to my breast. Ever awkward, I shift on bloodied haunches to find a place that hurts me less. Marta thumps the pillows. She lies down on the other side. She keeps watch over me and over it. The wee thing coos a gurgling sound. It sends a whush of calm, a steady thrumping heartbeat, a growing pulse of comfort and of warmth.

It Pod-sends, Loo.

My eyes close. Now I'm falling. Down and deep I go into dreamy rest with no help from any chemtreat. Pure exhaustion leads the way.

Roku: Spies and Sneaks

Nights, I soar high above the valley, free at last. I shake away those petty earthbound worries. I sink inside my mortal core and tune my pulse with the larger world around me, with all its wild and magical wonders. Nightcrawlers glow far below. Large hairy beasts huddle together for warmth. Smaller furries nest in clumps of leaves, in broken trunks of trees. Above them, flitting gnats and flies swarm thickly. Small bats gobble those up and frolic around the spires of brittle treetops. I fly past them all, and I cannot shake my joy to be stretching these cramped wings, hurtling myself up, twirling down stealthy through the velvet skies.

The other night guards creep and listen, climb tall trees and scent the brush. Two former Scouts are paired with dronebeets—the wee things can send over long distances to each other, much farther than we can. The dronebeets heard from their fiery brethren back at StarPod that something big is happening tonight. They say that ScanMans themselves are traveling nearby, and not just their Assassin militias. Practically unheard of! We are on high alert—a shuttle was sighted near the Red Soil Mountains earlier, and some activity was reported near the slaver compound to the west.

Whafa bring those skirted demons out from their safe caves? The other former Scouts are equally stunned. Clearly, they will be under heavy guard, Eights completely surrounding them. Dronebeets say the younger Scouts are all laid out in StarPod, exhausted after a chemfilled day—pure emo-drained from a full-frontal Send Down in the Great Hall.

"We have our spies," says one dronebeet. "We will learn just whafa. Carry me closer, birdthing."

I chirp sharply but it still laughs. It holds tightly to my feathers. Together we fall farther away from our own familiar lines, away from the other guards who shuffle land-tied far below. I fly, following the lazy chemtrails that mark the earlier passage of our beloved shuttles. *Formerly beloved.* I swoop further, lower, and I try to keep cover between my own stark shadow and this unfamiliar terrain. We graze the tops of trees to where a circle of lights marks a temporary gathering, some midnight marketplace, perhaps, or a traveling festival. A fire burns high in the circle's center, and private tents are assembled in angles around this hub. Two shuttles wait in darkness nearby.

"You will be seen," says the wee creature. "Drop me down close by and let me crawl around myself."

I fear this is a lot of responsibility for one wee critter. Perhaps I do not trust it yet.

"I read you, birdthing," it says. "Besides, you have no choice, really."

I swing low and halt. I stand solid on a tree stump outside the line of lights. The dronebeet shakes itself free and climbs down my perch. Off into the night with nary a winkle or wave. I decide to stay on the ground since I blend with the dark surroundings. Eights guard the tents marked with StarPod insignias: the great glowing eye of our mantra, *One Pod.* They are silent, motionless. The other tent is guarded by two large electrolls, such as the one Nadya and I found rotting in the deadlands. These, however, are alive and armed with large bashing stones and ragged whips. Neither one speaches, but loud voices and hearty laughs spill out from their tent. Shadows of the humanoid beasts dance on the walls of their tent. They are so easy to read—wee minds with hairy faces, large mouth holes that feed messily and slurp wine— all the while talking and joking with their own. They are soldiers from the slaver compound where Loo and Marta are being held.

I hop as close to the lighted area as I dare. Then I creep closer to the other tents, the deadly quiet ones. ScanMans lurk inside. I feel them. They do not feed or drink or laugh uproariously. They wait for the humanoid Leader, who finally leaves his men and walks across the circle with the electrolls on his heel. He is proud and tall for a man, but certainly no match for any of our Kind. He wears a long black cape. A metallic helmet covers his head and face. Gauntlets made from thick hide cover his forearms; his boots come past his knees. Her scent is all over him, no doubt about it. *Loo.* I nearly squawk, nearly fly at him and rip his little voice box from his neck, it pains me so. But I do not. I wait and watch him enter ScanMan's tent. The deal making begins.

Rustle: Agnosia

Neuronal damage reflects loss of information transfer functions. Severe agitation no longer detected. Specimen is almost somnolent. Attempt to surgically remove contraband download failed—software too entwined with organics. Program is likely too damaged to be of use in Lab or elsewhere. Specimen set for disposal.

This is my state, whafa recorded in my chart. *Full-frontal chronic iced,* we'd say in unit. And yet, here I am, still thinking, right? Still alive, ticking, some motor still running somewhere. The rest of me is crashed. Flatlined.

Two dronebeets come and wheel me through this wing of the Lab. They rub their feelers together, gurgle a wee bite in their foreign tongue. Sometimes I hear a word and I rememory back to the time when mouth holes opened and said meaningful things. The dronebeets stop the cot and disappear into some other room. One more appears, climbs right up the cot with me and chitters away. It prods me. This one tries to make me speach.

"What is your name," it says. "You are the swimmer, yes?" It likes this idea, I can tell.

Blaaty Kronk, I want to say, but nothing comes. Not out my mouth or mindcore or any other part. It jumps down, clearly annoyed with me.

The other two come back, dragging a bunch of transparent bags. They chuck them on top of the cot, right on top of me. The weight presses but I hardly notice. They wheel the whole contraption down a corridor, down into some cold, metal section I've never been. They press a button and a large grate opens.

"Stinks," one says, and wrinkles its feelers.

They toss one bag after the other inside the grate. After a few, they press another button and the thing shrieks into business; metal teeth clamp and tear the things inside it. The grate opens again. Now the bags are mangled flat. They toss in the last of the bags. Then it's me. They tug and tug at the sheet I'm wrapped in. Down I crash to the floor. They drag me over. My limbs don't work, not a bite. We wait until two more dronebeets arrive, and they each take hold of me, some part of my discolored, battered fleshcore, and roll me up and heave me over. I flop into the squish, into the sickly scented mess.

"I hate garbage detail," says one.

The grate slams shut but the teeth don't grind. Not yet. I am alone. I am broken. There is no comfort. *Well, I guess that's that.*

"'Ssup?" It's that dronebeet again. The one that speached me earlier.

I roll onto my back and try to stretch my bruised legs in the squishy, stinky dark. I can't move, really.

"Ah, hah hah. Can't swimmy in garbage, I guess." Its antennae twist and the yellow mandibles open. The feelers twitch. It's laughing at me.

Like the one I dreamed in the tunnel, so long ago.

"Oh," it says. "Well, you're a mess." Then that chuckling sound again.

I strain to bring my face closer. "Mmffgh."

It pushes my parts around with its energetic claws. "All fins and bones now, ya? Not so Warrior tough."

"Mmrrk." My mouth doesn't work. An idea shoots itself through my head, but it burns out before I can trace it.

"But you have some powerful friends now. Small and enslaved, but still powerful. Lucky lucky whafa's left of you. Stand up. We've got half a milli to crawl out of here before they start up the grinder. Move!"

I lurch and fall. One arm does not work at all. The dronebeet nudges me over the edge of the large metal container we're inside and drags me halfway down. Far away, a metallic whining starts. A closer motor noise kicks in.

"Hurry!" It pulls and bites me.

The machine's growl becomes a roar. I flop the other leg and over it goes, pulling the weight of my core along with it. I land in a pile outside of the container. I am mostly on top of something hard, flat. Something on wheels again.

"Now," it shrieks.

I only shrug as there is no commanding my limbs, not anymore. They only do what they will and at no direction from me. The dronebeet leaps up, clicking furiously at me all the while, and drops my heavy leg back onto the rolling cart. That is the momentum to push us forward. We roll into the stinking blackness, away from the grinding teeth of the compactor, away from the narrow strips of light that somehow lead back to Living Lab and to all those horrors. We roll slowly along some kind of track, the stone walls rising sharp on each side of us. Suddenly, we start to descend. Our speed picks up, and the syncopated bumps of the wheels on the track tell me we are faster; we are speeding; we are traveling headlong into some blackened disaster. My head, no doubt, is the crash pad for this contraption.

Full-frontal ironical, I think.

I'm so pleased I had this thought, this fiery spark of humor, and then I think, *Whafa funny?* Then there's no thought left, just a screaming, racing downhill panic and the dronebeet straddling my core.

I nod my head. I have overloaded my mindcore full-frontal this time.

Somepod spoons me porridge. *A spoon!*

Somepod wipes my bottom.

Somepod dusts my wiring, but I cry when I see it pulled out like that in a tangled, disastrous pile. I turn my head to the other side and sniffle loudly, while she checks it all and carefully spins it back into place. She stitches up the rippy webs between my toes, between my broken fingers, whafa ScanMans severed in the Lab. It doesn't hurt, but I just can't watch.

It's like my own private cozy corner. The faceless, nameless beetles—my servants—all tend to me and I allow them to, if that's their wish. I stare up and say nothing, send nothing. The dronebeets talk a lot. Sometimes I understand them. And so I hear about a great war they predict is coming, one that will pit pod against pod, and then some. And I hear how they plan to meet their sistren and fight in this spozed war. I hear about their hopes for the underground. For revolution.

We already are underground, I think. *Kronk, they're not too bright.*

They gripe and argue, list off injustices they've suffered and that their Ancestors endured.

Like it's a blaaty contest.

They glare at me, and one turns me back over on the ledge.

Rather roughly, I think. *And anyways, who even knew they had Ancestors? We'd certainly never given it much thought back in unit.*

"Why do we feed and bathe that monster?" says a particularly angry one. *The radical.*

Yes, why? I think. *Why bother?*

"We need her," says another, "to cross the water. You know we'll have a better chance."

Aha, I think. *How clever. But how will we get me to swimmy so good like before?*

"That's your job," says the first. "You figure it out."

I stare hard. *Can they hear my thoughts?*

"Yes. And believe me, they're not much. Now get cracking.

Start healing."

Aghast, I am. Silenced for the milli. What did I think? *What did they hear me think?*

They groan, and I imagine the layers of my repetition—those wildly propagating thoughts—circling us all, trapped in the space between our heads and the heavy rock tunnels. *Woah.* I shake myself clear.

Let me die. My first send in so so long.

Again, the angry one speaches. "Die for our cause and the righteous liberation of dronebeets everywhere, then." The others wavel sticky legs in solidarity.

I turn my neck. I look into its eyes.

"Swimmy if you can, or float. Either way, you'll carry us across that water." They click and whirl, waiting for my response.

And knowing now that they can read my sends, read all the thoughts in my feeble burned-out mind, I blank. To their great disappointment, I blank hardcore.

The pain manifests itself in my bellyparts. That's where they pour the hot liquid. Trails of it spin outward in shivering twitches, causing arms, feet to tremor.

At least the limbs move now, I think.

Dronebeets know their poison, though. They thrill with my every small advance, boast one against the next, and even place wee bets on how I might progress. Against my better judgment, I begin to breathe more deeply. I begin to sit and then to stand, begin to stretch and work on relearning these flailing parts of mine; that relentless survivalist program, subwired so deep that even ScanMans themselves cannot burn it from my mangled core.

Roku: Recap

After our shift and before we creep into our various dark nests, we update Red.

"You think they barter? That they trade together?" Red walks away from us, crossing the main hall. It's the same hall where Nadya and I first stood for hours while the Settlers decided our fate. Red leans on the open windowsill. She's thinking. I can see past her tall frame, past her long hair. The sun is coming up. Warm light spills through from the outside; it pools on her skin, dances when she shakes her head. "How can that be so?" She moves back toward me and the fiery lights leave her hair.

"My sistren witnessed with the eyes in her very head," says the other dronebeet. "ScanMans brought nasty, banged-up Scouts and gave them as gifts to the slavers. Brought them in a cage and sent them off, clickety clack!"

Red looks at us closely. The other guards shrug. They were far from this place and can't comment either way. She has to believe us or not. Red crosses her arms. She says, "I don't see how this affects us."

They are allies, I send. **They speached a long time, both sides under heavy guard. They made battle plans and trade treaties at great peril to Red Soil.** Inside, something tremors. I rustle my feathers. **They seek to storm the valley.**

Red does not comprehend.

They want your land, your water, your fertile feed. They may keep some of you for labor, but they'll kill the rest.

She laughs sharply, shaking her head.

The dronebeet says, "My sistren stayed behind to travel to the compound in secret. She will meet with those in prison and help to free them. Red, we must build on the unrest inside the compound and from within StarPod. Let those who want to come help us fight. Let them add to our own small troop."

I chirp at the dronebeet. Her plan is strategic and a far cry from the usual anti-Scout prop they often speach.

Red says, "You would trust a handful of battered and dirty Warriors to help our cause?"

The dronebeet clicks and hisses. "You do not see whafa coming, Red. It is big big and final." With that, she scurries away, off to meet with her other comrades in some darkened corner of the hall. They will, I know, be ready to act on this new information, even if Red and the others are not.

I twist my neck and stretch my tired wings. It was a long flight, a long night of scanning, listening, and keeping close cover. *And of worrying about Loo, thinking on our old unit: poor lost Pods.*

"Do you agree, Roku?" She looks as tired as I feel.

I nod. I feel a strain in me these days, especially whenever I'm around these two-legged types.

"I think, at the next council meeting, we can all agree on a new plan of action. You've been here for some time now, working hard and gaining trust. Your input will be important."

Please. Let a small guard militia tend to this. I look into her eyes. I feel-send just what is bottled up inside.

"That's not how we operate," she says quietly.

In two nights' time, the slaver compound celebrates festivities—that is the time to act. They will be distracted with their party.

"It's risky," she says. "We'll discuss it all together."

I hop away. Their discussions could easily take longer than that.

"It's important that we all agree on the actions we take, especially something as dangerous as this." Red also gets impatient with the process, but pod believes in it, whereas I do not. *That is the difference.*

I believe in the power and strength of my own core, of my mind and my spiritwind; I believe in the possible powers of others but not in the mouth sounds they constantly spill. Their vowels and consonants mean nothing to me anymore.

"Roku," she says. "We can't have secret missions here. We don't want to live like that, following orders from some false command. We also don't want to provoke those enslavers."

Yes, I send. But as much as you've chosen this life, this place, ScanMans have not. They will not change. And if they want to destroy you, they'll do it without an open forum. You won't have time to discuss a blaaty thing.

She says nothing, but her furrowed brow and the downward turn of her lips show me she is not pleased.

Don't you know they have been studying Red Soil? How do you think I ever heard of this place? They are biding their time and they will come for us all. We should be preparing our defense.

"No," she says at last. "We shouldn't. I don't think you are as important to their regime as you believe. Prolly they've given up on you and your few Scouts. In the end, it doesn't really matter to them. What matters is their system, and that will not stop for you or for any of us." Her cheeks blush with conviction. "You were cogs in the wheel, nothing more."

Perhaps.

I think on the download I stole, the one hidden inside Rustle's wee mindcore, and all the hopes I'd had for it. All the pod who might have been illuminated by its contents, once they'd been rememoried of our true Ancestors. How we were orphaned by these beasts, stolen, not Found, and then brought here all alone to become their private kill-servants, much like the trained dogs their type used on earth so long ago. I think of all the deprogramming that knowledge might have lead to, all the little mind liberations popping up like dried corn in a hot pan. The anger, the riots: the revolution that might have ensued. Where was that download now, if not rotting at the bottom of the sea? What good would it do the weeds and fishies below?

Hear me, I send. Some others will join me on this Mission.

Dronebeets want to come. They have sistren spying back in StarPod and at the compound. I look at her sharply. **I must go tonight, even if it means I won't be welcome back.**

She bites her lower lip.

I hope *you* understand.

"Very well," she says. "Let's convene with the others at once. I'll ring the bell." She turns and, when she walks away, her long hair swishes with irritation.

Loo: Bored and Lonely

Mornings, I take the podling and walk the full length of the compound, starting at my tower. I make my way through the men's living quarters, then past all the meeting and entertaining chambers, including that first round room we landed in, then along a quiet hall that runs above the slaves' living area and the manimals' stable. I look out that other tower window and rest; I can see clear across to my own small tower. I watch the servants doing their chores down below in the courtyard. While I nurse the wee thing, I take note of anything new, anything at all. After some water and maybe a bite of fruit, I walk all the way back. Then I prepare myself for the next feed.

Tonight I'm restless. I smooth out the fabric of the beautiful dress I'm to wear at the upcoming festivities—it's black and filmy, with silver threads throughout to bring out the shimmer in my hair and eyes. It hangs low on my bare back and shows the soft swell of my podbumps in front. I can't wait to have it clinging to my greedy flesh. I hang it carefully in the cupboard with all my other gowns, each one a gift from Volchok. Tonight I'm not tired, and tonight, again, I hate my solitude. Volchok is off with his men doing Kronk knows whafa. Marta is down with her stickly slaves, avoiding me since our fight.

I tuck the mewling bundle—still without a proper name—into

her basket. I cover her with a blanket. Tonight, I don't want her small breath on my neck, or my own warm milk spat back upon my flesh. She is fed and wiped and parceled into her place.

I won't be long, I think guiltily. *I'll be back.*

I wear two layers of dresses. It's getting colder outside, and even in my pretty chambers, a chill creeps through the stone. I wrap a scarf around my shoulders. I walk about the hallways. I stroll in and out of chambers until I come to a closed-off area that is guarded by one of the three large electrolls who carry the tall choppers. This is the only one I didn't hurt my first great day at the compound, and the only one whafa sometimes says hello.

I walk toward the door and raise my hand to open it. The guard moves quickly and blocks me.

"I'm looking for Volchok," I say with cold authority. I find I need more attitude with these stupid beasts now that I am no longer fat in the belly. "Let me in or get him for me."

He grunts and stands firm.

"I need him now," I hiss at him.

It won't even look at me.

I think about Marta's challenge—to push my boundaries in the compound and see how far my freedom really lies. *Maybe she was right.* I know this guard will not budge, and I'm in no condition to fight it like before.

"Fine," I say, forcing a smile. "Please tell our Leader that I wait for him to join me."

It nods at me and makes a sound that indicates it might understand.

I go back the way I came, but once around the nearest corner, I swear and punch the wall. *Volchok isn't in that room any more than I am,* I think angrily. I saw him leave with his helmet and cape, so I know he's out in the deadlands someplace, doing Kronk knows whafa.

I don't return to my wing. Instead, I sneak down two levels and head to the farthest side, where Marta stays with the other prisoners.

The air is damp. It smells of mold. Wee beetles and skittery things inch along the cold walls and in the darkened crevices along the floor. *Ugh.* I walk stealthy, though I don't expect to find anypod lurking about in these dank corridors. I'm not meant to be here. I open the heavy gate and slip my scarf around the closing mechanism. The gate will close but can't lock now unless the scarf is removed. The hallway narrows considerably and the air quality is even poorer. On either side are wooden doors with heavy bolts, some with barred windows.

A light flickers at the end of the hall. I hear whispers. My first few days at the compound were spent freezing and disabled on a filthy straw bed in that room, sometimes all alone and sometimes clinging to Marta as we wondered at our fate. I shudder. I stand unnoticed in the arched entryway. Marta sits in the far corner with several others gathered around her. They speach quietly, urgently, a clicking, whirling dronebeet in their midst. Suddenly, Marta looks up.

"Whafa doing so far from your pretty tower?" She gestures to silence the others.

"I came," I say, "as you requested."

"That was some time ago, Loo. We don't need your help now, or your interruptions." Her eyes glint. "I fear the worst has come," she says to the others. "She's bored, finally."

My cheeks burn.

"You are, aren't you?" Marta challenges me directly.

I stare back.

The dronebeet rears up on the back set of claws; its rotating eyes catch every small movement I make. "Has she got something to say? Something of value, some secrets perhaps?" It rubs its feelers: a shivery metallic squeak.

"Marta, come for one milli." I extend a pale hand, palm side up.

"No, Loo. Whafa have to say can be shared amongst this group or not at all."

"Fine. Stay locked inside with all your low-grade mates. I only thought you'd like to know that Volchok is gone with his men and will be away most of the night."

"Are you inviting us all upstairs, then?" The venom drips from her words.

I turn and retrace my steps. *Blaaty spietchka!* The slam of the heavy gate behind me echoes through the hall.

Rustle: Dead Destiny

The wee things decide I'm ready. Or that *they* are ready and that I must do. I am no prize. Rusted and slow, I can barely move on my own. We have yet to try me in water, so I hardly know if their plan will even work. They have trussed me up with long reins so that they can steer me, somewhat, like some floating sleigh.

"My mind is not—not—I cannot," I stutter.

"You don't need to think," says the feisty one. "Just keep your mouth shut and swimmy." They pull me along some barren track and, finally, out the wee hold of a new hidden cove, much like the one our unit escaped from so long since.

"After your mates ruined our last spot," says one. "Like, completely trashed it, and then we got the fiery paybacks from ScanMans."

The others grow quiet.

"So brutal," says another.

They stop to make a sign in the air; they murmur quietly amongst themselves, and one leads the others in some kind of rememory song, to honor their mates who were burned to death.

Kronk help them.

Later, I manage to ask the thing that has been nagging me all this time in the underground passage, all the time that they nursed me. "Why not hide on board a shuttle? It'd be easier that way, ya?"

"Yes, of course," says the one I think of as my fave. It's the angry one, the most militant of them all. "Until ScanMans modified us with flight trackers, we did that more often than by any other means. Now we can't. We set off alarms as soon as we come near the loading docks. Now, low-grades do all that heavy lifting, all our old work, coz they're too programmed to try and stow away."

It stands up on the back feelers and shows me a mutilated midsection, a gash with ugly wee scars crossed over. "See? I ripped that right out from my own blaaty core," it boasts loudly. "But I'll not leave the others, right?"

I nod, more impressed than ever.

They hustle me to the water's edge and instruct me to get right in. It looks bleak. It's cold and dark and doesn't bring me joy. Not like in my dreams or in my wishes, or when I was last here. It seems hopeless, but who am I to think or even struggle now?

The initial splash shocks my wiring—so blaaty cold, ya? It's the first sensation I've had in so long, I welcome it. I wallow clumsy while they get themselves settled. Three will ride in special pockets they've attached to my shoulders, two more lower down my back. Four more hang onto ropes they attach to my legs. Those four are the largest, the strongest, and they plan to kick and float on their own. I shake my head. *That'll never work,* I think. Then I'm pleased to have even *had* a thought. I perk up a wee bite and splash clumsily in the shallows.

Maybe the water is helping me after all.

The three eldest dronebeets stay behind since they prolly can't make the crossing. They elect to stay behind and teach the revolution to the others. They will guide the rest who might one day search for their own imagined freedom. *Good blaaty luck.* This is the awful part, their noisy goodbyes, their twitching feelers.

I realize I like them, grudgingly. I'm impressed by their determination to change their own lot. I mean, we followed orders and look where it got us, right?

I plod along, splooshing through the water, waiting for my inside changes to happen. I wait for my lungs to empty and shrivel up, wait for all those wee microscopic ducts to open and revive themselves, so that I may breathe and forage like my fishy friends. *Nothing happens.* I worry that ScanMans ruined that part of me, that they surgically removed it or damaged it forever. I paddle like any manimal might. I kick with my heavy legs but my head stays upright, my breathing stays the same. The wee things squirm and twiggle, weigh me down more than I'd have thought. The ones near my legs squeal when I kick—each movement drags them below the surface, jerks them around and threatens to drown them solid.

Stop, they cry and wavel their antennae.

I reach back and untie the ropes from my legs. I give them a longer leash and loop it around my waist, instead. Now they can try to keep themselves afloat. We're at the edge of the opening, the open sea just beyond. I worry how the wee things will stay above the surface once the rough waves and the strong currents hit us.

Now I feel stronger. My hair moves slowly in the wet. When I look down at my webbed hands, scarred or not, I see that the color is vibrant and my skin seems healthier than before. I almost smile. This water is slowly healing me and building my confidence. Suddenly, it kicks in. My watery self takes over and I plunge my face beneath the rolling waves.

I'll get there, I think. *Or at least die trying, like the dronebeet commanded.*

They must have known they couldn't all make it. *Silly wee things.* Here we lie on the far reaches of sand, washed up for good. Alive— the three who perched on my shoulders, and me. I might've laid a coin down and made some interest for myself, but it hardly seems the time to say so. Not even to the angry one, who is the first to talk of leaving.

"Can't I go with you?" I sound pathetic, even to my own hear-holes.

"No," it says, quickly.

It doesn't even try to make up a story about why I can't. It just doesn't care. The other dronebeets scurry up the beach a teeny bite. They're looking for shelter, to get dried out, get some feed. They'll have to rest up before they take off to find their renegade friends who live in a pretty valley.

"Whafa other rejected Scouts live there?" *Am I crying? Have I no pride?*

"Look," says the feisty one. *My favorite.* "We can't carry you and, anyway, you're seriously a pile of rust now. We don't need you anymore." It twitters a bite and scratches at the sand with one shining claw. "You understand."

I nod.

But I can't stop myself. "Please don't leave me. I'll walk. I'll carry you, I can. I promise." I try to wiggle my fingers as proof.

"All right," it says crossly. "If you're up and ready to go when we leave, then you can come. But we can't wait for you. We can't slow our pace."

I try to hug it in my bloated arms, but it leaps away. "Thank you," I gush. "Thank you so much, friend."

It harrumphs loudly and skitters over to join the other two. They leave me out in the baking sun, to dry, I hope. To dry my wires and collect my wits. *It's so nice to not be alone,* I think. Even though they don't give a blaat about me, it's comforting to hear them over there, making their driftwood nest.

I've been living a long time.

I've been a lot of places, seen so many strange things. Mostly I know this like some learned fact, as I can't even rememory it all in order, not since the whack job on my mindcore back in Living Lab. Mostly it's all gone—fried and stabbed and sliced, poked and terrified, right out of my wee head. But somewhere there are murmurs living on: in my scarred legs and up my battered arms, coursing through my feeble veins. My heart beats, those few dented synapses still firing off, despite everything. Why do I even want it anymore, right? Even after all this, I can't just Deplug myself. Not even like the monitor back at our lair in StarPod. I smile. That was a good feeling. Har har. *The look on Shona's face.*

The dronebeets are twittering away under some big soggy tree, up the sandy shore a bite. They're making their big big plans. They're going to the Red Soil Settlements, where pods rabble and carouse and further their own cause. One of their sistren is coming to take them. *Take us.* They're so excited to meet up with their old friends. I'm excited, too, although Kronk only knows whafa waits for me.

I stare into the hot sun until my sight blurs. My eyes are drying out. I wish I could flip over, at least, to extinguish my burning face in the sand. I note that the dronebeet carcasses entwined in the rope pile are starting to smell bad. I'm thinking I better start getting mobile soon. I better get less broken fast fast, or be left behind after all.

At first I think I'm imagining the sounds. I strain closer. Something is definitely crashing through the far-off bush. I can feel its stomping feet vibrate in the hard-packed sand. It breathes heavily and grunts. *Oh, why me?* I wonder. I smell it a millimile away, but I don't cry. I don't speach a thing, only to warn the wee dronebeets to keep quiet, or else.

When it stands above me, it blocks the sun. Whafa ugly! Worse then the autotron photos. *Ugly electroll whafa, and so stenchy!* I don't even struggle when it lifts me under the rusty arms. I only wonder, *Kronking now whafa?* It throws me on the back of a wagon and off we go, off through the stinging sands, the burning winds of—*have I been here before?* I wonder uneasily.

The dronebeets crawl out from their hiding spots, one by one. My favorite waves goodbye. *Sad sad.* At least, I hope it's sad to see me go, as I myself could weep. They're the only things that ever cared for me in so long.

Since Loo, really, and Solomon. Roku. Even Shona.

Well … maybe not Shona.

Roku: Mission

"That went all right," Nadya says. "Sort of." She smiles sadly.

We're standing near the Settlement bell at the center of the village. One or two pods help assemble our packs, filling them with food and weapons. The rest have walked away in anger.

Nadya, I know, is conflicted. She'd rather be here building her trade, learning from the elder Healers, than off warring again.

Stay, I send.

"Impossible." **One Pod,** she sends. She smirks when I nearly fall over in surprise.

"Still using that StarPod rhetoric," says Red briskly.

Nadya blushes. "It was kind of a joke," she says, awkwardly. She steps away to finish loading one of the packs.

I scan inside her guarded mindcore, try to find out whether or not she regrets this decision of hers.

"No," she says to me quietly. "I don't regret a thing."

I chirp. She reads me well, this one.

"Let's have our adventure." She hoists a small pack over her shoulder. "Come, Nadya," she says loudly. "You and I will fly that rusted shuttle." She jogs down the valley path.

Nadya lifts the larger food pack. "See you at camp," she says. She rests her warm hand on my feathered breast, just above where the organparts thrump.

I chirp softly.

She smiles, then follows behind Red.

I wish I was flying with her on my shoulders, like before. Instead, she and Red will steer the patched and dented shuttle, one found deserted in the deadlands two seasons ago. Settlers dragged it to the valley and nurtured it back into operation. It's a bandaged job on an out-modeled ship, lost forever by some ill-fated Scout unit. Dronebeets, the same who wanted us killed upon arrival, now my comrades in the evening guard, are coming, too. One flies in the shuttle and one with me.

"Like having extra tech," it says. "With spies in every crack."

This one insists on riding in a pouch that straps around my feathered chest, rather than hanging from my claws like before.

"In case you drop me," it says.

I'd be more worried about me eating you. I snort.

It quivers inside the pouch.

Then we're off, no fanfare, no bell ringing, no Warriors waving us into the sky. But flapping hard, curling and diving, climbing and looping high, thrills me into squawks of delight. My pulse speeds along; blood sings in my veins. I swoop around the shuttle and flirt with it, two flying beasts cavorting in the bright, cloudless sky.

Later, the dronebeet has to pinch me to beg for a land break. "The others want to set a camp to feed and rest," it whines.

So I concede. I circle slowly, easing our way nearer to earth, toward the spot where the shuttle sits quietly below. To where a curling lick of smoke begins to rise and meet us halfway. There we'll hatch the details of our rescue plan for Loo and Marta. And the dronebeets will fill me in on all their newly gathered gossip, whether they mean to or not. I'll scan them proper at the campfire.

That other campfire comes back to me now as I crouch around the flames. *Solomon dying, Loo tripping, Shona scheming.* I watch these newer faces, watch their gestures. I listen to Red and Nadya talk about the shuttle—how to improve the fuel line transfer, how to keep the weapons chute clear for faster response time. While they speach, I scan the dronebeets for their secret news morsels. They chitter away about their newly arrived sistren, lately escaped from StarPod. One says that they crossed the sea with a mangled Warrior, recycled from the trash bin. They laugh. They used her like a ship to sail them all that watery way.

Like she was some rusted old machine.

They think about Scouts the way we always thought about dronebeets, all through our Warrior training. Neither one relates to the other with any meaning.

Will we ever unlearn that?

In the dancing light, I watch them. I choke quietly on all that has come and gone before me. I back away from their chatter, from the sounds their mouths and fingers make when they eat, away from their intelligent eyes. I slip farther into shadow. I stray from them but I don't hunt. I perch and preen. I sing a mournful tune up in the bold branches of some sturdy tree. I call out to my old unit, out to wherever they may be: captive in some squalid cell, strapped and tied in Living Lab, buried in an earthen tomb, drowned along the ocean floor, or maybe dancing joyous up in Kronk's beautiful garden.

When night falls deeply, the others rest their cores. But not me. My vision clears; my claws retract. My growling empty bellysack prods me back to life.

Loo: Leaves Turn

Volchok stretches his arms above his head. Muscles ripple beneath his skin: forearms, biceps, triceps, shoulders, and so on down his back. I press myself against him on the bed, climb onto him and bury my face in his neck.

"Such a lovely party tonight," I say. "Do you want more wine?"

"Ah, Loo," he says, with a throaty laugh. He lifts me, shifts my weight, and I fight it a wee bite, push back into his solid strength to see how far he'll let me go without a tussle. "You're always wrestling."

I pin his shoulders. I smile into his face, playful and light, but inside I am testing my own strength. I exercise a little more each day and wonder how long it'll take me to get back to my former shape.

Volchok moves suddenly and I am flat on my back underneath his comfortable weight. He smooths my hair against the clean sheet. I kiss the end of his nose. I wrap my long legs around his. A tiny sound escapes his lips. I fuse deeply with him, kiss his open mouth and wave-send tingles as I pet and smooth his skin.

I'd be lying if I said I didn't like our times together. If I said I, like, completely hated him or his touch, or that he didn't bring me pleasure. He tries to, at least.

When I coo, he rolls to one side and begins to touch me in earnest. "Beautiful Loo," he whispers.

"Uh—" Marta stands in the open doorway, holding the podling. Her eyes sear mine.

"Not now," Volchok growls.

She drops the wee thing in her basket and quickly closes the door. She's gone.

Volchok turns back to me, undaunted. He seizes my hair, pulls me to his chest. I'm caught then. I'm halfway down the corridor sending some guilty peace offering to comfort Marta, who glared all night, never enjoying a moment of splendor, never eating a morsel of food. I can't even send that far any more, so I'll have to seek her out in person to apologize. My other half is still entwined with this human, this male beast, wrapped in the sheets but hardly able to enjoy.

"I've often wondered why you didn't long for your old home like the others," he says sometime later as we lie quietly.

I shrug.

"But now I know." Something about his voice chills me. "You're turning into a very expensive prize," he says thickly. He watches me from beneath half-closed lids.

"Whafa mean you with this tricky talk?" I soothe my own disquiet by stroking his wide chest.

"Your last masters seek you even now and offered me great sums to have you back. It seems you were as violent and untamed with your own kind as you were with mine." He leans toward me on one strong arm. My hand falls away from him. "Your ScanMans want you for some great and final punishment. Strange, isn't it, Loo?"

I swallow the panic that bubbles from my loins.

He touches a piece of my curling hair. He tightens it around his thick finger and tugs. "They think you're hiding from them. Is that the real reason you've stayed here by my side?"

"When were you with ScanMans?" I feel the air backing up inside my chest. It burns and pops and makes it hard to breathe.

"Don't worry. I paid them well to leave you be. I was owed some great favors by them." His smile vanishes. "They were surprised to learn how gentle and refined you've become. How very maternal."

Something bleeds inside—*they'll want the wee creature back to study in their labs!* Instinctively, I jump up and peer into her basket. She shivers and snorts. Her eyes focus on mine, and she makes her gurgling coo. She smiles.

"Volchok," I say. I try to clear the emo from my voice. I hold myself in tight to keep from signaling my deep distress. "Why don't they come and get their Scouts? ScanMans wouldn't let their prize Assassins rot in any prison or wallow on the ground to scrape your dirty pans."

"Oh, Loo." He laughs. "You think I stole them all? Well, I stole some. But at least half were gifts from ScanMans. They don't want the others back—just you. And when they told me what they planned to do to you—," he shivers in exaggeration. "Well, I just couldn't let that happen. Could I?"

I look at him closely. I scan through all those calcified emo stumps—hopes and joys, pleasure, affection—for the soft parts that might tell me where I stand. I am not hardwired inside him, not like with Rustle; neither am I synch-fused, like with Marta. I find cold, sterile compartments in him, all empty, and I can't gauge my powers or my influence, of late.

"You haven't answered me," he says, and now there is no pretence of niceness.

"I've been very content, Volchok. I didn't know they were looking for me still. I've hardly even thought of StarPod since my new beginnings here with you." It is partial truth, this, and the best I can deliver.

"Come to bed, Loo." His voice is a quiet measure of control. It unnerves me. "It's been a long and lovely night. And we have much to do tomorrow."

Like whafa? I think. *Like turn me over for another prize?*

I go to him, filled with silent terror that ticks inside my throat, and I lie down. I wait for him to sleep, but I myself cannot. I breathe deeply, try to calm myself, and think up a plan that my old Hunter self would like.

My favorite part is when his eyes fly open and he realizes that it's me, ending it all for him. That the thing I strangle around his neck was part of a pretty dress he once gave me. The slender hide belt—so slimming, so strong. The sounds that squawk from his ugly throat wake the podling. She cries and I almost lose my grip. My whole weight is in it now, and his eyes bulge in his fat red face.

Done.

Later, I roll the corpse off the bed. It lands on the floor at an odd angle. I try shoving it underneath the bed, but it's too heavy.

Too awkward. Instead, I push the bed and cover it that way.

Done.

I hold the podling close—I really must choose a name soon—and show her the bright moon outside my open window. The courtyard is still. Tables stand covered in dishes and cups; the leftover feed is still piled high; chairs and decorations are strewn about the ground. *Podslaves should have cleaned it up by now,* I think, distractedly. The guards are all asleep, well fed and too well watered, some lying in one another's arms around the mess. Shadows gather in the yard outside. Light glows from the smattering of twinklers. It spills across the bushes, with their scented nocturnal flowers that line the outer gate. I breathe them in.

I have to *think.* The things that Volchok told me have my fingers shaking, my mindcore racing. Prolly Marta will help me get rid of the corpse later on. *She'll be pleased, at least.* But if his men come looking for him, they will not give me a milli's peace until they find him. Unless he'd gone out on some private errand, some secret Mission. Then he would wear his riding clothes—the helmet and cape hanging just here, inside the room. *Hmm.*

I walk toward them quickly. I touch the thick fabric, the tall hide boots. I put the podling down and slip into Volchok's breeches. They're a bite big in some parts, but I am equal to him in height. I stuff rags in the end of the boots and pull them on next. I lace them tightly and practice striding about the room like a beasty man. For the top half, I simply slice one of my warm black dresses in two. To hide my podbumps, I wrap a scarf tightly around them, binding them flat. I put my newly fashioned shirt over that. Another scarf goes around my head to hide my pinky silver curls. I flick the cape over my broad shoulders and look into the long mirror.

I look really good. I smile at myself and at the wee pod, gurgling on the bed behind me. When I add the helmet with its lowered facemask, I almost scare myself. Ha ha ha, I think. *Whafa Marta see me now?* I can hardly stop staring into the glass. I stride about and copy Volchok's gestures—his wave goodbye, always more curt than his hello wave. Almost a salute. The way he dismissed the podslaves—a snap, a flick of the wrist, a jutting chin. I can't fool them with my voice, but if I could avoid speaching more than a few words …

It's settled. For now, I'll go find Marta and get her help with the corpse. She's likely outdoors, cleaning up our festive mess. As for tomorrow, when they call for him, it'll be me in charge, at last. I'll lead his feeble, wine-drenched guards about the compound and beyond. They'll be too ill from the festival to even notice my trick. This way, I can even lead the podslaves out to freedom. *Ha! They'll have to thank me after all,* I think, smugly. *Especially Marta.*

I round the tower stairs, carrying the podling, reveling in my long cape, my loud boot heels echoing on the stone floor. I can't wait to see her face when she discovers whafa done. It's hard to not laugh out loud, actually. The halls are dark, torches snuffed out; nopod is about. The round greeting room is also empty. Moonlight spills through the tall windows and I rememory my first day here, how I almost scrambled free. I couldn't do it now, especially carrying the podling. I kick open the heavy front door. Still, nopod is in sight. *Strange.*

Clanging chains and a squeaky pulley, hinges creaking—somepod's opening the gate. I see shadowy movement at the front.

"Halt," I yell in a low voice.

The gate is closing now, and as my eyes adjust to the moonlight, I see a large electroll lurching before me. It grunts and gestures to the small wagon it's pulling—much like the one Marta and I were rattled nearly to death in. There's a pile of bones inside. I shake my head—the last thing I need now is another half-dead slave. It grunts more loudly and rubs its belly. It grabs at the maimed creature and shakes a broken limb or two at me.

"No," I say. I squint, but can't see anything in the dark.

The podling gurgles. She makes a cooing sound. She sends—even I can feel it, though I can't really read her well.

The electroll scratches its nether regions and the bag of bones in the wagon twitches a finger. It tries to speach but only manages to croak a bite.

Whafa shameful mess, I think. *Should prolly kill it. Put it right out of its obvious misery.*

The poor creature lifts its swollen head and stares at us, at me in Volchok's uni and at the wee podling. I think it's sending to the wee one.

Hmm, I think. So it *is* the pod remains of some unlucky Scout. Hard to tell, she's so battered. "Throw her in prison with the others," I say, with authority. *Whafa Volchok would do, right?* Besides, Marta can see to her.

It lumbers forward, pulling the cart. *Whafa stink!* It rubs its hairy bellyparts again.

"Feed off the tables in back," I say. Kronk knows, there's plenty left over.

The electroll bellows, then disappears around the corner with its wagon. The podling starts to howl.

"Shh," I say. But I hardly notice. I'm wondering: *Where the blaat is Marta?*

Roku : Compound Courtyard

I settle into the twiggy branches, quiet except for the small crackling of dry leaves. Some fall, shaken from their perch. They settle on Marta's hair and shoulders below. She looks up and sees me—my eyes, at least: two orange moons in the darkened tree.

"Who's there?" She sounds scared. She quickly backs away. She strains to see more of me.

I came with Nadya, I send, the strength of which sets Marta staggering. **Sorry.**

"Who are you?" she says, backing further away from me.

Roku, formerly of Seventh Level. From Loo's unit. I'm almost afraid to ask. I smell Loo everywhere here, but she hasn't returned a single send. *Am I too late?*

"You're the Deformed one that abandoned Loo?"

I chirp. **Yes,** I send. **I never meant to, but yes.**

"So why are you here now?" Marta steps forward now, more defiant than frightened.

The compound door opens and a large electroll stumbles outside. It lurches straight to the tables, starts shoveling food into its greasy mouth. It doesn't even look at us. It tosses food into its empty wagon between mouthfuls. It steps over the bodies of the guards and keeps on feeding.

Marta looks over at the beast. "Good. The poison will kill it just like it did the other guards. One less manimal for us to worry about." She spits.

Are all the men and electrolls dead then?

She nods. "Poisoned by their wine and run through by my knife, just to be certain. Except the Leader, who eats and drinks from his own private source. He doesn't even know that his army is slaughtered."

This Hunter Warrior is hardened. To kill in self-defense is natural, especially for Hunters, but to shore up so much anger about it, so much bitterness, is not good.

I send, **I'm here to bring Loo and the podling to the Red Soil Settlement.**

"Good luck, Roku." Marta laughs bitterly. "She'd rather stay here and fuse with the enemy. She's their Leader's special pet, you see."

Hmm. It hardly sounds like Loo, but pod must prevail, and in dangerous times …

I send, **Why aren't you on board the shuttle? The prison is already empty. They're ready for take-off.**

"If you think I've come back for Loo, you're wrong," says Marta. But her face says otherwise.

She's hoping Loo will come along. I read her softly, gently. Pod has been through many indignities in this place. She has lost her unit, seen some mates killed. She's survived the journey through the deadlands, the electrolls, and Kronk knows what else. She's been a Leader to the others in prison, and now she's tired. She's wiry on the outside, but badly bruised elsewhere. It's whafa fills her to the hearholes with hate.

You want to kill that man in charge. I don't ask; I already know. I see the long blade in her hand. Whafa wee beasts use to carve their meat. I rememory that tall man striding toward ScanMan's tent, his black cape flowing at his heels. He had Loo's scent all over him and I, too, had wanted to snap his tiny neck.

"Plus, I want the podling. Loo would let it starve," she says, "from lack of attention, if not feed. I won't leave it here to become some compound slave."

A wee pod growing up at Red Soil, free from ScanMans, free from prison chains. Now that would be something. Never to have to unlearn all those Rules and Regs, all those lies.

I'd coo to this Marta if I could. She could use some healing. *Nadya could help her,* I think. **Go to the shuttle,** I send. **I will try to convince Loo. I'll bring her wee pod. And I'll gladly kill the Leader, too.**

"I'd like to do it with my own hands," she hisses.

It'll be hard to carry all three of you back to Red Soil. I ruffle my feathers.

"You won't have to," says Marta. "I tell you, she's not coming."

She'll come if there is nothing left for her here.

Marta shrugs.

I worry she isn't strong enough to make the kill, but this Warrior is stubborn and the Leader is only human, after all. **Then, good luck to you, Marta. I'll fetch the podling. Meet me back here at this tree,** I send.

She nods. She walks toward the compound, shoulders set, knife flashing in the moonlight. The electroll pauses, sniffs the air when she walks past, but goes back to the cold feed piles and slurps a jug of wine.

I picture the podling from images stored in Marta's mindcore, from the descriptions given by the other podslaves. I feel a powerful send growing—it's unfocused, all emo, no text, but that could be her. I follow it. I flap my wings and lift myself into the night sky.

Rustle: Gray Stone, Black Night

I'm plopped in a shivery pile of myself on the cold stone floor. The prison is empty, except for me. *Alone again!* It's still barred solid, the other so-called podslaves long gone. *Prolly froze to death and crumbled into dust,* I think, miserably. At least I'm thinking, though, right?

I wonder where my wee dronebeets are now. I wonder if I can move. I wonder how long I'll lie here, rusting. *Rustle's rusting. Rustle's rusting.* I think it fast fast. It makes me laugh. *Har har.*

I breathe deeply—not much else I can blaaty do. There definitely were Pod-kind here. Smells like the mangled pod in Living Lab, though. Starvy sticks with blank faces, not the strong Warriors we used to be. Better than nothing; better than no nice smells at all. I roll to one side and wish I could finally close my eyes. There's nothing to look at here but the gray stone of the walls, the very color of Loo's cold eyes. I leak an emo-send, an impulse full of all that grief and pain whafa fills me up when I think about her now. In fact, I realize that to think of her right now is suicide. I need whafa wee hopes I can muster if I'm to make it through this black black night. Instead, I blank, and hope to never wake again.

Shadows gloom in the cold cellar. I'm still lying on the floor. I roll over again and notice a pretty green blanket over in one corner. It's the color of the weeds I once fed on at the bottom of the sea. I wish I could crawl over and wrap myself in it, but I'm almost too weak to move. My tongue lies heavy in my dry mouth. My lips crack when I open them to cough, to clear my swollen throat.

There is one large open window about three podlengths above the blanket. Out the window, there's a sliver of sky, black with a few twinklers in it. Nothing else to look at but the cold gray stone. Some emo waves me and I send, piteously; clumsy and blubbery, I send all kinds of dementoid wishings. I think, *Oh, that stone is just like the color of Loo's eyes,* and then I think, *For Kronk's sake, I already thought that, didn't I?*

I groan.

I may murder my own annoying Self long before I give up on living.

Then, black fury catches me: a movement in the sky, a wild, shrieking sound. A large winged creature wheels about and descends not one milli from the window. It roosts on a jutting rock ledge. Hot wind from its wingbeat dries my face. The thing ruffles its powerful wings, then tucks them away, standing taller on the perch. And all the while its orange eyes shine steady from the dark mammalian face. The magnificent beast pins me with its stare—nary a twiggle or wink—daring me to search the depths of its wide, rolling eyes. It holds a rope in its claws and dangles it through the open window.

Rustle, she sends. **I hear you. I thought you were the wee pod.**

I am transfixed. *Huh?*

It's me, Roku. Let me take you away.

I can't mouthspeach. My sends are full-frontal wonked, and I may not be able to crawl across the floor. But I think—*I think*—I know this pod.

Roku? I used to know a Roku Pod.

The bird slowly nods its massive black head. **One Pod,** she sends, and dangles the rope to the floor. **Come, grab this, Rustle. Then we'll go get Loo.**

Loo? It can't be! But I inch myself along the gray stone floor.

Roku is so patient. She chirps to me as I make my long, painful haul to the window. She waits as I roll myself over and slowly tie the rope around my waist. She settles her impossible feathers; then, in a wink—*we're gone!* Into the black night. She sends while she flies, but I don't get it all. It's too much for my feeble mind and my broken self. Instead, she mindsweeps me like that other time back at StarPod. She presses into my mind and tries to sort through the bungled rememories to find out exactly how damaged I am. Still looking for her precious download, prolly.

Poor Rustle, she sends at last.

At least I understand that, I think.

We're rounding a tall tower that's at one end of the gated compound. The bright moon spills onto the courtyard below. There are two figures: a blond Scout and the black-caped beast whafa sent me to the prison cell. The beast is carrying a small bundle. The Scout holds a knife.

Roku screeches and dives down between them. **Sorry, Rustle,** she sends, and drops me unceremoniously onto the hard ground.

Ow.

Roku squawks. She is Kronk-sized, and the black-clad beast nearly falls right over when it sees her great wings stretch and slap the air. Roku's shining claws rip the small bundle from the beast's arms. She reels and flaps away, a sudden feathery flash followed by a shining silver one.

The beast seems confused. It stares after Roku and doesn't even look at the angry blond, doesn't even protect itself against another slice.

"Where is she?" screams the Scout. She stabs again at the beast's torso.

The beast falls to its knees. I'm lying on the ground, nary a podlength away. I can't move. I can't even close my eyes. I can only drink it all in.

The beast throws off that shiny, full-faced helmet and says, "I'm here, Marta." The long knife juts out from her bellyparts. Her breath comes shallow and quick. Her profile sets off a bomb in my stuttering core. She falls to one side, closer still to me, and her eyes meet mine.

It's Loo. *Mother of Kronk.*

She stares, not recognizing me in my battered state. She doesn't return-send. Those mutable silver eyes flash cold as Marta's knife.

"Loo," I say. "It's me. R-Rustle." I am right beside her now, suddenly touching her, my mouth agape, my fingers trembling. She stares at me and doesn't say a word.

"Loo!" The other Scout shrieks in disbelief. She rushes close and tries to stop the blood from pouring out Loo's front. "I thought you were Volchok," she sobs. "Oh Kronk, whafa do?"

"Volchok's dead," says Loo softly. "I was coming to find you." She doesn't move her gaze from mine. "Rustle?" She moans. "It's really you?" That composed brow still masks her thoughts; she is stabbed now, yet as inscrutable as ever.

Loo—I start to send but the other Scout interrupts.

"She can't send properly any more. You have to use your mouth."

And I can hardly speach. *Full-frontal ironical.* My eyes plead silently. This sudden emo-rush might finally do me in: too much salt in my septic wounds.

"I thought you were long gone," she whispers. Her cheek is paler than I've ever seen it. Her hand is on my face, my ugly, swollen face.

I nod. **I was.** The places where her fingers touch my skin are the only ones that exist. I tell myself I will not cry. *Not here, not in this strange place. Not now.* But I'm a liar.

Marta shouts for Roku. She rips her own dress to use around Loo's wounds. She's flailing to undo her kill-strokes, but I have a feeling it's too late. It had never even once occurred to me that after all of this—the desperate flights, the endless pilgrimage— that I might finally find Loo, only to hold her cooling core to my brokenhearted self. Heat flames my face and a sickness surges in me. I sway. I coo her name Pod-style. The notes are pure. The sound of lost love fills the courtyard, spills over the stony wall, and far beyond into the sandy plains. I fall to my knees before her, my bloodied arms outstretched.

Loo: Swansong

"Roku?"

How can she be here *now* when she wasn't all those times I needed her? She chirrups a strange low sound at me. I see her outline against the starry sky. She drops the wee pod right on me, right on Rustle and me.

Rustle—not dead and drowned, after all—arrives just in time to weep and watch me die. *Full-frontal ironical!*

Loo, sends Roku. She blinks and, for the milli, she is gone. No orange signposts to her face. She opens her eyes and there they are again, headlights that plow into me. Roku hops closer. Her scent is strong. Hot, like some heaving beast. Fresh from the wind and the grassy nests she builds. Wild from the bloodied pulp of her mangled feed: carrion traces. I feel the power of her send but I don't get the meaning.

The warm wet on my bellyparts is red. It's blood, I realize. No wonder I hurt so much.

"Keep her safe." I hand Rustle our purple-haired podling. I kiss her tiny waving fist.

The wee thing knocks me back with her unruly emo-send. She's angry and frightened; she's sad, and there's something else: love. And in that milli, I rememory the name of the mother I left behind. *Kalista.* My first send in so long is also my last. I send this legacy to our wee pod and she suckles it right up. No longer nameless, then. And not orphaned, after all.

I look from Kalista's wee face to Rustle's. *I fuse you, Rustle Pod.* I fuse.

It's cold, I think. So cold. And dark. There is movement. Feathers rush the wind. They're gone.

Roku: Black Flag

It's far from perfect but it feels right, more or less. Poor broken Rustle hobbles in a corner. She watches Kalista play in the sun. It makes her think about Loo. I feel her emo-send, quiet though it is. Rustle walks a bite farther, feeds a bite more, and slowly grows more interested in the new world around her, with every passing day. *Remarkable.* Kalista engages her without even trying. And Rustle can't help but recognize her own genestrands twisting through that miraculous young core.

Born of Rustle and Loo, this creature defies all our old Rules and Regs. She breaks the very fundamentals of our StarPod teachings. I marvel that she even exists. She, oblivious and pure, is living proof that they don't know everything about us, and they, therefore, cannot ultimately control us *or* our destiny. A joyous chirp escapes my beak, and the wee thing sputters a wet coo back.

She has your sense of humor, I send.

Kronk help her, sends Rustle.

Rustle snorts and Kalista copies the sound. Kalista looks up, laughing. She tosses sand into the air; it is the future. She grabs at it with her chubby fist. She is wild: wavehoned to the earth beneath her, the sky above, the waters just out of reach. Seemingly untouched by all those previous worlds, the commanding StarPod prophesies mean nothing to her. They are irrelevant for the milli. We other creatures marvel at her daily. She is fearless, proud, and she wavels a stick into the air, shouting with delight.

Nadya watches us from the hillside. She laughs, too—musical and light. Then she bends back to the herb garden. She clears it of mud clumps and rocks. Marta works nearby, helping to dig up the last of the root-feed harvest. She works slowly. Her spiritwind is low. Healers sit with her and try to ease the ugly scars she holds inside her tightly. She says digging helps more than mouthspeach, so they let her go back to the fields each day. Besides, the Settlement's winter survival depends on bringing in the harvest, so nopod can rightly complain. Cause for a cheersong, that.

Nadya. *She is happy,* I think. Not a word we used in StarPod. Not something we even understood. There was satisfaction. There was pride, especially in competition and success, but not happiness on its own. I don't think so, anyway. *Oh, that time.* So far removed, so long ago. How I struggled to make sense of it. She turns to me again and smiles. When I think of her, she feels the warmth of my send and knows my soft intention. She clearly doesn't return the feelings, though, and that makes me even more awkward around her these days.

Red busies herself at the main fire pit. Then Nadya is not far away. There is some sparking chemistry between them, building. My beak smells it. They'll mate and fight and hunt and, someday, I suspect, grow gray and argue less. They are bound to find it all. One brushes the other with a limb. They tremble and blush. So would I, if it were possible!

I peck the ground and slurp up juicy worms and a beetle or two. Hunger fuels me, drives me ever forward in this strange world. *What lies ahead?* A grumbling belly, for sure. An empty gullet. A hacking cough. I hop and land on a twizzling stick. It's adronebeet's feeler and it's still attached. Two of them roll out from under the bushling, mating as well! I choke back my laugh. I'd say they smiled, but perhaps they didn't even notice me.

Well, I think. They all have their place. They are learning their new roles, finding their new lives. But I am restless here and lonely, dandystill. There's nopod here for me, and it's clear I don't belong on the star-baked soil, red or otherwise.

I peck through a pile of seeds fallen from a luscious yellow flower. This pretty world is peaceful in the now. *But for how long?* The slaver compound is dismantled; the men and electrolls are dead. ScanMans lie quiet for the milli, but I can't believe they'll let this colony bloom and prosper on its own. No, I don't trust in this tranquil comfort, this temporary bliss.

Just as before, when I cowered and slunk about the underworld mines and tunnels of StarPod, I think again: *Whafa good am I here?* This cannot be my place. Elsewise, I wouldn't feel so alone, so separate from all that I know in my breast to be true: that this is only the beginning. Adventures call me out and, yet, will call me back. I couldn't leave forever, but I can't stay here now.

Silence, for a milli. Then wind blows the grasses and some faint music trails the air. Scents abound: flowerweeds, groundweeds, dirt and sweat, and the fresh-hewn smells of wooden planks for the new hut. *The newcomers' home.* Not mine, though. Never mine. Beyond that, I smell something frail and wild, and fusey and unknown. The wind stirs quick. My feathers twitch. I am up, then, before a note leaves my beak. Up and into the big big sky, past the filmy fluffs of cloud, into the deep, clear blue. I spread wide. I am anything; I am nothing already known. The future calls me, and my dark shadow flies high above them, black and free, flapping like the freedom flags of yore.

Acknowledgments

The author wishes to thank the Ontario Arts Council for its financial support.

Sloppy kisses to all my dog friends—you know who you are. Big props to Mark McAlpine and Hilary Cameron for insights on earlier drafts, and for irreplaceable friendships, and to Milena Soczka for the love. Leslie MacDonald, Gwen Bartleman, the Mabel's Fables writing crew and the West End Literary Salon—thank you for your encouragement. Nalo Hopkinson was teleported by Kronk herself to edit this book: her insight has been essential. I would like to express deep gratitude to my parents for their unconditional support, and also to Peter Carver, aka Yoda, my long-time mentor and friend.

photo courtesy of Jen Black / www.jenblack.net

Kristyn Dunnion is the acclaimed author of *Missing Matthew* (2003) and *Mosh Pit* (2004). She studied English Literature and Theatre at McGill University. Her passion for children's literature and wigs led her to the University of Guelph where she completed a Masters Degree in English. She likes big boots, shaved heads, and loud music!